"You have any di

Suddenly, I was one part pleased and nine parts panic. Flirting with Van under the innocent guise of playing basketball was one thing. But going on a date with him, alone, with Ket out there, was suicide. Or murder, depending on who Ket would kill, Van or me. Or both. I looked around at the group. "I don't know. Have we made any plans?"

Undaunted by my sudden reserve, Van grabbed my hand and pulled the phone away from my ear. "I was thinking, we could make plans. You and me." He pointed to me and then him. "Just the two of us. Eating together somewhere nice. I have the feeling you're a local girl. You could suggest somewhere. I could pay."

I turned to stare at him, my heart melting to mush. "Are you asking me out? Like for a date?"

"Yeah. Like for a date."

My phone beeped. I had a text message.

The dude 2 ur right wants u. Tell him ur mine. Im watching u. —K

SPY GAMES

GINA ROBINSON

ZEBRA BOOKS
KENSINGTON PUBLISHING CORP.
http://www.kensingtonbooks.com

ZEBRA BOOKS are published by

Kensington Publishing Corp.
119 West 40th Street
New York, NY 10018

All Kensington titles, imprints and distributed lines are available at special quantity discounts for bulk purchases for sales promotion, premiums, fund-raising, educational or institutional use.

Special book excerpts or customized printings can also be created to fit specific needs. For details, write or phone the office of the Kensington Special Sales Manager: Attn. Special Sales Department. Kensington Publishing Corp., 119 West 40th Street, New York, NY 10018. Phone: 1-800-221-2647.

Zebra and the Z logo Reg. U.S. Pat. & TM Off.

ISBN-13: 978-1-4201-0473-8
ISBN-10: 1-4201-0473-X

First Printing: December 2009

10 9 8 7 6 5 4 3 2 1

Printed in the United States of America

For my wonderful family;
I've been truly blessed by having all of you in my life.

ACKNOWLEDGMENTS

Writing a story is a solitary endeavor. Seeing a story become a book is not. I owe a debt of gratitude to so many people:

To my husband, Jeff, who's always my first reader and my creative sounding board.

To my children, Janelle, John, and Jennica, for the joy you give me and for keeping me young. And particularly to Janelle for helping me with my research and introducing me to IMDb, John for lending me his Bond book and sharing his love of all things spy with me, and Jennica for sharing her love of fastpitch, basketball, and track with me.

To my many writing friends for their advice and encouragement.

To my husband's parents, Don and Berta, for introducing me to the Puget Sound area, this wonderful part of the country where I now live and write.

To the staff at Kensington for all the work each of you put into my books.

And to my agent, Kim Lionetti, and my editor, Peter Senftleben. You're both a joy to work with.

Chapter 1

My panties were in a bunch.

Literally in a bunch. Piled à la mode on the overturned contents of my suitcase on the red and gold, diamond-patterned carpet of my hotel room.

Not just one or two pair, either. Every luscious new pair I'd brought with me and neatly tucked into my suitcase to bring to Fantasy Spy Camp, Seattle, Urban Ops—three thongs, three boy shorts, three briefs, three bikinis. I'd taken FSC's packing instructions at their word. They *had* said, "three pair of underwear, any style." What style of panty does a girl wear with fatigues?

I stood rooted in place in the doorway, key card in one hand, car keys dangling from the other.

I'd signed up for spy camp to increase my odds of survival should my psycho, stalker ex-boyfriend Ket get out of prison. If he made good on his threats, he'd dramatically shorten my lifespan. Three days of target practice, spy techniques, and self-defense training were motivation enough to get me past the distaste of wearing fatigues. Camo on the outside, lace on the inside. I was half hoping I'd meet a hot, adrenaline-addicted thrill seeker who wouldn't be scared off by a wacko like Ket.

I took stock of the situation, hating that Ket still had the power to scare me. I tried to reassure myself. This was probably nothing more than a camp prank. A setup to test our spy capabilities.

The DO NOT DISTURB sign dangled from the outside doorknob where I'd left it before heading out for a late afternoon meal with my fellow campers. The weepy-tearjerker TV channel for women that I'd left on to give the impression the room was occupied still chattered away inside. That alone should have been enough to scare off any male prowler.

The Goldilocks of room trashing was *obviously* not still on scene. Ket couldn't have done this, I told myself. Nicki, my victim counselor, would have warned me if he was out of jail. So why was I shaking so badly? At that moment, I hated Ket and his power over me with an intensity that scared me.

The reassuring din of my fellow campers floated down the hotel corridor. Several of the group jostled and joked, and insulted one another as they returned to their rooms for a pit stop before our first official Urban Ops meeting.

I was aware of Van, who had dreamy, intelligent brown eyes and was considerably more restrained in his enthusiasm about playing tough-guy spy for a week than the rest, pausing across the hall in front of his own door. Honestly, although I'd only met him a few hours ago, my pulse raced whenever he was near me.

"Reilly?" he asked.

I looked over my shoulder at him, relieved by his presence.

He stood in the dim light, gazing at me with a quizzical expression. With his height, dark hair, and intensity, he looked as if he could scare away the boogeyman. "You going to lurk in that doorway all day?"

I opened my mouth and shut it without saying a word.

"Hey, you okay?"

I pointed into my room. "Take a look."

He crossed the hall in a single stride. As he brushed past me into the room, he knocked my keys out of my hand and onto the floor. The brief brush of his touch sent a shiver of attraction through me. I was too busy watching his reaction, not to mention his very nice, sculpted backside, to bother stooping to pick up the keys.

"Whoa!" He stopped short just inside the doorway, then turned to glance back to see how I was taking things.

I don't know what he was looking for. Hysteria, maybe? Whatever he expected of me, he was clearly excited by the turn of events.

"Anything missing?"

"I don't know." I paused, mulling over the possibilities. "Why would anyone bother with my room?" Anyone other than Ket, I added to myself. "Everything worth stealing is in my purse." I rattled the handbag slung over my shoulder. With Van in the room, I relaxed.

"Want me to take a look?" He pointed into the room, clearly eager to search it.

"Knock yourself out," I said with just a touch of flirtation and relief in my voice.

The bathroom was to our immediate right. He gently pushed the bathroom door full open with the toe of his boot.

I put a hand on his arm to stop him.

He turned to me with his eyes sparkling. "You think Freddie's hiding in the shower?" His grin was infectious. He wasn't scared at all.

I was actually wondering if I'd left any embarrassing feminine products lying around that I didn't want him to see. But I couldn't admit to that. "Maybe you should take a weapon with you," I said to cover. "I have a baseball bat in the closet."

I didn't mention the gun in my purse. Or the pepper spray. I liked the bat better. The gun and the spray were actually a bit scary. For dire emergencies only.

"No, thanks."

"Suit yourself." I pawed through my purse, looking for my self-defense whistle. I held it up for him to see. "I'll just whistle for help if you run into trouble." Humor may have been my coping mechanism of choice, but I was only half joking.

"Yeah. Do that." He stepped into the bathroom and looked around with me peering over his shoulder like a bumbling stooge.

"I don't see 'redrum' written on the mirror in blood," he said, stepping back into the entry in front of the mirrored closet.

And I hadn't seen anything he shouldn't have seen.

"I think we're good." He slid the closet doors open with a sudden movement.

I jumped, hand to heart. "Don't do that."

He laughed. "Don't do what?"

"Make sudden moves."

"Jumpy?"

"Maybe."

He poked his head into the closet. "No skeletons. Your bat's still here, slugger." He handed it to me and headed for the main part of the room.

Bat cocked, I followed him, wondering if he was one of those guys with a photographic memory. Photographic memories come in real handy, I'd heard. For spies. Not for victims of violent crimes. Not when you can't stop reliving the event in minute detail.

His quiet perusal of the room, with its "dainties on parade" decor, made me uncomfortable. This wasn't exactly how I'd imagined showing them off.

I spoke just as his gaze lit on my hot pink thong panties. "Okay, so I know what you're thinking."

"I don't think so." His grin was full of innuendo.

Yeah, from his tone, I think I did. And it made my pulse speed along like a happy racehorse. "I was going to say I ignored the packing directive. I brought just a few more things than they recommended."

He stared at my large pile of clothes and accessories. "Yeah, the bat tipped me off."

I laughed and made a move to step around him, ostensibly to clean up, but mostly because I hated not being in control. He deftly blocked me with a well-muscled arm. "I haven't finished with the room yet."

I smiled at him and his protective instinct. I liked the heroic type. I stepped back out of his way. "Don't forget to check beneath the bed."

He looked under the bed and behind the curtains. When no one popped out from either place, he shot me a triumphant look. "All clear."

A female character on the tearjerker channel screamed. We both jumped. Van flicked an annoyed glance at the TV.

"Shut it off," I said. "I only had it on for security purposes."

"Next time try Spike TV." As he flipped the TV off, he gave me a look that couldn't have been more clear if he'd rolled his eyes. "Give people the idea there's a man in the room."

"I'll keep that in mind."

He tried the adjoining room door. "Locked tight. No signs of jimmying." He turned back to the room. "Nothing's broken. Are you thinking what I'm thinking?"

I nodded. "You mean do I think FSC did this?"

He smiled. "You got it."

I set my bat down on the bed. "You'd better check your room."

Before Van could move, a string of curses broke out in the hall.

"Holy shit!" I recognized Jim Martin's voice with its loud growl of dismay and menace. "Some asshole broke into my room."

Van shot me an excited look. "Let the games begin."

I darted into the hall, ready to sing the hallelujah chorus. I hadn't been singled out. Ket hadn't found and terrorized me.

"My room was ransacked, too!" I yelled down the hall, trying to calm Jim while not sounding *too* elated.

Huff, Cliff, and Steve, who were still talking in the hall, came running to have a look at my room.

"Wow!" Steve, the whiny sidekick of the group, braced his hand on my shoulder as he peered past me into my room. "Cool. How'd you two get so lucky?"

"Luck?" I said. "How much you want to bet your rooms are tossed, too?"

Huff retrieved my car keys from the floor and handed them to me. A woman would have to be dead not to notice how attractive he was—six feet, blond, dancing blue eyes. Despite Ket's best efforts, I wasn't dead yet. So I noticed. Even so, Huff didn't quite set my pulse on its ear like Van did.

"Thanks. I'd forgotten I'd dropped them." I needed to remember to be more careful.

"Where's the damage?" Huff asked.

"Straight ahead." I stepped out of his way.

"Whoa!" Huff let out a whistle. "Nice panties."

I rolled my eyes. "What is it about panties?"

"You have to ask?" Huff shot me a leer.

Steve and Cliff dashed off to their rooms like young hounds on the scent. Huff smiled at me, winked, and ambled off, a study of easygoing sex appeal.

People often wondered how I could still like men after what I'd gone through, was still going through, with Ket. I called them the one-bad-apple believers.

Not me. To me one bad apple was just one bad apple. Toss the apple out of the barrel and you're good. There were plenty of men who were good fruit. Some, like Van, were even luscious ripe fruit. The kind of fruit a girl like me who'd been living like a monk-ette was just dying to try.

Van went across the hall to his room, yelling at another camper, Peewee Canarino, four doors down. I knew Peewee slightly. He worked out at Ket's gym. Even the slight association was enough to make me leery of him. "Canary, your room tossed, too?"

"Shit, yes!" Canarino replied.

"See if anything's missing and meet us in the hall," Van called back to him.

Less than five minutes later, the seven of us gathered in front of Van's door. I was the only woman in the group. I'd grown up with brothers. I could handle it. But it would have been nice to have a confidante.

"They got us good." Cliff, the movie director, had his hands stuffed into his shorts pockets. He sounded amused and excited. Short, not more than five foot nine, soft, with hairy legs, and a scraggly beard, Cliff was not on my list of men to ogle. Unfortunately, he liked the sight of me. Short men always did.

"What do you think they wanted?" Steve crowded in.

"Information." Huff leaned casually against the wall. "Anything they can use against us in camp."

Van nodded his agreement. "They're looking for

weaknesses." His gaze flicked to me, amused. "And whether we can follow directions."

I smiled and shrugged.

"Anyone leave anything incriminating in their room?" Van scanned the group, landing his gaze on me.

"Don't look at *me*! I had my purse with me the entire time. The only thing they learned from me is that I don't have a favorite style of panties."

"Nice to know," Huff said.

The discussion continued until we determined FSC had succeeded only in scaring us. Me, mostly. We split up and headed back to our rooms.

In my room, I reassured myself of my safety. Just like I did practically every day of my life now. My room was above the fifth floor, which made it statistically less likely to be burgled. And away from the stairs. The farther away from the stairs, the riskier it was to get to me. I wasn't going to make things easy for Ket.

I had my trusty Louisville Slugger, my gun, pepper spray, and a self-defense whistle. No one but my parents, Grandpa, and Nicki knew where I was. I was on a floor full of macho guys who wanted to be spies. For most of camp, there'd be three well-trained instructors to watch out for me. Ket was locked up for contempt, a guest of the California penal system. He wasn't Vapor Man. He couldn't just glide through the bars at will. What could possibly go wrong?

I carefully picked through the mayhem, gently refolding clothes and packing them back in my suitcase, ready for flight, like always. I could have hung my things in the closet, packed away my lingerie in the drawers, lined the bathroom counter with my cosmetics. Only I didn't.

I lived like a butterfly perched on a flower—always poised for flight. I kept a packed bag in the car. One at the office. One here. Better to be prepared than end up pinned to an exhibition board.

I sighed. Without paying much attention to my work, I smoothed out a pair of panties and picked them up to fold. A matchbook tumbled out of the crotch.

Madam Lou's Martini Bar.

I flinched and jumped back as if I expected the matches to spontaneously combust and consume me. My mouth went dry and I began to tremble uncontrollably.

Ket!

Lou's was Ket's favorite Seattle bar.

Before he'd gone to jail, Ket had broken into my home, my office, my best friend's house, and anywhere I was or was likely to be. He always left a calling card. A little memento to let me know he was watching and had the upper hand. *Always.*

I rubbed the scar that Ket had given me on my chin. Beneath my breath, I cursed him to the fieriest recesses of hell. He wouldn't win. I wouldn't let him ruin my life.

I pulled at the collar of my blouse, fighting off claustrophobia. I shouldn't have put Van in danger by flirting with him and letting him into my room alone. I needed a new room. I needed a new one *now*!

Chapter 2

With trembling hands, I scooped up the matchbook with a tissue, grabbed my purse, and headed for the lobby. I couldn't stay in that room another second. Not one. For just an instant, I considered leaving, abandoning my vacation. I discarded the idea just as quickly. If Ket was out, nowhere was safe. At least FSC advertised that it had submachine guns on the premises.

Trying to appear reasonably calm, but doing a bad job of it, I slipped up to the front desk and asked the clerk for a new room, leaving out the part about being stalked by Ket. That never went over well with people.

"Reason for the switch?" the male clerk asked, typing away without looking at me.

"Reason?" I had a very good reason. One I couldn't tell him. I took a deep breath and forced a shaky smile. "Allergies. Something in that room bothers me. Look! It's given me the trembles. And I feel flushed and nauseous." I held out my shaking hand for him to see, thinking all true. But definitely not the hotel's fault.

"I'm sorry for the trouble." I put on my apologetic look while appealing to the old "the customer is always right" credo.

In victim counseling they teach you to yell "FIRE!" when you need immediate help. More people jump to the rescue at the threat of leaping flames than any other plea. I've learned you don't tell people you *think* you're being stalked. Not unless you want to be labeled a flighty, paranoid nutcase or a conspiracy theorist.

"Just give me another room and I'll be fine." Let him think I was a hypochondriac. Hypochondria was a lot more benign than paranoia.

He hesitated, then began typing again. "Right now I don't have anything clean and available." He looked like he hoped I wouldn't take his head off. "We've had some late checkouts and we're still cleaning. If you could check back in a few hours, I'm sure we'll have something."

"Fine." Okay, I'd have to live with it. I'd be out all evening at the FSC meeting anyway. Surrounded by men with guns. Men who knew how to use them. I handed the clerk the matchbook, wrapped in the tissue for safekeeping. Nicki taught me to save all potential evidence. The tissue was my idea. I'd watched enough *CSI* to know better than to smear the prints and contaminate the forensic evidence. "Drop this in the safe for me?"

He looked skeptical of my sanity. But at that point, he wasn't prone to argue. He reached for the matchbook.

"Thanks. I'll be back." I really didn't mean to sound so Terminator-like.

"Oh, one more thing," I added like a casual afterthought, but it was completely, wholly deliberate. I had plenty of practice with this part of the procedure. I pulled a three-by-five picture of Ket from my purse and slid it across the counter to the clerk. Distasteful as it was, I kept a stack with me.

"My ex." I sighed. "Bad breakup. I'd really appreciate it if you'd notify me if you or any of the staff see him around? I'd like to avoid a scene . . . and him."

The clerk nodded knowingly, almost sympathetically. People are so much more forgiving of relationships gone sour than ones gone stalking.

I left the desk and took a seat in the lobby in front of a mega-size gas fireplace and, hands still shaking, called the California jail where Ket was being held for contempt. The authorities were *supposed* to notify me before they released him.

In a timely matter. Like in less time than the ETA between the jail and wherever I was at the moment. Like I had a lot of faith they would.

Ket was refusing to testify before a grand jury about one of his clients knowingly using steroids. Sounds selfless. Except Ket's a personal trainer, and he probably sold the client the alleged steroids in the first place.

I punched through the jailhouse menu until I finally reached a live person. "I'm calling to verify that Ket Brooks has not been released and is still being held for contempt?"

Some typing. "Yes, ma'am."

"You're sure?" I couldn't keep the uncertainty from my voice. "He hasn't escaped? They were supposed to notify me—"

"No, ma'am, he hasn't escaped." The operator sounded testy.

I couldn't blame her. I *was* questioning the accuracy of her information. But only out of insecurity and the need for reassurance.

I took a deep breath, thanked her and hung up. Just because Ket didn't personally put that matchbook in my room didn't mean he hadn't hired someone to do it.

Ket. It *had* to be Ket. He collected matchbooks from every bar he visited. He'd taken me to Lou's years ago. And later beat me up for flirting with a stranger who sent me a drink. Need I say, I wasn't flirting? Heck no. I sent the drink back. Didn't matter to Ket. Once his jealousy reared its ugly head, he wanted blood.

Anyway, who else would put a matchbook in my panties? Why would FSC do that?

No, Ket was trying to scare me and doing a great job of it. Just how had he found out where I was?

My mind ticked off the possibilities. In the possible but not probable category—Peewee "Canary" Canarino. He worked out at Ket's Los Angeles gym from time to time. Everyone at the gym knew the situation between Ket and me, and where Ket was right now. The Canary could have sung to Ket. I doubted it, but he could have. Most probable—Ket had hired someone to tail me. Scary. But why not? He'd done everything else. I glanced at my watch. Time for my FSC meeting.

* * *

Except for its unique, Northwest name, the Sasquatch Room was like every other hotel conference room in the world—tables covered in white cloth and set with water pitchers and dishes of hard candy. Your basic uncomfortable conference room chairs in forest green. A podium at the front. Refreshment table with coffee and cookies in the back.

Every society has their mythical beasts. In the Northwest, we love our Sasquatch. And why not? He's big. He's hairy. He's scary. He doesn't photograph well. He's rarely seen, but he leaves behind impressions of his visit and a bad odor. Kind of like Ket. Ket wore a size thirteen shoe, too.

Ket. If I could spit his name from my lips and never utter it again, I would. He may have hired someone to scare me. But I was certain he'd save all the really good torture, the part where he would rape me, then beat me senseless, for himself. He wasn't out of jail. I was "safe" for the day. And furious that from over a thousand miles away, he still had me looking over my shoulder.

The conference room was empty when I arrived, as was the hall and the entire wing of the floor. It appeared that Fantasy Spy Camps had rented out a sizeable portion of the hotel for our vacation pleasure. Even empty, I preferred the conference room to my hotel room. I chose a seat near the door.

Huff showed up first.

"Going for drinks with the gang later?" He sat and scooted his chair far enough back from the table to lounge casually, and openly appreciate his view of me.

I never have minded a man admiring my form. As long as he takes my cues when to back off. I didn't mind Huff's attentions at all. "And ruin your boys' night out?" I replied, with a hint of flirt.

"Ruin? It'll be no fun without you." He leaned toward me. "I'll buy you a drink."

"Any drink?"

"Anything you want."

"Deal." What would one tiny drink hurt? Flirt with enough different men and maybe it would draw Ket's fire off Van.

Van entered the room. I did my best not to look at him, but he was a hard man not to ogle. To both my relief and severe disappointment, he took a seat in the front corner of the room.

"You look so damn familiar," Huff said, bringing my attention back to him. "You ever play beach volleyball?" He put just enough salaciousness in his voice for it to be flattering.

"Only on the pages of a magazine."

Huff snapped his fingers and grinned as if he'd just had a lightbulb moment. "I knew it! 3D Sportswear Girl. The face, or should I say, the body of 3D." Charmingly lecherous eyebrow wiggle. "Am I right?"

I nodded, flattered that he remembered. "Used to be. Now I work behind the scenes in corporate marketing."

"Man! I can't believe it." He slapped the table. "I've lusted after you for . . . years. *Sports Illustrated.*" He whistled. "Hot."

"Stop it. You're making me blush."

He kept grinning. "You didn't play beach volleyball? Another fantasy dashed."

"Don't look so disappointed." I laughed. "I played regular volleyball. And basketball. And softball. I went to the University of Washington on a full ride fastpitch scholarship."

"Damn! I knew I loved lady jocks." His eyes danced as he surveyed me. "Let me guess your position. Tall, gorgeous. First base or pitcher."

"Pitcher, big shot."

He shifted in his chair. "If I buy you *two* drinks will you show me your change-up?"

"For two drinks I'd have shown you a curve or two."

"How about I change my mind?"

"Too late. A deal's a deal."

"What if I throw in dinner?"

I smiled enigmatically.

He grinned back. Was that a tiny trace of a frown I noticed from Van out of the corner of my eye?

The room filled as Steve, Peewee, and the movie moguls, Cliff Wilkins and Jim Martin, filed in. Our instructors showed up at the last minute, carrying boxes of what I assumed were our uniforms.

They positioned themselves in seats in the front of the room by the podium. One by one, they greeted us and introduced themselves. Ace, former Army Ranger, crack shot, served in Iraq, good-looking, and full of possibilities. Kyle, retired Air Force, married, kids, blond with receding hair. And Warner, War as he preferred to be called. Definitely the head guy. Fortyish. Former Ranger. Sniper. CIA experience. Shaved head and ramrod posture that would have made a boarding school mistress proud. They were the kind of guys you'd want on your side, battle or not.

I felt safer just being around them. No way they'd let Ket get to me.

Sure enough, the boxes contained our uniforms. War and company issued us our gear—one set of digital camo BDUs, battle dress uniforms; three black, moisture-wicking T-shirts; one digital camo boonie hat.

The T-shirts were standard men's style—boxy, high neck, square shoulder—completely devoid of female flattering flare. I was an executive of 3D Sportswear; those tees were utterly offensive to me. Clothes, be they evening or sportswear, should flatter the body.

When War handed me my three tees, I handed them back. "Keep them. I brought my own. With curve hugging spandex." I winked and smiled at him.

"They better be black."

"But pink looks so much better on me," I said, pulling his chain.

"Career trainee!"

"Black. Yessir." I gave him a little salute and smiled. "I work for 3D Sportswear. Talk to me later. We can cut you a deal on women's moisture wick gear. Unfortunately, we don't make camo." I returned to my seat.

Each uniform came complete with personal name tapes and patches. Only the name tapes were actually more like first-initial-tapes.

"Career trainees, listen up." Kyle called us to

attention after everyone had their gear. "From now on we'll refer to you as CTs. Your code names are on your name tapes. Get used to them. From here out those *are* your names." Hard, serious, broach–no-questions stare. "As a spy, it's important to get used to answering to anything but asshole. Regularly. Consistently. Naturally." His gaze danced around the group. "Any ideas why we picked these code names?"

Steve bounced in his chair with his hand up until Kyle called on him. "Because they're short and sweet."

Kyle remained impassive and unimpressed. "Anyone else have a theory?"

I raised my hand, playing cool like a Bond Girl, all slink and seduction.

Kyle called on me. "R?"

"MI6," I said. "Ian Fleming based Bond on World War One British spy Sidney Reilly." Yes, I was aware of the coincidence of my name. Only I was named after my grandmother's maiden name. "Reilly was a special informer for Scotland Yard, whose chief inspector was William Melville, code named 'M'." Personally, I held Steve's theory about this code naming being a cop-out. But it originated with Scotland Yard, not FSC.

Kyle gave me a barely perceptible nod of approval. "Correct, R."

Kyle went on to describe the purpose of Urban Ops. "FSC is a division of Fantasy Camps. FSC runs a variety of extreme, fantasy spy vacations nationwide and internationally. Each camp focuses on a different aspect of the spy industry.

"Urban Ops's focus is on the exciting and important aspect of self-defense and escape for the spy or urban warrior. CQB, close quarter battle techniques, reflexive shooting, and even hostage rescue, which includes learning techniques to survive a hostage situation.

"This is the Bond action stuff—the shootouts, the hand-to-hand combat, the escaping from the clutches of MI6's archenemy Blofeld and rescuing the gorgeous girl action."

Exactly the kind of thing I needed to know so I wouldn't end up *being* the girl who needed rescuing.

Kyle stood at the front of the room, calm and unmoving. He wasn't the pacing kind. "We'll be training in our indoor urban training facility, a mock city built with input from the Army's Special Forces Group and designed by a Hollywood set designer who worked on one of the Bond films.

"Breakfast is at oh seven hundred. The bus will pick you all up and transport you to the facility at oh seven thirty." He turned the mic over to War. Then he and Ace left the room.

War was the pacing kind, the intense pacing kind. "You're a bunch of quiet birds tonight. Not a squealer in the group. But I happen to know that someone broke in and trashed each and every CT's room this afternoon." He scanned the room. "No talkers?"

No one moved.

War continued his speech. "After each session we'll have a mission debrief. Consider this your first.

"The savvy spy, the one who makes it to old age, assumes he's under surveillance twenty-four-seven. He takes precautions to protect himself and the mission. He knows how to react if his position is compromised or threatened." His piercing gaze slid over each of us. "He must have his out planned."

Yeah, I knew that. I spent every day looking over my shoulder and planning my out. Take right now. I was pretty sure my position had been compromised. But what was I going to do about it?

"Took the three of us less than half an hour to turn seven rooms. On the one hand, I have to compliment you, CTs. We didn't get much in the way of cover-blowing crap. On the other, only one of you used any security techniques at all. R!"

"Yessir!" I sat up straighter.

"R left the TV on and put the 'do not disturb' sign on her door to make it look like she was in her room when she was not. Good work." He reached beneath the podium, pulled out a rolled up black polo shirt, and unfurled it before us. "The coveted FSC 'I've been spied' shirt." He tossed it to me. "Consider yourself rewarded."

I caught my prize and set it on the table in front of me. "Thank you, sir."

"What's the baseball bat for in your room?" War asked.

"Protection."

He shook his head. "We'll teach you how to use anything handy as a weapon, CT. However, R is at least *thinking* about protecting herself. Any questions? Yes, C?"

"How about telling us how you got into our rooms?" Cliff looked smug.

Before War could answer, the door slammed open

and two armed men dressed in black and wearing ski masks burst in.

Startled and shaking, I instinctively reached for my purse and protection.

"Leave it! This is a hit." Huff grabbed me and pushed me beneath the table. "Crawl for your life," he whispered, shoving me along between table legs and out into the aisle near the wall. "There's a service door at the front of the room. Reach it and we're free. No way they're taking me." Huff let out a string of curses beneath his breath.

Even though I hoped this was just another camp test, my heart hammered out of control. The submachine guns they carried looked real. Real dangerous.

I scurried in front of Huff as fast as my knees would carry me. My mother said I was one quick crawler when I was a baby. Look away for a second and I'd be gone. Only I seemed to have lost some of my baby speed.

Just as we passed Van's table, the intruders yelled, "Freeze or you're dead."

Staying alive being my main goal in life, I froze.

"Ignore them. Keep moving. Stay here and we're dead," Huff whispered, crawling for the door.

Van stared hard at me. "Do what they say and they won't hurt you, R."

I was torn between two men and their advice.

Huff tugged me forward by my sleeve. Van leaped from his chair and threw himself between me and the bad guys, shielding me with his body. "Fools, they're going to kill you for sure now."

Chapter 3

"No way." Huff got to his feet and reached for the doorknob. "We're out of here."

"You're already Swiss cheese, hot shot," Van said to him. He grabbed me before I could stand, and whispered, "You're a woman. The only woman in the room. You still have a chance. Don't look at the gunmen. Don't give them a reason to pick on you. Stay calm. Wait to be rescued. We'll be fine."

My gaze bounced between Van and Huff. I glanced at the gunmen. One of them ordered the other CTs to the corner of the room, where he kept them covered. The other one moved forward, with his gun trained on us. My heart hammered away so fast that I couldn't think straight. My hands shook. I just wanted out. I just wanted away. I panicked.

"Cops don't always save people." I gave Van a big, swift shove in the shoulder, trying to push him away from me.

He grabbed my arm. "Put your hands on your head. Lie down on your stomach. Show the gunman you're not a threat. Quickly."

I shook my arm free. "Get out my way. I'm getting out of here."

Huff was cursing now as he rattled the door, ramming it with his shoulder. "The damn door's locked."

I stood and threw my shoulder into the effort with him. The door didn't budge.

"He's coming for us." Van grabbed me around the waist and pulled me to the floor, pushing me forward onto my stomach. "Get down."

The gunman reached us. Huff turned from the door to face him, poised to lunge. The gunman pointed his gun at Huff's head.

"No!" I screamed, popping up. "Nooo!"

Huff hesitated. The gunman lowered his rifle aim and shot Huff in the chest before either of us could move. Without missing a beat, he took aim at Van. I knew I should move. I knew I should *do* something. But I was paralyzed with fear. The gunman rapid-fire shot Van, then me, in the chest, dead center.

"Ouch!" The blue pellet that hit me stung. I grabbed my chest and rubbed it, trying to take the sting away, trying to digest that I wasn't dead and there was no blood, looking frantically between Huff and Van, both of whom looked peeved, but fine and completely intact. Huff was cursing.

"No 'I've been spied' shirt for you," Van said to Huff, who scowled back at him.

I let out a relieved breath and tried to stop shaking. Just stop shaking. And breathe.

Our fellow CTs huddled in the corner, watching us "die."

Behind his podium, War frowned. "Game over. Three dead. Four"—he shrugged—"possibly alive. If the gunmen don't panic."

"We never panic." Ace pulled his ski mask off. "Sorry, guys," he said to us. "If we'd been real terrorists and this"—he shook his rifle—"wasn't an Airsoft gun, it would have been two to the head for each of you." He grinned slowly and pointed to where he'd made his entrance. "From way back there."

Still shaking, I looked up at Ace. "You guys really know how to get the adrenaline pumping." I was breathing hard. "I figured this was a simulation, but still." I tried to smile and held out my trembling hand so Ace could see. "Look at me."

Across the room, Kyle pulled his mask off and let the others go.

Huff bent and picked up the toy bullet from the floor where it landed after bouncing off his chest, and cursing, tossed it at the wall. "So close."

"And yet so far," Van added, tossing up and catching his bullet, showing great restraint in not saying, "I told you so."

My heart was still racing. I was shaking, and totally frustrated with myself. This had only been a simulated attack, and I'd gone to pieces and done everything wrong.

Van handed me my bullet. "A souvenir." He paused. "You okay? We're theoretically in heaven now. You can calm down."

"Or hell," Huff added with a wry note to his voice. "In which case . . ."

I put my head in my hands. "I'm so sorry. I got

you both killed." I tried not to sound as upset as I felt.

Van shrugged.

"Live free or die," Huff said. "No way they were taking me hostage."

Ace slapped his hat against his leg. "I really hate shooting women. They never take it well." He looked directly at me. "Do you need to sit a minute longer?"

"I'm fine." I wasn't exactly fine, but I was calming down.

Ace offered me a hand up.

On my way back to the table, I bent to retrieve my purse. My Beretta had slid partially out. Its black muzzle peeked above the rim, giving my purse the appearance of a snout. I slid my lethal darling back out of view as I scooped up the purse, hoping no one had seen it.

About the gun—only my gun dealer and the government knew for sure. If I ever needed to use it, I wanted the element of surprise on my side. Despite oodles of target practice, I wasn't sure how good my aim was going to be under duress.

Honestly? I had a love/fear relationship with my piece. After a gun safety course and diligent hours at the firing range, I'd almost lost my fear of it. Almost. Mostly, I depended on it as a last line of defense. Equal force be damned. If Ket came after me again I was going to use it and face the consequences later.

Seeing it now brought back the first fleeting seconds of the intrusion. What if Huff hadn't grabbed me and knocked my purse out of reach? Would I have grabbed the gun? Used it?

A brief flash of horror, starring me shooting Ace and Kyle, flitted through my head. I was still trembling, but determined to overcome my fear and become a kick-ass woman totally able to protect herself, as I fell into my seat, clutching my purse.

Huff returned to his spot next to me and shot me a concerned look. "You okay?"

"Fine."

He looked skeptical as he poured me a glass of water. "Drink this. You'll feel better."

I doubted it.

"You. You. And you"—War was back at the podium and on the warpath. He pointed at Van, Huff, and me in turn—"failed this hostage pretest. If this had been a real situation, you'd be dead.

"In the event you're ever taken hostage—stay calm, do *not* make any sudden or suspicious movements, comply with all demands, never challenge a hostage taker . . ."

After War's lecture, the seven of us went directly from the meeting to the hotel bar to unwind, carrying our bags of uniforms with us. It was Sunday evening and the bar was quiet. Just the odd business traveler or two. We pushed two tables together, set our BDUs on an adjacent table, and ordered a pitcher of beer. I was flanked by Huff on my right and Van on my left. Steve immediately began bending Van's ear.

"How do you think they did it?" Peewee asked the group-at-large from across the table.

Peewee wasn't called Peewee for no reason. He

was a short guy with short-guy syndrome—cocky, full of himself, and belligerent. He was one of those dark Italian men who'd benefit from having his back waxed. I'm all for hair, but I think moderation is the key. I sure wouldn't want to clean his bathroom. Think Drano in the industrial size.

I'm a quarter Italian, which means I'm used to descriptive nicknames. All my Italian relatives have them. And they usually have to do with height or food.

Despite the expensive cut of his clothes, Peewee had thug written all over him. He looked like he'd be more comfortable wearing one of my cousin Ceci's "damifino" baseball caps. His last name was Canarino, which meant canary in Italian. His uncle was Sil Canarino, a notorious Hollywood PI who was currently in jail awaiting racketeering charges. Sil was probably Mafioso, so the story goes. I had no reason to doubt it. Which made Peewee dangerous. Ket had always been impressed by him, which tells you something right there.

Just my bad luck that Peewee was at the one FSC session that had a last minute opening for me. If I'd known in advance that he'd be attending, I might have backed out. Unfortunately, I was stuck with him.

"They who? Did what?" Jim Martin asked. Jim was mid to late forties. Thin, like a runner. Receding hair. And a lawyer. He asked the question with the theatrical quality of the Spanish Inquisition.

"Broke into our rooms," Peewee said.

"Bribed a maid, stole a universal key card or paid someone for it," Huff said.

Steve looked up from his intense conversation

with Van. "I bet they hacked into the hotel computer and created their own key card."

Personally, I found all the possibilities frightening. Was it really that easy to get into a hotel room?

Huff's cell rang. He excused himself to take the call.

Jim let out a noise of disgust at the theories set forth. "Occam's razor. *Entia non sunt multiplicanda praeter necessitatem.* Given two equally valid explanations for a phenomenon, one should embrace the less complicated formulation. The hotel simply let them in because FSC has an agreement with them as part of our vacation package.

"We signed a waiver when we paid our fees. If you read the fine print, you saw that FSC has the right to spy on us and invade our privacy using whatever means they deem appropriate. And we've agreed to hold them blameless." Spoken like a true, smug lawyer.

Peewee looked at Jim as if he wanted to wipe that arrogant expression off Jim's face with a good right hook.

Cliff ordered another pitcher of beer and complained about the uniforms. "No shorts. The weather's warm and no shorts."

"That's what scissors are for," I said.

"You want to come help me make some cuts?" Cliff shot me a leer.

"You wouldn't like the kind of cuts I'd make." I gave him a slow smile to soften my rejection. Cliff, unattractive as he was, wasn't used to women turning him down. I imagine he used the director card to his advantage whenever possible.

"I might. Try me." He held my gaze as he swigged his beer.

"No, thanks."

Cliff turned to Jim. "Why do the young, attractive women ignore me unless they know who I am?" He spoke as if I wasn't right there where I'd have to be deaf not to hear him.

You only had to have a pair of eyes to know why. "I know who you are," I said.

Thank goodness Huff returned and eyed my glass. I'm not usually a drinker, but I'd already downed a beer without much trouble and was working my way through a second, and beginning to feel pretty relaxed and slightly flirty. Not smashed enough to go for Cliff. That was about a keg off into the future. But a light buzz always made me flirty. Flirty, then sleepy. Yeah, I was a lightweight. Tonight I was glad for it. I wanted to forget the day. Forget it all and just have some fun.

"I promised you a drink," Huff said. "A real drink. What'll you have?"

I never drank the really strong stuff. Never anything straight up or neat. I preferred unsophisticated girlie drinks with lots of rum and fruit, capped with whipped cream. In other words—dessert.

"I'll take a strawberry daiquiri."

"That's not a Bond Girl drink." Huff grinned as he flagged the waitress.

"You can tell them not to stir it if that makes you feel any better." I smiled back at him.

Just after my drink arrived, a local quartet of the lounge-lizard variety began playing easy listening favorites from the seventies, along with a touch of disco. I didn't like the music selection.

"Dance with me?" Huff's eyes sparkled with flirtation.

I shook my head.

"Come on." He stood and held out his hand to me.

"My mother never taught me the Hustle," I said.

He motioned me toward the tiny, square dance floor.

"Or how to disco."

"Neither did mine," Huff said. "We'll wing it."

The beers had relaxed my inhibitions. Not to mention Huff looked damned enticing. Against my better judgment, I stood and let him lead me out to dance.

"Alone at last," he said as we reached the dance floor, pulling me toward him and taking me in his arms. He smelled of a woodsy, expensive cologne I should have been able to name, but couldn't, not with his lean, hard body next to mine, chasing away coherent thought. "I've been angling for this all day."

I looped one arm around his shoulder. He caught my other hand in his, cuddling it between us, keeping one arm around my waist.

A disco ball spun overhead, casting its multicolored light over the deep green vinyl-covered booths and wooden tables surrounding us. We were the only couple on the dance floor. As Peewee hooted at us from the table, I felt suddenly conspicuous and exposed. As always, fear of Ket watching and catching me intruded. I stiffened.

"Relax. Lighten up." Huff squeezed my hand. "The band's not that bad."

"I'm sorry." I started to pull away.

He held me firm. "Did I do something? I don't think I've stepped on your toes yet."

I looked at the floor and shook my head. "It's not you." I paused. "It's . . . it's my ex."

Huff tipped up my chin and raised a brow, giving me a look I assumed was asking if I still had feelings for Ket. "Ah, the ex . . ."

"No, not that." I laughed nervously. "I hate the guy. It's just . . . Ket's the jealous type." My words came out in a rush. "He's promised to kill anyone he catches me with. And by his definition, dancing is almost 'with,' probably deserving of a sound beating." There, I'd said it. Ket had just ruined my chances. Again. "I shouldn't be out here with you. Peewee's pals with Ket." I scowled.

Huff chuckled. "I'll take care of Peewee. Now relax."

"You're either very brave or very foolish." I smiled back at him, admiring his moxie. "Peewee's uncle is Mafioso."

"I know." Huff grinned.

"You know and it doesn't bother you?"

"Not in the slightest."

"You're crazy. How about this—Ket, my ex, is a personal trainer and steroid-using junkie."

"You have good taste in men." Huff's eyes danced as he teased me.

"Had. Tastes change."

"Don't worry about me," Huff said. "I'm a PI. I

carry a big, bad gun. I've dealt with characters like your ex a time or two. I can handle myself."

Huff seemed so confident and unconcerned that I believed him. I relaxed enough to keep dancing anyway. "A PI?"

"A damn good one, babe." His voice was sympathetic and convincing. "An ace at tracking, and watching people's backsides. I could watch yours. I'd like that." His tone made my heart flutter.

"I'd like that, too. Though what I'd like best is Ket Brooks's head on a platter."

"Vicious."

"What can I say? Sometimes my Salome tendencies just pop out."

"I've always liked Salome." Huff tucked a lock of hair behind my ear with the attentive gentleness of a lover.

"I don't know what that says about you."

"I like women who can dance?"

I laughed.

The song ended. As we parted, Huff grabbed my arm and pulled me aside. "R, I need a favor."

"Yeah?" I paused beside him just off the dance floor. "Just ask."

"Two things." He paused. "Two top secret things."

"Top secret? You're not working for FSC, are you?"

He shrugged and shot me an enigmatic grin.

"Are either of them immoral, illegal, or fattening? 'Cause I don't do those."

"Fattening, definitely not. Illegal, no way. Immoral?" He shrugged. "I have my fantasies."

I smiled at his innuendo. "What do you want me to do?"

He shot me the grin again. "Hide a small flash drive in the ladies' room here in the bar." He gave me instructions.

"Hide a flash drive," I said. "What's on it? The secret to cold fusion?"

He laughed again. "No questions. The less you know, the better."

"Oooooh, mystery and intrigue. I love mystery and intrigue, and I need a powder. I'll do it," I said when he finished. "And number two?"

"Mail a letter."

"A letter?"

"A simple letter." He patted his pocket. "It's right here."

I pursed my lips and made a big show of thinking about it. "I don't mail explosives, threats, illegal substances, anthrax, or chain letters."

"Chain letters?" His grin was practically heart-stopping. He obviously found me amusing. Amusing, fascinating, mysterious . . . I could go on.

"Hate those," I said.

"That makes two of us. No chain letters. Just a letter to a friend."

"Okay," I said, nodding. "So I hide the drive and mail the letter and then what? War gives me a lecture about the dangers of doing a drop in the ladies' room? No worries 'cause I always wash thoroughly, and use a paper towel to open the door when I leave."

Huff laughed again. "I like you, R."

"Wait!" I said as inspiration hit me. "I know. A

bunch of double-agents come after me?" I raised a brow, begging for him to continue the gag.

He took my chin in his hand and smiled as he slipped the flash drive into my hand and whispered instructions on where to hide it without any embarrassment at all.

My eyes popped open at his knowledge of ladies' rooms. "You sure? Not every one has them."

He nodded, and continued. "And, Reilly, if a bunch of thugs or nasty double-agents come after you, give me up. Show them where you hid the drive." He pulled me into a hug, and slipped an envelope into my tight back pocket. The man had magic hands.

"Give you up? You sure? I'm a good liar."

He nodded. "Yeah, give me up. Whatever you do, be careful with that Beretta you have in your bag."

I was so startled it took me a minute to speak. "You know?"

"Saw it this evening."

"Don't tell me you're like that *Psych* detective and notice everything!" I wondered if anyone else had seen it.

"It's my job."

"Yeah?"

He nodded again.

"I have a permit to carry concealed."

"I don't doubt it."

"I know how to use it. I have Bond Girl skills, you know."

He nodded, smiling suggestively. "I'm guessing they're not necessarily of the firearm variety."

He'd guessed right there. I gave him a playful smile back.

He laughed. "You don't want to use that gun."

He smiled at the expression I gave him, confirming his guess. "R, I won't let anyone hurt you. Not any devious double-agents, not your ex. I have your back."

"Good." I flashed him another bright smile. "While you're at it, could you warn Peewee he'd better not report anything he sees here back to my ex?"

"Done."

I squeezed the drive in my hand. "Well, there's no time like the present."

Then it was off to the ladies' room to do the first deed. It's true what they say about beer—it goes right through a girl. As I headed toward the powder room, Huff returned to the table and said something to Peewee. It may have been my imagination, but I thought Peewee paled. PIs, they had something on everyone.

There was a line in the ladies' room. A long one and I was dancing. If I hadn't been on a mission, I would have ducked into another one. Where had all these women come from? The bar wasn't that busy. I had a feeling they were spilling over from some other function and hogging the bathroom that I was entitled to by way of actually patronizing the bar. Cheaters.

I stood in line, impatiently hoping the third stall in from the door magically opened up to coincide with me taking the lead spot in line. Huff had told me specifically to make the drop in the third stall. Guess he hadn't been counting on the crowd in here. I was wondering how he knew there'd even be a third stall. I didn't like the ideas that bounced into my head, like security cameras or men lurking in corners. I settled for hoping the person on the other end of the drop was a woman and had scoped out the scene ahead of time.

Even in desperate times with a spy mission hanging over my head, bathroom etiquette must be observed. I had to wait my turn. It was the first time in my life that I actually wished I was a mother with a small toilet-training child in tow. Yeah, not the thing most of us dream of. But you can always push to the front of the line if you have a kid hanging on to you, crying she has to go potty.

Just my luck the third stall opened up for the broad-beamed broad in front of me.

Crying child! Why didn't I have a crying child?

I glanced around madly, but there didn't seem to be any I could even beg, borrow, or steal. Not that stealing a child was a good idea, especially when you're on a covert mission.

Broad-beam ambled into the stall with all the speed of a turtle. When she shut the door, the whole row of stalls shook.

Almost immediately, number two opened up. Reluctantly, I passed and let the girl behind me have it, making a lame excuse about how I could wait. Then number one. I passed again.

Someone turned on a faucet behind me. Suddenly, all I could hear was running water. I couldn't block it out. I crossed my legs.

Number four opened up.

"Be my guest," I said. My words came out sounding choked. In trying to hold everything in, even my vocal chords seized up. I silently cursed Broadbeam with every foul word I could think up. What was she doing in there?

On second thought, I didn't want to know.

The lady behind me shook her head. "Look, you look miserable. Why don't you go in?"

"No, thanks. I'm waiting for number three."

"What on earth for?"

"Three's my lucky number."

She sighed and shook her head again. "Believe me, this in no place to get lucky." She went into number four.

This waiting was so not covert. Just as I reached the point of actually thinking about dragging Broadbeam out of there, she threw open the stall door and staggered out, leaving a bad odor behind her.

Grimacing, I slipped in. All this waiting meant I had to do my business first. I set the drive on top of the feminine protection disposal receptacle, as Huff so elegantly and technically called it.

The automatic toilet flushed as I reached for a seat protector. It flushed again before I could sit down. I had to get another seat protector and move quicker this time.

I finished my business, stood, tidied myself, and scanned the stall. This was a high-class establishment. It had seat protectors, a room freshener, a feminine protection disposal receptacle, and the rare find—a sanitary protection disposal bag dispenser of lady-safe bags, all in satin finish chrome. Wow!

I was supposed to hide the drive in the bottom of the feminine protection disposal thing beneath the liner bag. I grabbed a piece of toilet paper and picked up the drive. Now that my hands were dirty, I couldn't touch the drive. I tried the lid. Stuck. I tried. I pried. I shook the stall. The toilet flushed.

Someone squealed, "What's going on in there? Do you need help?" in a pitch just below only-dogs-can-hear-it range.

The lid was bent and totally stuck and I was shaking the foundations and taking more time in the stall than Broad-beam had. The natives were getting restless. Never stand between a woman and her stall. I had to get out of there.

I thought back over Huff's instructions. He couldn't have meant to hide the drive in the disposal bin. No way. That's nasty. I had no desire to reach in there. Not without some heavy-duty gloves.

I glanced at the lady-safe bag dispenser. Yeah, he must have meant that, the sanitary protection disposal bag *dispenser,* not the receptacle. Men were likely to mix these things up. I'd straighten him out later. I reached into my purse and found a bandage.

Using the toilet paper as a glove, I slid the drive up into the dispenser and tucked it so it rested on the inside lip. Then I carefully secured the drive in place with the bandage.

Mission accomplished, I left the stall under the watchful glares of several dancing women.

Chapter 4

Back in the bar, I slid into my spot at the table next to Van with Huff's envelope burning in my booty pocket. Van looked up as I scooted in my chair. His conversation with Jim came to an abrupt halt.

"Sorry. Didn't mean to interrupt," I said.

"You weren't," Van said. "We were just marveling that you managed to dance to a lounge-lizard classic."

"Hey," I said. "It had a beat."

"Sure," he said.

Jim grinned, but I noticed he kept glancing over at Cliff and Huff.

"What did I miss?" I asked eagerly. I was a girl. I liked gossip and hated to miss anything juicy.

"Jim was just telling me about his practice in LA," Van said.

"LA? Don't tell me you're an entertainment lawyer?" I asked, addressing Jim.

Jim took a swig of beer. "You don't like entertainment lawyers?"

"I have my beefs with them. Too many celebs get

off because of celebrity lawyers." I was thinking of Ket, who was only a minor, local LA-type celebrity, but who'd gotten off with a slap on the wrist for beating me practically into a coma.

"I represent celebrity clients."

"I'm very sorry to hear it. Divorce lawyer?" I took a sip of my daiquiri and set it back down. The ice was melting. It was too watery for my tastes.

"Divorce. Scrapes with the law."

"A celebrity criminal defense lawyer." I spit the words out like the anathema they were.

Van looked startled by my outburst, but Jim laughed.

"Don't hold back," Jim said. "Tell me what you really think."

"Sorry," I said, covering. "But if the Bruno Mali fits . . ."

Jim laughed again. "I can see it's going to take some work to convince you we're not all bad."

Huff got another call. He looked at the number and gave the table a thump to get our attention. "Hey, I've got business to attend to. I'm calling it a night. See you all in the morning. Seven sharp. And you"—he pointed at me—"owe me a change-up."

"Find me a softball," I said, disappointed by his sudden departure.

He winked. "You got it."

As it so often goes, once someone leaves the party, everyone else follows. Steve, Peewee, Cliff, and Jim took Huff's lead and begged off, leaving just Van and me. I would have headed out myself, but it seemed rude to leave a hot guy like Van hanging alone.

There was a moment of awkward silence after the others had gone. As was my nature, I had to say something. Only I was trying to steer clear of questions about Van's line of work. When we'd all first introduced ourselves, he'd mentioned that he was a professor of mathematics.

I've always been pretty good at math, but that didn't mean I wanted to waste precious getting-to-know-you time discussing imaginary numbers, polar coordinates, and negative infinity.

So instead of discussing math's imponderables, I said, "Van. Is that short for something?"

"Van-Rex."

"Unusual name. I bet you don't find it on toothbrushes and key chains."

"Not all that often, no," he said. I liked his smile. "It's a family name."

"So you're Van the second, third, fifteenth?"

"None of the above. Dad lucked out and dodged the name. I'm named after my great-great-grandfather or something. He was a war hero."

I nodded. "Well, I like it. Reminds me of a dinosaur. Very powerful."

He looked bemused by my comment, so I explained. "You know, T-rex? Van-Rex?"

"Ah, now I see the correlation. What about Reilly? You probably have to order special from Lillian Vernon to get that on a toothbrush."

"Lillian Vernon! You shop there often?"

"It's Grandma's favorite store."

I laughed. "Reilly's my grandmother's maiden name. Mom thought she was having another boy. I have two older brothers."

We made more small talk in which Van revealed very little about himself.

"You're a softball player?" he said, referring to Huff's comment about my change-up.

"I was. I pitched for the University of Washington." I downplayed my ball career in case he wasn't a big fan of lady jocks.

"I like softball players," he said and I couldn't really tell if he was flirting or not. "Jenny Finch. Cat Osterman. Hot." He grinned. "I've always liked tall girls."

"So you're a pitcher, first baseman kind of guy?" I asked, flirting back. Hey, if mark number one bails, it's off to mark number two. Not that Van was necessarily my second choice.

"Give me a girl in a ponytail any day."

At that outrageous comment, I had to laugh. "We use them for intimidation, you know," I said. "Stretched out to my full five ten with a high ponytail giving me several inches I can really psych out a batter."

"It's all those crazy ribbons in the ponytails you softball girls wear that distract me. They turn me on." He grinned like a bad boy, but I could tell he was teasing about the ribbons.

"You have a thing for schoolgirls?"

"No, I like the grown-up kind of girl. And for the record—bet you couldn't psych me out."

Bet I'd like to try.

"I'll rise to that challenge. If Huff finds me a softball, I'll make you eat your words."

"You're on. But I warn you—I was a hell of a

Little Leaguer." He paused. "And I played college baseball on scholarship."

Even better. I knew there was a reason I liked him. I had a thing for baseball players.

"What position did you play?"

"Guess."

"First base."

"Bingo."

We discussed the finer points of baseball and softball, stats, our favorite teams and players, and the merits of serving garlic fries at stadiums.

When the discussion heated to the point of becoming a no-win argument, he changed the subject. "What do you do now?"

"I'm vice president of sales and marketing for 3D Sportswear."

I told him about the company. How we'd started out making athletic gear for women. Our ace in the hole was a line of sports bras for full-figured girls.

"Most sports bras only support up to a C cup," I said, giving him my spiel. "We make comfortable, moisture-wicking, well-supported bras for the D cup and beyond. No woman wants to be a joggler."

"Joggler?"

"A jogger who jiggles."

Talk about breasts and a man will naturally be tempted to look. I couldn't help noticing Van's gaze flicking between mine and my face. And, yep, I was a double-D cupper myself.

"Double D, I get," he said. "Where does the third D in 3D come from?"

I smiled. Boys!

"The three musts for an athlete—drive, dedication, determination. Those are our three Ds. Yours is a common misperception."

He didn't even have the good grace to look embarrassed. "When are you going to confess to being the 3D Sportswear Girl?"

I laughed and stared into my daiquiri. "I *was* the 3D girl. No longer." Since the scandal with Ket, I'd been forced behind the scenes. I left the thought there and tried to forget about the scars.

"*Sports Illustrated* swimsuit edition two years ago. Your 3D ad was opposite the first page of the swimsuit spread. Straight up I thought you should have been the centerfold."

I smiled down into my watery drink and stirred it idly with my straw to hide my embarrassment. "Thanks. Paid ads don't make the centerfold."

"They should."

I had to bite my tongue to keep from blurting out, "You think I'm pretty!"

I remembered the ad he referred to all too well. The picture was a side shot of me squatting. I was wearing a red sports bra and boy shorts. Very tiny boy shorts. And tennis shoes. And glistening with the glow of exercise. My hair was pulled into a high ponytail. My right side faced the camera.

And for good reason. My left arm bore a bruise the exact replica of Ket's handprint, so clear a crime scene investigator could have dusted it for prints. My left eye was black, covered by makeup, my hair, lighting, and the angle of the pose.

"Reilly?"

I hadn't been aware I'd been lost in reverie. "Sorry.

Just reminiscing about my glory days. You're the second guy tonight to remember me in *SI*."

He regarded me silently, ignoring my reference to Huff. "Playing softball and modeling for endorsements, that's some life."

I suppose it sounded that way to a math professor.

"Yeah, a real fairy tale." I came off too bitter.

He cocked a brow, obviously surprised by my reaction.

"Sorry." I laughed to cover. "That came out wrong. Modeling for 3D wasn't really an endorsement, not like the big athletes get. I just sort of fell into it." Back when my life was charmed.

"How does one just 'fall into' an international modeling campaign? A talent scout for the Ford Agency showed up at the diamond one day?" He was ribbing me, probably thinking I was being falsely modest.

"Almost right. My neighbor did."

Van looked like he was expecting an explanation. You know me, I fill silences.

"Before she founded 3D, Dara Light lived across the street from my parents," I said. "She was a big fan of mine when I played for Kentwood High School." Thinking of Dara, I smiled. "Dara's a lady jock, a buxom fireplug of a woman.

"My sophomore year in college I was playing summer ball, giving private pitching lessons, and working at the U's softball summer camp for girls. One day when I was home visiting, Dara popped over. She'd been working on a sports bra for the full-figured woman. She was putting together a brochure to take to potential investors and needed a 'hot, young, athletic thing' to model it and I fit the bill. Plus I worked for free.

"Dara got her financing thanks, she claimed, to how sexy I looked in the bra. She insisted that I was *the* look of 3D and kept me on as 3D took off. She started paying me, gave me free sports bras and I just kept modeling for her. Things grew from there. I quit modeling last year and helped Dara run the campaign to find the next 3D girl." I'd reached the unhappy part of the story. I didn't feel like talking anymore. I glanced at my watch. "It's getting late. I should turn in."

"I'll walk you back," Van said.

I was hoping he would. Safety rule number one for stalking victims—never go anywhere alone.

"Great! Would you mind swinging through the lobby with me? The desk clerk promised me a new room."

He looked at me quizzically.

"Mine smells of smoke," I said, covering. "I asked for nonsmoking. I'm allergic." Well, I'm allergic to matchbooks left by stalkers. Plus I needed to mail that letter.

In the lobby, I slipped Huff's letter from my pocket into the mail drop in one swoop. Stealthy as I tried to be, I didn't have Huff's dexterity. Van caught a glimpse of my postal action.

"Mailing postcards already?" he asked.

"There's nothing that says 'I love you' like a free postcard. Mom likes that I remember her."

"Geez! Your mom's easy to please. Maybe she could talk to mine."

I shrugged. There was a different clerk at the desk than the one I'd spoken to earlier. I gave her my name, saying that I was switching rooms, hoping I didn't have to re-explain everything. But the other guy seemed to have taken care of things and filled her in.

"We have three rooms available," she said. "Room one forty-two."

"That would be ground floor?" I asked.

She nodded.

"No, thanks. I don't do ground floor."

"Room seven fifteen?" She looked optimistic.

I made her show it to me on a map. "Next to the fire escape. No good."

"That leaves . . . six twenty-three." She sounded hesitant. "But that's on the same floor. You may experience the same allergy problem as before—"

"She'll take it," Van said, looking from her to me. "That's right next to mine."

I agreed and the girl made my new key.

"You'll have one more entry on your old key, to allow you to gather your things and move to the new room," she said as she handed the key over. "That'll complete your transfer."

"Great. Thanks so much." I debated whether to dismiss Van. Only I couldn't quite make myself do it. Which gave me no choice. I had to speak again to the clerk in front of him. "I need you to keep my new room number confidential. Can you make a note not to give it out to anyone? Not even my mother. Not even me."

Evidently, the girl didn't feel like asking questions was part of her job. She'd probably heard it all. She tapped something in on her computer and that was that.

"I'm surprised you didn't ask to speak with the hotel security manager," Van said as we walked away toward the elevators.

"Tips from *Oprah*," I said. "A woman traveling alone can't be too careful."

"This has nothing to do with winning another 'I've been spied' shirt?" His tone was light. I don't think I threw him off the scent, though.

When we reached my old room, my hand shook as I tried to insert the key card.

"May I?" Van took the key card and opened the door.

"No!" I grabbed his arm as he prepared to enter.

He paused and gave me a curious look, which I ignored as I scanned the room from the doorway. Ket had a bad habit of sliding warning messages under doors. Fortunately, I didn't see any.

"Okay. Looks like FSC didn't pull any more tricks," I said, trying to slide past Van. But he held me back.

"I'll go in first. You stay here until I give the all clear. Here, hold our uniforms." He was polite enough not to call me a big, fat chicken as he handed me our new wardrobes. For all he knew I was overreacting to the staged break-in.

I kept an eye on him as he stepped into the bathroom. "Everything okay in there?"

"Nothing here but soap, towels, and toilet paper." He stepped back out and checked the closet.

I noticed he was frowning. "Something wrong?"

Dear God, don't let him have found another calling card from Ket, I thought. My heart raced with fear at the mere thought.

Van slid the closet door closed without comment and I relaxed a little. He took a step into the room and spied my packed suitcase sitting on the suitcase stand by the dresser and turned back to look at me. "You're certainly prepared. Everything zipped up and ready to go."

"Yep. That's me."

He picked up my suitcase. "I'll carry this for you."

"You mean, wheel for me?"

He grinned. Across the hall, he performed the all-clear inspection in my new room before taking the suitcase stand from the closet, setting it up, and depositing my luggage on it. "There you go," he said, "you're all settled in."

Only I wasn't quite. I'd set our uniforms down and had my back to him. Ignoring him, I inspected the deadbolt lock and security latch on the door.

He came up behind me. "More *Oprah* tips?"

"A girl can never be too careful."

"Let me take a look. I have some experience with locks."

I stepped back out of his way and over to my luggage. I know it was cowardly, but on the off chance that Ket, or someone, had stuffed a little present in my suitcase, I wanted to open it while Van was still there. Fortunately, my suitcase came up clean and so did the locks.

We finished our inspections simultaneously. Van came over to where I stood in front of the luggage rack between the dresser and the adjoining room door.

"The locks are good," he said, standing very near me, crowding in on the heart of my personal space so close I could feel his body heat.

"Great." He was distractingly good-looking. He smelled delicious, too. Scientists say that if you like someone's scent it's a good indicator of compatibility. Well . . . I loved his. And the best part was he smelled completely different than Ket. The smell of Ket's signature cologne was an automatic turn-off. I rejected any man who wore it. "Thanks." I felt almost shy and suddenly nervous as I looked up into his eyes.

"You going to be okay here tonight by yourself?" His question sounded more like concern than a come-on. I wasn't sure if I was disappointed by that or not. Part of Ket's legacy was that I didn't trust my judgment in men anymore.

"I'll be fine."

He reached an arm past me and thumped the adjoining room door. "I'll be just on the other side of this door. I'm going to unlock my side. If you need anything, come on over."

I nodded. Up close, I could see the golden flecks in his eyes. Our lips were so close, it would have been too easy to lean into a kiss. Only I panicked and looked down.

He took his cue and stepped back. "Until tomorrow then."

I walked him to the door and locked up behind him, thinking what a big, scared dummy I was. One little kiss, what would that have hurt?

The thing was, I liked Van. Probably way too much for having just met him. Though he looked like he could take care of himself, he was a math professor, not a cop or an FBI agent or something. Not someone who was equipped to deal with a maniacal Ket.

I sighed. I'd had very few dates, and no real relationship, since Ket. And it was going to be hell starting one if I rejected every guy I genuinely liked because I feared I was bringing danger their way.

I hated being scared and vulnerable. By the end of camp, I intended to be a stronger, more confident woman.

I eyed the adjoining door. Thinking of Van getting ready for bed on the other side, I smiled.

Chapter 5

Breakfast at 0700 seemed cruelly indecent after the night I'd had. The beer-daiquiri drinking mix from the night before was a definite do-not-repeat combo. Dreams of Van are best not interrupted by visions of Ket in slasher mode. I woke frustrated and tired. And too scared to go to the hotel weight room for my usual morning exercise.

I preferred getting up, working out, and grabbing breakfast—an energy bar and a skinny, nonfat, sugar free, vanilla latte—on the fly. I've never been haute couture or world class and maybe my eating habits explained why.

I would have bagged breakfast altogether and headed for the bus at 0730, but I got the feeling that I'd need a protein hit to get through the day. Plus I didn't like the thought of all the macho men being at breakfast, leaving me to a mostly deserted hotel floor.

So I dragged my butt out of bed, pulled my hair into a high, intimidation ponytail, and hit the showers. When I got out, I dressed in my form-hugging

3D black, moisture-wicking tee, combat boots, and BDU. I decided against the natural look in makeup and went with smoky and hot. One thing I'd learned from my modeling days was how to apply makeup for just about any occasion. When I was satisfied that I looked reasonably like Lara Croft, Tomb Raider, and was ready to kick some spy-wannabe boy butt, I prepared to head out.

But first, I locked my purse in the in-room safe. I tucked my key card and a lipstick in one of those travel neck pouches and slid my cell phone in my pocket. *Now* I was ready.

When I opened my room door, Van was lounging just outside it, waiting for me.

"Ohmygosh! You scared me to death," I said, hand to heart. And it was only a slight exaggeration. I don't know what was worse, the fact that Van had caught me jumpy or realizing that Ket could have just as easily been lying in wait. "What are you doing skulking in hallways?"

"Waiting to walk you to breakfast."

"Oh. Thanks." If I hadn't been annoyed with myself, I would have tried to sound more appreciative. Maybe even flirted.

Van looked tousled and dewy-eyed and I liked my men that way. He looked way more attractive in his BDUs than I did in mine. Face it. BDUs were designed with the male physique in mind.

"You shower and clean up quickly . . . for a woman." He was grinning.

I didn't have to ask how he knew that. He'd probably been listening to the shower.

"I didn't wash my hair," I said to be flippant.

"When we don't have to wash, condition, and dry yards of hair, we can be just as fast as men."

"That's what I'm counting on," he said. Only the way he said it implied another meaning.

I ignored him and ran off at the mouth. "If you want to keep hair healthy, you should only wash it two or three times a week, tops."

"I didn't know. *Oprah* tell you that?" he said as we walked to the elevator. "You forgot to complain about how women have to put on makeup. If they went barefaced, that would save a lot of time, too." He pushed the button to call the elevator. "I'm not complaining. I like what you did with your eyes."

I couldn't help smiling. At least that effort hadn't been wasted.

Breakfast was supposed to be served in a small, private dining room off the main restaurant. To get to it, we had to take the elevator down from our floor and walk through the lobby.

When the elevator doors opened, I barely recognized our stop. The lobby looked like the invasion of the Seattle Women's Fair—wall-to-wall ladies, hundreds of them and more arriving by the minute, their lavender-wheeled suitcases and sample bags trailing behind them. A welcome table had been strategically placed by the hall to the main conference area. A line snaked around it. At the table, a heavily bejeweled woman handed out name tags and goody bags.

My first thought was Mary Kay Convention. Only there was a shocking lack of makeup and pink. However, what the women lacked in makeup, they made up for with a profusion of jewelry dangling off earlobes, looping around necks and waists, and cuffing wrists in coordinated sets.

Beside me, Van hesitated before stepping out of the elevator. Probably overwhelmed by so much estrogen. I thought he mumbled, "Holy shit."

Before we could move, we were accosted by one of them.

"Cindi Lou Jewelry. Cayla Smith, regional director." A tall, brunette woman about my age approached me and extended her hand. Her gaze flicked between Van and me as she obviously tried to make out our relationship.

"R," I said, shaking her hand, thinking how great code names were. I made it a habit never to give out complete personal info to strangers. Like full names. Maybe I was a bit of a worry freak. But so be it.

Cayla's eyes held the hint of a question, but her smile didn't waver. She was too busy appraising me, taking in my battle gear garb and distinct absence of accessories.

"Nice to meet you, R. And this is?" She was looking at Van. Well, in my opinion it was hard *not* to look at Van, not if you appreciated masculine eye candy. So I forgave her. "This is V."

"You're not here for our convention, are you?" She was talking to me but still looking at Van.

"No," I said, trying to draw her attention back to me. "I suppose my lack of jewelry gave me away?"

She laughed. "You could say." Her gaze ran over my garb. "Military?"

"Vacation."

She didn't have to voice her thoughts. As she

twirled her long, loopy ribbon and bead necklace around her fingers, you could see the wheels turning. What kind of a vacation required camo and combat boots? I had the feeling she thought we were some kind of paramilitary freaks. Or maybe white supremacists who'd escaped from the wilds of Idaho for a vacation in the big city. But the real question was written on her face—how in the world was she going to sell jewelry to GI Jane? Would GI Joe buy it for me?

"We have a very nice line of military-inspired jewelry," Cayla said, undaunted, a hint to Van in her voice. She produced her card from her oversized purse and handed it to me. "Are you staying in the hotel?"

"Uh-huh."

"Great! We're having a benefit show tomorrow night that's open to the public. Free admittance. We'll be showcasing our new fall line. Half the proceeds benefit breast cancer research. Be sure to pop by. And if you'd like to take a look at our selection before the show, stop by my room, six twenty-two."

Maybe it was just me, but I thought she put in a big hint to Van there.

Then it struck me—622!

Curses! She was staying in my old room, the matchbook-haunted one. Which didn't bode well on two fronts—one, it was right across the hall from me. I recognized the light of rising to a challenge in her saleswoman eyes. I'd just become her next project. Or maybe Van had. Or both of us. Anyway, she was sure to find out where I "lived." And two—I suddenly had a horrible vision of Ket breaking in in the dark and mistaking her for me. Not that she looked like me, but she fit my basic description. Huddled under the covers with her brown hair peeking out, she'd pass for yours truly.

One of the sickest things about being a stalking victim is the guilt you feel for always putting others in danger. It makes for a lonely world.

I tried not to look too shaken and assumed my woman-to-woman-word-of-advice tone. "You shouldn't be giving out your room number or answering your door for strangers, or even hotel staff."

She looked skeptical and like I was probably a jealous hag over Van.

"Let me guess—*Oprah* tip? You just saw a show on safety for women travelers?"

Poor Oprah! She always gets the blame.

"Not exactly," I said, hoping I wasn't coming off like a crackpot alarmist. "I overheard the hotel staff discussing some jerk who's been hanging around and trying to pick up women in the bar and lobby. He's . . . overly persistent. And he's been seen following them to their rooms."

Her eyes widened and I decided I'd better soften things up a bit, so I added, "So far, he's been chased off without doing any harm."

I couldn't help pausing for dramatic effect.

"I wouldn't open my door for anyone, not unless I was sure it was someone I knew well. And beware tall, dark, handsome strangers."

Her gaze flicked back to Van. Yeah, she definitely thought I was being territorial. He *was* tall, dark, and handsome. But so far he didn't seem like a jerk. Besides, he wasn't mine. I really was being altruistic with my warning.

I didn't mean to sound like Madame Reilly, the all-knowing prognosticator of doom. I really didn't. Nor did I mean to scare Cayla. But what could I do? I had to dispel her of the jealous theory. I had to keep her on her guard.

I gave her a loose description of Ket. Just as Cayla and I fit the same general description, so did Van and Ket. But they didn't look the same. Not at all. Ket had several inches and thirty pounds or so on Van. I hoped she'd see the difference and take my warning to heart.

I finished by saying, "You might warn the other women."

It wouldn't hurt to have a couple hundred more pair of eyes keeping a watch out for Ket. For her sake and mine.

Cayla nodded. "Thanks for the tip."

Her thanks was so insincere, she may as well have done the heavenward glance. She'd barely tolerated listening to my warning. And I'm pretty sure she thought it was bogus.

"You *will* be at the benefit, won't you?"

Only I think she was looking more at Van than me.

As we walked away, Van caught my arm. I paused to look up at him.

"What's this about a man hanging around? Since when did you hear the staff talking?"

I shrugged and started walking. "I dunno. Must have been yesterday." Which was kind of wiseass because when else could it have been?

"Something or someone has you spooked."

Despite his intimidating, penetrating stare, I didn't validate his accusation. I didn't deny it, either.

"You don't strike me as the flighty, high-strung type so I'm going out on a limb and saying it's not the FSC break-in gag. If I had to guess, I'd say it's a six four, two hundred twenty pound, dark-haired man . . ." He went on to repeat my description of Ket.

By the time he finished, we'd reached the breakfast room.

"Let's eat! I'm starving," I said, ignoring his question. I might have been leery of having a fling or anything else with Van for his own safety, but I didn't feel like scaring him away completely by telling him about twisted Ket, the celebrity trainer/gym owner turned stalker, just yet. Van wasn't a big, bad PI like Huff.

Our run-in with the jewelry queen in the lobby made us late for breakfast. When we finally arrived, all the boys were present except Huff.

"There's two more." Cliff sat at a table, eating a half of grapefruit. Taking my suggestion, he'd commandeered a pair of scissors from somewhere and hacked off his camo pants at the knees, exposing his stumpy, hairy legs.

I should have kept my mouth shut about the scissors.

"Huff with you?" Cliff seemed edgy.

"No. Isn't he here?" I asked. "Nice shorts."

Cliff mumbled a thanks.

"He's probably just sleeping in," Steve said, standing in front of the buffet with a look of disgust on his face as he surveyed the breakfast offerings.

I glanced at the clock on the wall over the buffet. It was 0715 already. "If Huff doesn't hurry, he'll miss out on the chow." Such as it was.

"He'd do better to join us at the bus," Steve said.

I took one look at the breakfast spread and agreed with Steve. "Continental breakfast? Where's the real food? I need a protein fix."

Van and I grabbed a plate and started through the line. The spread was disappointing, heavy on sweets and carbs, and lacking in substantive protein.

I turned to Van. "Do you think they swapped our breakfast with the jewelry ladies'? They're probably complaining about eggs loaded with cheese, nice fat sausages, and stick-to-the-ribs oatmeal. How are we going to go to combat on this?"

Van just smiled, looking like he could go to combat on an empty stomach.

I finally settled for a cup of yogurt, some granola, and fruit. I think I'd have been better off with my energy bar.

At 0728, we all headed to the FSC bus that was waiting for us out in front of the hotel in the passenger pickup zone. Huff still hadn't showed. Van asked the driver to wait and ran inside to the front desk to have them ring Huff's room. Peewee and I tagged along after him.

When the front desk got no response to their call, Peewee tried Huff's cell. "Voice mail. I think he's got it turned off."

Out of options, the three of us headed up to Huff's room to smoke him out.

Peewee banged on the door with a fist that could've doubled as a meat tenderizing mallet. "Huff, you lazy son of a bitch." He let loose with a string of cursing. "Get up and answer the damn door!"

I would have used politer language. But I wasn't willing to step in as Miss Manners, not when Peewee was that hacked off. Besides, I had the feeling that foul language was his mother tongue.

A guy in the room next door poked his head out. "What the shit's going on out here?" That was the genteel part of the spew of curses that followed. Brave, or maybe foolhardy, soul.

Peewee gave him a look that would have silenced me for life. "None of your business."

Van stepped between them and apologized before things got uglier.

The guy finally ducked back into his room with a slam of his door.

Van turned to us. "Let's go. Huff's not here."

"Where do you think he is?" I asked, frustrated as we gave up on rousing Huff from the hopefully not dead, and headed back to the bus before the driver gave up on us.

"No idea. I'm sure he'll turn up eventually. He's a big boy. He can take care of himself," Van said, but I noticed he kept glancing back at Huff's room as we walked to the elevator.

"He better not be off screwing around with one of the jewelry ladies," Peewee said, sounding more like someone who's been double-crossed in a business deal than a concerned buddy and fellow CT. Annoyed didn't even begin to describe his tone.

As I pressed the button to call the elevator, Peewee flicked a glance at me as if he'd suddenly remembered who was with them. "Sorry about back there. Huff's not a one-woman man. Better you know."

I blushed, not happy that Van overheard.

"Yeah," I said distractedly. I had a bad feeling about Huff's no-show status. A guy didn't spend thousands of dollars on an extreme vacation, fly up from California to take it and then just blow off the first exciting morning of it. Not even for a quick screw with a babe clad only in fabulous costume jewelry. I turned to Van. "Maybe we should leave word at the front desk to call one of us if Huff shows up."

Yeah, I'm a bit of a mother hen with a side of worrier thrown in. A habit born from too many years of worrying about adventurous, irrepressible brothers.

Van raised a skeptical eyebrow at me.

As the elevator doors opened at the lobby, I turned toward the front desk, intent on following through.

Van caught my arm. "I'll take care of it. You two go hold the bus for me."

Obedient to a fault, I headed toward the bus. At the top of the bus stairs, I paused to look back into the lobby and caught a glimpse of Van flipping open his cell phone before he turned his back to the bus. Now whom would he be calling?

Chapter 6

"No luck?" Jim asked as Peewee and I boarded, and Van ran for the bus.

Peewee scowled his answer and headed for the backseat of the small, airporter-type van.

I fell into a seat across from Jim, my eyes glued out the window on Van. Whoever he'd called hadn't been the chatty type. I'd bet his callee wasn't a woman. My relief shouldn't have been so palpable, but I was a woman only *potentially* on the make. Until I could at least fully commit to the chase, I didn't need any competition from unseen women on the other end of phone calls. Things were complicated enough.

I watched Van appreciatively. The man had such fine running form, my toes curled. Ask anyone. I'm a sucker for gracefully moving muscles and sinew. I watched a lot of track and field. I loved instant replays in slow motion. Anyway, Van was barely breathing hard as he swung into the stairwell and boarded the bus.

Jim cleared his throat. "Get the *Chariots of Fire* theme out of your head, girl."

"*Chariots of Fire*, are you kidding? I'm not that sentimental," I said, grinning as I turned my attention from Van to him. "Where do *you* think Huff is?"

Jim shrugged, noncommittally.

"Huff has a flare for the dramatic," Cliff chipped in with amusement, and only a slight hint of annoyance, in his voice. He flashed a knowing, and undeniably pleased, look at Jim that could have doubled for a wink. "He'll probably be waiting for us at the warehouse."

"Or show up late in a limo to make a grand entrance," Jim added, also in good humor.

I wondered at their apparent pleasure in Huff's absence. Just what did they know?

Van walked past. "All taken care of," he said as he took the seat behind me.

"Where do *you* think Huff is?" I asked him, sounding like a one-question-wonder, as he settled in and pulled out a pocket-size Sudoku book.

"Swimming with the sharks." He was grinning.

"Stop it," I said. "I'm worried."

He arched a brow. "You think he's in trouble?"

Despite Cliff and Jim's buoyant mood, I *was* concerned that something horrible had happened to Huff. Something in the form of retribution from a celebrity trainer gone mad. Accepting a public hug and dance with Huff yesterday had been flirting with danger.

"Why wouldn't he show up for the exciting first day of spy camp? Tell me that. This is the premier, action-packed vacation in the country. The brochure says so." I gave Van a pointed look.

"He hasn't missed the day yet." Van opened the book and pulled out a nub of a pencil. "Maybe he doesn't like buses."

"He never mentioned it."

Van gave me a look that could have been construed as either slightly jealous, or just plain sarcastic. "Lying in a ditch syndrome."

"What?"

"You heard me."

"You sound like my brothers."

"Yeah? Probably because I have a mother and two older sisters who are always imagining the worst. Can't say it's an attractive trait." He grinned and pretended to be engrossed in his puzzle so that he could ignore my glare.

Which left me to admire the top of his head, covered as it was with his thick, wavy, finger-stroking good hair. "It's better than indifference."

Van grinned and gestured toward his book, making me an offer. "Puzzle?"

I ignored his meaning. "Yes. This business is, isn't it? Now if only we could work together to solve it." I put a finger to my lips, posing in the thoughtful look. "But wait! That would require your participation."

He refused to rise to the bait. "Sure? Numbers will keep your mind off your troubles."

I gave him a seriously skeptical look. "The only numbers I want right now are the four-one-one." I leaned over and whispered again, nodding toward Peewee behind Van. "What do you make of Peewee?

He's been huddled back there looking like the Black Spy and making secretive phone calls since we boarded."

Van didn't even look up. "Everyone has their own way of killing time."

I thumped back in my seat. "You're no help, you know that?"

He kept grinning and working on his puzzles.

To divert myself from my own worst imaginings, I feigned interest in the passing scenery, and listened in to my fellow CTs' conversations.

Jim and Cliff chatted, falling quickly into a discussion of business matters. Cliff complained to Jim about one of his bevy of ex-wives bleeding him dry. Jim promised that he had things under control and soon they'd be able to legally outwrangle her.

From time to time, both Jim and Cliff cast glances at unsociable, cell phone engrossed Peewee. They were obviously acquainted with him and viewed him as an intruding tagalong on the vacation. A barnacle that attaches himself to the action and can't be shaken loose without a whole lot of prying.

Steve sat in the seat in front of Cliff, waiting for his chance to insert himself into Cliff and Jim's conversation. Obviously, he was a big fan of Cliff's. When Cliff hazarded to mention his current film, Steve belly flopped right in, drenching any remnants of their old conversation with his own fawning opinions about movies, Cliff's in particular.

Listening to them for just a short while, I was able to determine that Cliff had directed a slew of successful action/adventure flicks. Nothing I'd seen or was likely even to rent.

Eventually, I couldn't contain my curiosity about Cliff's choice of vacation. I interrupted, with feigned admiration. "Cliff, your life sounds far from mundane. What brings you on a vacation like this?"

"Sacrifice for the craft." Cliff winked at Steve, as if the girl is hot for my bod.

Feigned admiration was not the same thing as flirtation. With Van handy, although admittedly busy putting numbers one through nine into little squares, which would have been horribly dweebish if he so obviously wasn't, would I really resort to flirting with the roly-poly dough spy?

"Experimenting," Cliff added. "Putting myself in a scenario where *I* feel what the characters will feel. So that I can then convey those emotions to my actors."

"You're filming a hostage movie?" I guessed.

"Begin shooting on Monday. Right after I get back from Seattle."

"Wonderful," I said. "When will your new flick be released?"

"Next year about this time."

"Oh." I sighed. "It'll be a long year waiting for it to come out."

"I'll send you tickets to the premier," Cliff said.

"Can't wait."

I turned to Steve wondering aloud at his reasons for attending FSC Urban spy training.

"My ex-wife is back at court asking for more child support and alimony. If I don't blow my cash on fun, that bitch gets it." Then he shrugged.

* * *

The trip from the hotel to the FSC facility took roughly half an hour. Conversation came to a standstill as the bus pulled to a stop in front of a warehouse. The camp brochure said the training facility was thirty thousand square feet, complete with a firing range and mock city scenes. From the outside, it looked like a big, ugly box.

We all piled out and filed into the building. Inside, the warehouse was like a miniature Universal Studios, a great big playhouse for adults.

"It *is* just like a movie set," I said with a bit of a gush. "Main Street meets *Rambo*." I turned to Cliff for verification.

"It's good," he said as War walked over to greet us.

"Welcome to FSC City," War said, encompassing the facility with a sweep of his arms. "You like?"

"I think I speak for all of us," I said, "when I say, gee, it's big and huge and . . . look it has cars and streets and everything. What's not to like? Really."

Next to me, Van rolled his eyes. "Laying it on a little thick, aren't we?" he whispered as War extolled the site's features.

"When was the last time you saw cars and streets inside a building?" I asked him. "Not to mention an indoor firing range capable of withstanding submachine gunfire?"

"Point taken."

"You could have fought a little harder," I said, goading him for fun. "The Boeing facility in Everett has whole planes, great big ones, inside. It's probably even better. You should take a tour."

"I'll remember that for next time," Van said, grinning.

I think he liked me.

If Cliff and Jim were expecting an exuberant greeting from Huff, they were sorely disappointed. He was nowhere in sight. And believe me, it was obvious everyone was looking for him.

"Someone's missing," War said, suddenly realizing the group was small.

"Huff didn't show up for the bus," I said.

War didn't look happy. "No one's seen him?"

We all shook our heads.

War wrinkled his brow in consternation and excused himself to call Huff's cell and then the hotel.

"We already tried that. No answer," Steve called after him.

War simply waved him off. He returned a few minutes later. "If anybody hears from H, let me know immediately." Then he launched right into the program, giving a brief overview of the day ahead.

Boiled down to its essence, the day was equipment issue—helmets, body armor, radio, pistol, ammo, and MP-5 submachine gun. Instruction on handling the equipment. Lunch. Weapons firing and classes. Bus ride back to the hotel. Free time. And a whole lot of eager anticipation and speculation about Huff. Not that War mentioned that.

I'd been fitted for my body armor and helmet and was feeling a bit like Bat Girl, cool, black, and invincible, when my cell phone played "Take Me Out to the Ball Game" from my pocket.

War shot me a dirty look.

I shrugged. "Guess I should have remembered to put it on vibrate."

His glare didn't stop me from stepping away from the group and answering it. "Take Me Out to the Ball Game" meant a call from one of the group of girlfriends I used to hang with at Ket's gym back in the day. We'd been a tight group. We kept in touch.

I looked at my screen. Julie White. Hadn't heard from her in a while. It figured she'd catch me at a bad time.

"Jules, hey! It's been a long time—"

"He's out," Julie said, no preamble necessary. The fear in her voice told me who.

"What?" My suddenly hammering heart must have interfered with my normally wicked hearing. I clutched the phone until my knuckles went white, trying to maintain control over something.

"Ket's out." Julie sounded worried and incredibly apologetic, like, hey don't shoot the messenger. "I just hung up with him."

I cursed under my breath.

"Rei, I'm worried," Julie said. "He sounded, you know . . . charmingly pissed. Like he was just calling to chat and catch up, find out who you'd been seeing—"

"Out? How in the world did he get out? Did he finally talk?"

"Some kind of legal snafu," Julie said, trying to sound calming. "I'd just heard it on the local news and was going to call you when he called me. The court didn't confirm the contempt order within the required number of days after jailing him."

I cursed inept court officials under my breath, hoping it would make me feel brave and tough.

"If the court affirms the contempt order, they can still throw Ket back in." Julie's voice wavered, giving away her optimism as false.

"If they can find him." I balled my fists, feeling like hitting something and crying at the same time. I'd hoped he'd rot in jail until his anabolic steroid use sent him to an early grave. Shot his liver or ruined his heart like prolonged use was *supposed* to do.

"He asked me to deliver a message to you," Julie said softly, timidly.

My mouth went dry. The clever jerk. If he *could* somehow find out my new cell number, he knew I'd never pick up his call. "Oh, he did, did he?"

Julie hesitated. "He said he loves you. That he knows you love him, too—"

"I don't love Ket! I hate him. Hate him with every fiber of my being." I took a deep breath, trying to calm the trembles that had come over me. "I wish I didn't. Really. I'd love to be apathetic."

"I know, Reilly. I have to tell you the rest." Poor Julie, I could tell it was the last thing she wanted to do. "He said he's coming for you."

"Coming for me? To make amends, I suppose?" I said with all the sarcasm I possessed. "Like slapping me with another restraining order?" I snorted, letting my anger chase my fear away. "That bastard—"

War drowned me out by barking out a command that started with "CTs, listen up!"

"Where are you?" Julie asked. "Basic training?"

"Someplace safe. Let's leave it at that."

"You'll be careful?"

"Always. I have to go now," I said. "Thanks for the warning." I disconnected and blew out another sigh before dialing Mom and Nicki with the news.

Neither was in. I left messages and put my phone away.

Van left the knot of CTs gathered around the ammo table and approached me. "You okay? You look like you've seen a ghost."

More like my future at the hands of a demon.

"I'm fine," I lied, wishing things were different, wondering if Ket would *ever* leave me alone.

I studied Van, liking the fine, sleek line he cut, the defined, natural shape of his musculature un-marred by steroid use. His intense expression of concern. How could I have ever backed away from his kiss last night? And yet I knew how. Or at least why. Ket.

"War's about to issue our submachine guns," Van said by way of tempting me back to the present. "You don't want to miss that."

"Submachine guns can blast bad guys to hell, right?" I said, fantasizing about a spray of bullets and a dead Ket.

"At the very least, purgatory."

"Good enough." I smiled, feeling less shaky and maybe a touch stronger and safer with Van there. "You're right. I don't."

As we walked back to rejoin the group, I looked

around for Huff. An irrational chill of worry for him ran down my spine. I shouldn't have flirted with him. Not in public. "Huff still hasn't shown up?"

"Not yet," Cliff answered for Van. He sounded surprisingly angry.

Chapter 7

Ace and Kyle joined us. We followed War to the firing range at the far end of the building. Van walked beside me silently, casting sidelong, inquiring glances my way. I think my comment about sending bad guys to hell had tipped him off that all was not well in vacationland. I replied with what I hoped was an enigmatic smile and not a cheesy, faked grin that would give my panic away. The truth was, I was spooked. Ket coming for me meant nothing good.

Fear clung to me like the sticky remains of a cobweb I'd inadvertently walked through—unseen, but felt, even after I tried my darnedest to brush it off.

My phone rang again, playing "Take Me Out to the Ball Game" for the second time in less than an hour. I jumped, pulled the phone out and set it to vibrate without answering, flashing the others an apologetic look. I barely glanced at the number that popped up on the screen. Sheila. I didn't have to pick up to know what she was calling about. I couldn't handle a second account of Ket on the loose with as much relative aplomb as I had the first time.

Damn him! Ket was calling everyone with dual-fold purpose—intimidate and find me.

And his diabolical plan was working well on the first front of attack—intimidation. Suddenly there was movement in every shadow. Eyes watching me from the rafters. Goose bumps on my arms. Even surrounded by three well-trained former military guys and five other healthy men, I felt defenseless and scared.

Ket could be calling from anywhere. For all I knew, he was already in Seattle. He had friends with private planes and even a commercial flight from LA took only a few hours. In fact, I was certain he was in the city somewhere, prowling my hometown for me. It was only logical.

Still I had no call from the California penal system telling me to hide, young Reilly! Run!

"Not in a chatty mood?" Van asked beside me.

When I stared at him blankly, he nodded toward my phone.

"Pesky friends," I said. "They're dying of curiosity about my vacation. Why would any sane woman go to spy camp?"

"Good question," he said.

I didn't answer.

"You're not going to berate me for apparently questioning your sanity?" he asked.

"I'm here for the same reason as the rest of you— for the adrenaline rush."

"Then why do you look so pale and frightened?"

"Are you calling me a scaredy-pants?" I said, trying to muster up some real indignation.

"That's my girl. That's more like it," Van said, not at all perturbed. "I like spunk." But he was still giving me the questioning look.

"A girl should know how to protect herself," I said. I was spared from further explanation.

We'd reached the firing range. War opened a gargantuan gun safe that looked like it housed the complete arsenal of Manuel Noriega.

"War'd better not let ATF find out about that," I whispered to Van, pointing to the safe. "We'll have another Waco on our hands."

"I'm guessing he has permits," Van replied.

War began giving instructions on how to handle the weapons. He started with the M9 pistol he was about to issue us. The M9 is a lightweight Berretta. Standard Army issue. It had a longer barrel than mine, but it shot the same 9mm rounds. I didn't anticipate any problems handling it. War referred to it as a "personal defense weapon," which somehow sounded less scary and more politically correct than gun. In theory it could be anything—pepper spray, a loud whistle, a billy club, a karate chop, even a really good, stern look accompanied by a scream.

War issued us each a PDW, then went on to explain how to handle, operate, and clean it before moving on to the next PDW, which was so much stronger, he could have referred to it as a mega PDW. I did.

"This is the MP-five submachine gun," War said, removing one and holding it up.

It was a real James Bond–type weapon. All the

guys were lathering at the mouth over it like it was a *Playboy* centerfold. I eyed it with caution and a certain amount of fear. You could do serious damage with that thing. In the wrong hands . . .

I leaned over and whispered to Van. "I'd like it better if it came with Pierce Brosnan as an accessory."

"A Bond Girl would be better."

"You think so? I disagree. I don't think you guys would even notice a Bond Girl right now. I could strip my shirt off and do a pole dance and not one of you would pay attention."

"Prove it." He flashed me a grin. "Go ahead, prove your point."

"Pervert," I said, grinning.

"Coward!" he said.

War kept talking. "The MP-five is designed for accuracy, fifteen to thirty rounds of nine millimeter caliber destruction." War patted it affectionately. "Black. Sleek. Small. You can holster it for covert use."

Assuming you wanted such a superbly deadly weapon next to your skin. Probably a rush for some people. Van would look hot with the MP-5 holstered beneath an Armani suit coat, gun carefully concealed.

Me? It wasn't my first choice of a fashion accessory. Thoughts of Van gave me a bigger rush.

I forced myself to relinquish my daydreams of Van as Bond and to pay attention to War's instructions on how to use the weapon. The old MP-5 would be a great equalizer between Ket and me. If

I could overcome my fear of it. Sadly, the odds were running against me.

I've been somewhat afraid of guns since I was eight and Grandpa Dutch, the very definition of the outdoor sportsman, taught me how to shoot beer cans off fence posts with a .22. Despite my gun shyness, I'd trained myself to be a pretty good shot with my Berretta. Fear of Ket had proven a great enough motivator for that accomplishment. But overcoming machine gun squeamishness was another matter altogether.

"Right hand on the pistol grip," War demonstrated. "Left hand on the forward handgrip. Thumb of the right hand sets the selector to 'safe.' Cocking handle is pulled to the rear with your left hand and hooked into the retaining notch. Insert magazine and clip home. Left hand uses a chopping motion to release the cocking handle. Right thumb sets the selector to single shot or automatic." He demonstrated each step, then stepped to the range and aimed at the target. "Aim and fire!"

The sound of automatic gunfire erupted. By the time War had dispensed his magazine, his target was thoroughly punctured in the center.

"When the magazine is empty, the working parts stay closed," he said. "Repeat process."

All the guys were grinning, their irritation at Huff's disappearance momentarily forgotten. I was playing tough, but the slender webs of fear still clung to me.

"We'll begin our shooting practice with the pistols," War said. "The M-nine is a great weapon in close quarter combat."

When it was my turn, I stepped up, donned the ear protection, and fired off two rounds with confidence.

"Two to the head," War said, looking over my shoulder as I took off the earmuffs. "Impressive. The FBI hostage rescue team could use you."

"Huh?"

"That was a compliment," War said. "Two to the head should be their motto."

"Whatever happened to negotiations?" I asked, feeling definitely uncomplimented.

"Nah," War shook his head like that was sissy stuff. "That's law enforcement. That's why law enforcement officers don't make good HRT men. They're used to dealing with distraught spouses and bank robbers. You can negotiate with those; wait them out forever. HRT deals almost exclusively with terrorist situations. Two to the head to whomever you encounter. Think Jack Bauer. He who hesitates is dead."

"Well, it's easy with a paper outline man," I said, self-deprecatingly. I felt a tiny stab of relief. As War had just said, Ket could, in theory, be negotiated with. Negotiation had worked last time. Sort of. "Paper man doesn't move. You don't see his soul in his eyes. And he's in a permanent state of hesitation."

"Still not easy to hit his head," War said.

"Why not go for his torso?" Steve asked. "It's the largest target."

"Not always as lethal. Not as quick a kill. Gives time for the terrorist to yell out and warn his fellow terrorists of an intrusion. Two to the head."

"Nice to know," I said.

We fired the pistols for another half hour, then War showed us how to clean them. Next he moved on to the submachine guns, going through the handling instructions again as we practiced with him. The pistol I could handle, this PDW, not so much.

Next to me, Van seemed perfectly comfortable with his.

"Have a lot of submachine gun experience?" I asked him.

He seemed startled. "What?" He laughed. "No. But it's a sleek instrument."

"I don't like it."

"Why?"

"It's too . . . too mobsterlike. Like modern-day Al Capone." I made some machine gun noises, which drew me a scowl from the instructors.

"Mobsterlike, that's an interesting comparison."

"Yeah, well, someone could get carried away. You know, just start shooting up the place."

Van held out his hand. "Give me the weapon. You obviously can't be trusted."

I spun it away from him. "I'm just kidding."

"Uh-huh."

"It's like walking through the china department," I said, returning to studying my PDW and practicing loading the magazine.

"Your logic is so easy to follow," Van said, heavy on the sarcasm. "Maybe you could just fill me in on the meaning."

"Haven't you ever been walking through the fine china department and had to put your hands in your pockets to stifle the urge to run through with your arms outstretched knocking dishes and crystal glasses to the floor?"

"You're a sick woman," he said, but he was smiling.

"And you're in denial. Everyone feels that way."

"And I still don't trust you with the weapon. Maybe I should tell War."

"Right." I grinned back. He was obviously teasing. "But I am worried about the kick."

"The kick. Afraid of being knocked on your butt?"

"Afraid of an accident."

He looked confused so I explained.

"Yeah, an accident, smart aleck. They had one at the firing range in Bellevue a few years ago. A woman was shooting. The gun kicked, sending her hand up over her head and back behind her. She still had her hand on the trigger and kept firing. Fortunately, no one was hurt. Can you imagine what would happen if someone did that with a sub-machine gun?" That was a true story, but I was rambling to get his goat.

"Urban legend," he said.

"Honest to God true fact," I countered.

"Use two hands, you'll be fine."

"Oh, I'm not worried about me," I said casually.

Chapter 8

Since the unseasonably warm fall weather continued unabated, the FSC staff decided to serve lunch al fresco on the terrace. Sounds fancy, but it meant we'd be eating at metal picnic tables on a concrete slab outside the warehouse, with a scintillating view of train tracks, miscellaneous equipment, other equally architecturally uninteresting warehouses, and to the south, towering over the tops of it all, Mount Rainier. Besides a great view of the awesome mountain, the terrace's only redeeming quality was the basketball hoop at one end and an ample supply of balls provided by FSC. For me, engaging in athletic activities has always been a fantastic way to shed stress. I shrugged off my camo jacket, snagged a ball, drove for the hoop, and dropped in a layup.

As I spun around for a repeat performance, I nearly collided with Van, who crouched in a guard position as if he'd been lying in wait for me.

"Up for a little one-on-one?" He'd lost his camo jacket, too, and looked not only game ready, but totally delectable. I liked a man with a challenge in his eye.

I made a point of sizing him up as I dribbled to the top of the key, letting my gaze linger where I liked. For as long as I liked. And I liked the strong set of his shoulders and the tight squeeze of his butt. Liked very much. Sizing up is always a good idea, especially when you like what you see. Size up the right way and you can even psych out.

Van was doing his share of size-up/psych out, only his gaze lingered in the vicinity of my double Ds, which were nicely showcased in my black 3D tank with built-in shelf bra, which had the same fine push-up, shove-together qualities as a top quality Victoria's Secret underwire number, only with more freedom for bounce. Actually, he wasn't so much psyching me out as budding me up. And grinning at his own power.

"Think you can take me, number boy?" I said and drove left around him toward the hoop.

"I think I'd liked to . . . take you," he said, close behind me, trying to reach around and knock the ball loose.

I laughed at his innuendo. "Shameless. Catch me if you can."

He was quick, but I was quicker. I put one up left-handed before he could check me.

"The girl's fast," he said as he retrieved the ball and bounced it back to me at the top of the key.

"You wish." I flashed him a grin as I crouched into position on the balls of my feet. I had a couple of choices—shoot from where I was, or drive past him. Driving had worked once. I faked left and drove right.

But Van was smart and had court sense. He was on me, blocking my every move and reaching playfully around for the ball, tossing out flirtatious jibes as I flirted back and drove around the court looking for a shot.

"You move like a girl," Van said.

"And you like it," I shot back.

He grinned. He reached in for the ball. I spun away. But not before his arm brushed my breast.

"You missed," I said.

"No I didn't." From the coy grin he was wearing, the breast brush was intentional.

"I meant the ball. Keep your head in the game," I said.

"Believe me, I'm trying," he whispered in my ear as he reached around again for the ball.

"Hey!" I slapped his hand away. "No reaching in."

"No slapping," he retorted as he reached around and knocked the ball loose.

"Foul!" I said, scrambling for the loose ball. "You caught my arm."

"I caught something, but it wasn't your arm," he said, coming up with the ball and taking it back to the top of the key.

Yeah, my breast again. Which is what had distracted me. I scowled at him.

"Lodge a complaint with the ref." He leaned low, dribbling slowly in place as I got into position to guard him. "You going to whine that this isn't a fair fight?" he said with mock compassion in his voice. "That I've got five inches on you so I should go easy?"

I rolled my eyes. "I've played taller than you. My brothers are six six and six seven." I smiled back at him. "Besides, I like it hard." I paused to let him digest that comment. "I have two points on you. Now put up or shut up."

He took off. I was right on him, swerving with him, tracking him, waving my hand in his face.

He laughed, spun around, dribbled back out and put up a long shot. "Swish!" He grinned, egging me on. "Two points."

"Lucky shot." I took the ball and dribbled back to the top of the key.

"Yeah, I'm a lucky guy." He caught the ball I tossed him. "Only I'd like to be luckier."

"Stop it."

"Am I making you lose your concentration?" he asked, eyeing my bounce. "Face it, you like the thought." Then he took off for the basket.

I got in front of him and boxed him out. He dribbled around playfully while I stayed in front of him, facing the basket, with my back and rump toward him.

Boxing out was a whole different maneuver the way Van played. With his hand on my butt to keep me away from the ball . . . and distracted. Definitely distracted. I'd play this game all day if it meant Van kept his hand on my booty.

"Intentional butt grab," I said, backing into him. "That's an offensive foul."

"Never heard of it." He gave me another playful squeeze.

Our heights were such that as I stuck my butt out to keep him back, it nestled directly into his crotch. His very hard crotch. Which gave me an all-over body tingle.

"Hey! Enough of the bump and grind out there!" Steve called from the sidelines. "Some of us have cash on this game. Someone score!"

"I'm trying," Van called back with a grin. He put up a shot, but it swirled around the rim and out.

I grabbed the rebound. Back to the top of the key and off to the basket again.

Van picked me up, hanging with me. I spun away from the basket, deciding to back him to the hoop. Only he was on me, literally. He had his hand on my butt as he checked me. I liked that, too. I liked it so much, I slowed my advance and stuck my butt out, right into his hand. Okay, it was part a distraction play. That's how I justified it, anyway.

"You like that," he said in my ear.

"No hands on the booty," I said, continuing my backward assault into him.

"Fine by me." He removed his hand, putting them both in the air so that I bumped directly into his . . . front booty.

I felt myself flush. "It's warm here in the sun," I said to cover.

"Scorching."

I twirled to go around him and take a shot. As I went up, his hand was in my face. As I came down, my bounce was in his. Instead of moving out of the way to let me land, he grabbed me with his arms around my legs just below my booty, my chest still in his face.

"Put me down." Only I didn't sound as decisive as I should have. His face nestled in my breasts was way too distracting. I was getting tingly all over, especially in my female region. "Put me down," I repeated.

"You missed." He slid me down, slowly, so that I felt every hard inch of muscle on his body against mine.

"Faster," I said, trying to sound commanding.

"Harder?"

"Stop it. The guys are watching," I said.

"Let them."

When we were eye to eye with my feet dangling several inches above the ground, he stopped. We locked gazes.

"I believe catching the shooter midair is a personal foul," I whispered. We were both glowing with exercise. Our lips moved very close, almost with minds of their own. "Though personally, I've never seen it done before."

"Personally, I don't think I have, either." He sounded thoughtful, and sexy. "What's the penalty?" He was angling in for a kiss.

"Has to be a big one," I said, eyeing his mouth. "You could be expelled from the game."

"Sounds good to me, if you come with me."

"Lunch is served," Ace called out, killing the mood from where he stood in front of a puke green army surplus table.

"Looks like you get your wish," I said to Van.

"Yeah." He sounded sorry.

Van set me down. I was relieved that my jelly legs held my weight. Van definitely had a knee-weakening effect on me.

"Gather round and grab your MREs. You two on the court, get over here," Ace barked. "Once everyone has a meal, I'll demonstrate how to heat them. Lady first."

"Excellent." I stepped away from Van in hopes my normal breathing pattern would soon return. He had me completely off-kilter. With relief, I took first place in line, noting that Ace was not bad-looking himself. So much male eye candy at camp, but the only one who sent my pulse into orbit was behind me in line standing a little too close.

"We'll continue the game later," Van whispered in my ear. "I owe you a free throw."

"Next time we'll play horse," I retorted, thinking it was safer . . . emotionally anyway. Before Van could respond, I turned to Ace and looked over the selection of packaged MREs before me. Anything to distract myself from Van. "What's on the menu today? Are we all eating the same thing or do we have a choice?"

"We have an excellent selection for your dining pleasure, ma'am," Ace said, waving his arm over the stack.

"Ma'am! How polite. How formal. How old it makes me feel! Call me R. Please." I gave him my helpless, flirtatious, pleading smile. I couldn't help myself. Van had toyed with me, turned me on, and now men looked good. Period.

"Done." Ace was all grins.

Yes, I am an equal-opportunity flirt.

"You were saying?" I asked. "The selection?"

He made a high-class waiter-type gesture and put

on the voice. "On the menu today—beefsteak with mushroom gravy—"

I made a face. "Mushrooms, ugh."

"Not a mushroom girl?" Ace smiled. "We have a fine selection of other entrees—ravioli, BBQ pork rib, hamburger patty, chili with macaroni, veggie burger—"

"Oh, for heaven's sake," Van said behind me, teasing. "Just give the woman the veggie burger and be done." He leaned in to whisper in my ear. "Some of us are starving."

"Chauvinist." I didn't bother to turn around and look at him.

"Are you going to tell me you're a big beef eater?"

I couldn't help myself. I finally did turn to face him. "I'm going to tell you I just burned as many calories as you did." I heaved a big, dramatic sigh and put on my Scarlett O'Hara voice. "But I'll leave the artery-clogging beef to the big, strong men." I fluttered my eyes, squeezed his bicep, and grabbed the veggie burger. "Enjoy."

I turned with a flip and bounced off to take a seat at the empty picnic table next to the one where Ace served the meals. Van grabbed a meal and took a seat next to me. "You're pretty good on the court," he said.

"I'm pretty good everywhere," I said, conjuring a mixture of tease and flirt.

"I believe it." He had a twinkle in his eyes. "You played high school basketball."

"Four-year letterman," I said. "You?"

"Same."

I nodded. "You know I lettered in softball. I also lettered in volleyball."

"Seems we have a lot in common," Van said.

"You lettered in volleyball, too?" I teased, knowing there is no guys' volleyball in high school.

"No, but I loved to watch the girls play. I bet you looked great in your volleyball shorts."

The others joined us at the table, cutting our conversation short. When we all had our meals, there was still one left at the serving table, a stark reminder of Huff's absence.

Ace showed us how to use our FRH—flameless ration heater—and took his seat at the instructors' table. Yes, we were a segregated society. You can take the man out of the military, but you can't take the military out of the man, being the operative phrase here.

Silence fell as we waited for our FRHs to heat our meals and I was strongly aware of Van's radiant, hot, hot heat next to me. Cliff's gaze kept flicking to Huff's lonely MRE. If Cliff could have sent out an AMBER Alert for Huff, I'm sure he would have. I had the feeling, given the chance, Huff's disappearance was going to become the lunch topic of the day. In my own warped little mind, Huff's disappearance was linked to Ket. I didn't want to dwell on either man.

"Isn't this a lovely setting for a meal?" I said to break the silence and keep my mind off the fact that Ket was loose in the world. I put on my announcer voice. "Here we are, nestled among the train tracks and weathered industrial structures in the beautiful warehouse district of south Seattle,

just off the scenic, sluggish, and only slightly industrial, Duwamish River."

"We look like the lunch crowd on an old *M*A*S*H*
rerun." Cliff had been growing grumpier by every
minute that Huff didn't drive up in the promised
limo to make a grand entrance.

A seagull squawked overhead.

"Look! Wildlife," Van said, his eyes dancing with
tease.

"Someone's in the spirit," I said.

"Anyone have any Alka Seltzer?" Jim was staring
at his warming meal.

"Oh, naughty boy," I said. "Gulls are nasty, dirty,
annoying birds. But you don't want to explode
them with Alka Seltzer. That would be fun, but
wrong. Definitely wrong. And I'd have to report you
to PETA."

"I meant for us," Jim said.

"Of course, you did."

"All right, CTs," Ace yelled from the next table. "I
believe our meals are ready. Chow down!"

"I guess that passes for a blessing," I said, staring
at my ostensibly warmed, not so appetizing-looking
veggie burger with BBQ sauce.

"Wow! Meals-rejected-by-everyone. Materials-
resembling-edibles. Meals-rejected-by-the-enemy."
I looked around the silent group staring back at me.

"Oh, come on, everyone! I'm tanking here.
Don't tell me I'm the only one who did my research
before coming to camp? This is supposed to be a
bonding experience. Our first MREs. Join in. Someone? Anyone?"

Van gave me a wry look. "The three lies—it's not a meal; it's not ready; and you can't eat it."

"Excellent! That's the spirit." I smiled at him with lust in my eyes before looking demurely down at my meal again. "This stuff is supposed to have a longer shelf life than a Twinkie. And it's made to withstand a twelve-hundred-foot parachute drop. Now that's a substantial meal." I poked at it, hungry, but not certain if I was hungry enough. "Crackers, cheese, peanut butter, main course, dessert. Ohmygosh! Twelve million calories of death. I can't eat this. I'll be a tank if I do."

"Twelve hundred," Van said. He seemed to be the only other CT capable of speech. "Stop exaggerating."

"That's two-thirds of my daily allowance. For one meal. And I already had breakfast." I pawed through the contents of my MRE. "I'll trade my cookie for someone's Charms candy." I playfully elbowed Van.

"Charms are bad luck, R," Ace called from the next table before Van could respond.

"Okay, thanks for the warning. I withdraw my offer." I made a pouty face at Van.

"More urban legend. You know I'd give you my Charms any day," Van said with a wink.

"No way. I'm not taking any chances with giving someone bad luck." I forced a smile. "My oatmeal cookie's up for grabs."

"I'll eat your cookie, R." So much innuendo in Van's voice!

"You got it. Anyone want my gum?" I cupped my

hand around my mouth as if I was talking aside to an audience. "I hear it's laced with laxatives."

"Urban legend, R," Ace yelled over.

"Everything's urban here. Thanks for setting the record straight."

We fell into silence again, nothing but the sounds of eating everywhere. Miss Manners would probably say that checking phone messages at the table is bad form. But since she wasn't present, who was going to rat on me? Anyway, I was dying of morbid curiosity. Which isn't, actually, the best way to go.

I'd just opened my phone when Van, who sat to my right, cleared his throat.

"Something on your mind?" I asked, staring at the phone. Ten new voice mails! Ket had been a busy boy.

"I was wondering," he started.

The morbid won. Almost against my will, certainly against my better judgment, I was dialing my voice mail. "Yeah?"

"You're not eating your meal. Maybe you'd call it stirring or playing, but definitely not eating."

"Uh-huh." A call about Ket. Delete. I listened to my messages with half an ear and Van with the other. I would have given him my full attention— he was definitely full attention worthy—but those darn messages were like a siren song calling me to my own destruction. I needed to know if there was anything new. If anyone had seen Ket in the flesh or knew where he was. Finally, the eighth call in, Nicki, my VC, called with the startling news of Ket's release. That inspired my trust. Half of LA knew before she did.

"You're probably going to be starving later."

"Yeah, probably." I nodded. Nothing new on Ket that I could tell.

"You have any dinner plans?" he asked.

Suddenly, I was one part pleased and nine parts panic. Flirting with Van under the innocent guise of playing basketball was one thing. But going on a date with him, alone, with Ket out there, was suicide. Or murder, depending on who Ket would kill, Van or me. Or both. I looked around at the group. "I don't know. Have we made any plans?"

Undaunted by my sudden reserve, Van grabbed my hand and pulled the phone away from my ear. "I was thinking, we could make plans. You and me." He pointed to me and then him. "Just the two of us. Eating together somewhere nice. I have the feeling you're a local girl. You could suggest somewhere. I could pay."

I turned to stare at him, my heart melting to mush. "Are you asking me out? Like for a date?"

"Yeah. Like for a date."

My phone beeped. I had a text message.

The dude 2 ur right wants u. Tell him ur mine. Im watching u. –K

Chapter 9

I looked around slowly, feeling my pulse rise like a tide in my ears. Ket could be anywhere. *Anywhere.* Across the train tracks. On the roof of the neighboring warehouse. Hiding in the wooded area across the road with his high-powered binoculars trained on me. I felt the hairs on my arms stand up and shivered despite the afternoon heat, wondering how in the world Ket got my new number. I was petrified he'd threatened one of my friends.

"Reilly?" Van stared at me. "Earth to R." He waved his hand in front of my face. "What's wrong?"

"I can't go out with you. I'm sorry." I spoke like an automaton, still slowly scanning, watching for Ket.

Van pried the phone from my hands. "Who the hell called you? And what in the hell did they say?"

"Is it Huff?" Cliff leaned toward me. "What's happened to him?"

The instructors were on their feet and at our table in a second, crowded around me, a great big barrier of men.

"What's going on?" War asked as Van read my text message.

Van handed the phone to War. "Who's K? The guy you warned that Cindy Lou to look out for?"

I nodded. "Yes. Ket Brooks, my ex-fiancé."

"Possessive bastard," War said.

"Brooks? Owner of Brooks Gyms?" Jim asked.

I nodded.

Jim squinted in the sun and frowned. "I thought Brooks was in jail for contempt."

"He's out. Yesterday evening or early this morning. Some kind of legal mistake. Someone didn't file the charge in time or something." I was rattled, weighing my options and coming up empty.

War handed my phone back. "Brooks is obviously watching R. He's seen us react. He's getting a kick out of watching R panic and the rest of us respond. He feels like he's in control and pulling the strings. The longer we stay out here, the more power we give him." War paused and looked around the group. "If we move inside, we frustrate him."

War nodded to Kyle and Ace, who helped me to my feet and closed in to shield me. "CTs, form up around R."

Van rose and War shoved him back down with a hand to his shoulder. "You're the guy on her right. You stay in the center, under cover."

Once inside the building, War showed me to his office and closed the door as the others watched. He ushered me into a chair by his desk and got me a bottle of water. I guess that's what you do for upset people, hydrate them.

War went around to his side of the desk, took a

seat, and pulled a file from his in-basket. He opened it and slid out the picture of Ket I'd sent him before coming to camp, spinning it around for me to see. "This the guy we're dealing with?"

I nodded. "I'm so sorry. I just found out. That call I took earlier—"

He held up a hand to silence me. "No apologies necessary."

"I'll go home." I didn't want to go home!

War pierced me with a look. "There will be no going home, CT. This camp is designed to teach people how to protect themselves. Most people come here for fun. We rarely get the opportunity to help someone in real need. You mentioned when you signed up that this Ket character has stalked you. How dangerous is he? Has he hurt anyone?"

"Other than me?"

"I'm sorry, CT." War sounded like he meant it. His voice was laced with compassion.

I sighed. "He got into a fistfight with a guy I dated a couple times after we broke up. I stopped seeing the man in question. Other than that, no. Ket's threatened to kill anyone I'm with. But that's it." I took a deep breath. "Though it's hard to tell what Ket would actually do. I've pretty much avoided dating because of him."

"Since you broke up has he . . . ?"

I shook my head, no. "He's harassed me. Tried to scare me." I laughed bitterly. "Succeeded in scaring me." I told War about the matchbook I'd found, and my theory that Ket had someone plant it. War didn't jump in to say that FSC *had* planted the matchbook, verifying my assumption that Ket was involved. "I'm worried about Huff. I danced with him last night. Before . . ."

War nodded. "Don't beat yourself up. You didn't know. Personally, I don't believe Huff's disappearance has anything to do with you. It doesn't fit the pattern you've described." He paused, watching me fiddle nervously with my hands in my lap, obviously weighing whether he should confide in me. "We had someone at the hotel check Huff's room," he said at last.

I simply stared at him, waiting for him to continue.

He ran his fingers through his hair, looking tired and frustrated. "You all signed a waiver giving us permission."

I nodded. "I know. I don't blame you. What did you find?"

"Nothing. Everything's gone. His wallet, keys, clothes. All gone. No sign of a struggle. Don't worry about Huff. It looks like he left voluntarily."

"But he didn't check out. The front desk would have told us when we asked about him." I paused, mulling things over. "He didn't check out, right?"

War shook his head. "No. He didn't check out. He may be planning to return."

"It's odd, though." But I had to agree with War that Huff's disappearance didn't fit the pattern of him being attacked by Ket. Now if they'd found Huff beaten unconscious . . .

"Maybe we should file a missing persons report on Huff?" I wondered aloud.

"We can file," War said. "Doesn't mean anyone's going to go looking. Not without any physical evidence of violence."

I sighed and nodded my agreement.

War changed the subject back to Ket. "Do you have a restraining order against that bastard ex of yours?"

I laughed the bitter laugh again. "No. He has one out against me."

War gave me a quizzical expression. "The crazy bastard! He put a restraining order on you?"

I nodded. "Wild, huh?"

"You didn't fight it?"

"And play into his hands? Go broke paying legal fees? No thanks. He filed in California after I'd come back to Washington, hoping to draw me down there. The order is a nuisance. Nothing more. Anyone who's known me more than thirty seconds knows I would never voluntarily go anywhere near Ket."

War gave me another sympathetic look. I was so damned tired of being the object of pity.

War picked up on my mood. "We'll help you get your life back, CT. I'll call the hotel and alert them. I have a few friends in the department. I'll call them and give them a heads-up about Brooks. See if they can send someone around to patrol the area. In the meantime, I suggest you call your lawyer and get a restraining order here."

I nodded.

"I'll personally oversee your training this afternoon. Should this guy come calling, you'll be prepared."

War made copies of the photo of Ket to distribute to the group. After he and I made our calls, we met up with the others in the mock city. War sat me in an overstuffed chair inside a mock living room in a mock apartment in the mock city, and passed out Ket's mug shot. Actually, it was more of a publicity photo that Ket looked damned good in. Seeing his handsome face threw people off. How could such a gorgeous, charming-looking man be evil? It didn't compute. Ket's appearance worked against me. Women fawned over him. Men? Their reactions varied from envy to dislike.

Nestled within the apartment's three walls, I felt secure and homey in a creepy, gothic sort of way. The others gathered around, filling the sofa, the chairs, even the floor, waiting for War to make the next move. I watched their reactions to Ket's picture.

Peewee tossed it aside and threw me a dirty look, mouthing, "I didn't tell him." Van studied it thoughtfully. Cliff and Jim took a cursory look. Steve stared at it for some time.

"Listen up. Time for debrief, CTs." War stood behind me.

Everyone stared at me.

"Sorry for ruining lunch, guys." I settled back in my chair, trying not to appear nervous. I hated people knowing about my situation with Ket. It always changed the way they viewed me. And not for the better.

"The MREs ruined lunch," Van said.

"You provided the excitement," Steve said. "What do we do now? Call the cops?"

"This is not a camp game, CT." War put a hand on my shoulder and squeezed before praising the men for their quick action and the way they obeyed orders, and giving them a quick rundown on the situation with Ket. "Slight change in the afternoon plans," War said in closing. "R will come with me for some advance lessons on hand-to-hand combat. The rest of you will go with Kyle and Ace for more practice at the firing range before we begin our instruction on reflexive shooting.

"Ace, Kyle, or I will always have our eye on R while she's here. I expect the rest of you to watch over her at the hotel. If anyone gets any word on Huff, notify me immediately."

War and I remained in the mock living room after Kyle and Ace led the others away. War sat across from me, ostensibly coming up with a way for me to defeat big, bad Ket in a fight where I was out of my weight class.

"Done much fighting?" he said at last.

I shook my head. "I've always been more of a pacifist. If battle must be done, I prefer to use words. I'm pretty quick with an insult."

He raised a brow. "No experience at all?"

"I have two older brothers so I have to lay claim to my fair share of horseplay."

"How'd you come out in that?"

"When I squirted them with my perfume, I was pretty victorious. They tended not to like that a lot. No boy wants to be a girly-smelling guy."

War nodded his approval and smiled at my attempt at levity. "A squirt to the eye with just about anything can be temporarily disabling and give you time to escape. Anything can be used as a weapon,

R. Keep that in mind at all times. Do you ever carry hairspray with you?"

I nodded.

"Good. Hairspray is particularly effective when sprayed into the eyes or directly into the mouth or nostrils," he said.

"Good to know," I said. "And, now that I think about it, patently obvious. All the boyfriends I've ever had have run for cover whenever I've pulled out the old hairspray. Men fear it."

War smiled and tapped his temple. "Way to think like a warrior. Any other experience? Think vicious." He laced his voice with sinister to emphasize his point.

"Right, Reilly Vicious." I paused, nodding. "Think eeeviill." I pursed my lips. "My mom tells me I was a biter when I was young. But I haven't used that skill since I was five and bit my cousin at his birthday party. I got punished for that, by the way."

"Different social situation. Different protocol." War rubbed his chin in thought. "Biting's a skill you'd be wise to recover. In this case, I'd reward you for defending yourself with a good chomp."

I nodded in understanding. "Gotcha."

"I'm not kidding."

I must admit, he sounded serious. "Neither am I."

He nodded. "Good. Ears are an excellent target for a bite. They're readily available and he won't be expecting it."

I nodded again.

"Ears are a good bet in other ways, too, if you can get to them. Clapping both your palms simultaneously over Brooks's ears will produce a nasty numbing pressure change to his brain. It's even been known to cause unconsciousness. A quick, sharp movement is best." He demonstrated the motion, though not on me.

"Is it more effective than the Vulcan shoulder pinch?"

War grinned. "Much." He gave my shoulder a re-assuring squeeze. "From what you've told me, you have good, natural fighting instincts, R."

Bless his heart, he was trying to bolster my confidence.

"Maybe I did as a kid."

"Then think like a child. Let go of your socially imposed restraints. Trust your basic instincts in a fight," War said. "The key is to keep your attacker off guard and fight dirty. There's no such thing as a fair fight when you're fighting a bully or for your life." He gave me a penetrating look. "Got that?"

"Got it."

"Good. Now look around this room and tell me what you could use as a weapon."

"Lamp?"

"Sure. What would you do with it?"

"Swing it like a bat. Or crash it over his head."

"Okay. What else?"

"Chair. Use it as a shield."

"Fine."

I scanned the room. "Ashtray." I paused. "Ashtray? Not many of these left anymore. Maybe in a bar."

"What would you do with it, R?"

"Whack them with it."

"Or throw the ash in their face." He raised his brows in a look that asked if I was following him.

I nodded.

"Fireplace ash would work as well. You could use the ashtray or a coaster as a Frisbee-type missile. What else?"

I looked around the room. It was pretty sparse. I shrugged.

"Newspaper or magazine," War said, picking one up. "Roll it up and use it as a baton. It's a great weapon to use to fight off a knife attack."

"Oh," I said, feeling inadequate.

War tapped his head. "Think like a warrior."

"Right." I nodded again. I was doing so much nodding I felt like a bobble-head doll.

War stood and reached into his pockets, pulling out a handful of change. "I don't recommend getting into a fistfight with Brooks. He'll have the advantage on you there. Most girls fight like girls. No wallop to their punches. But if you absolutely have to, a fistful of change will add weight to your punch."

Then he showed me how to make a proper fist and throw a blow. Which he followed with how to use my elbows, knees, heels, and feet as weapons.

"Ever wear a belt?" War asked me.

"Only as fashion dictates," I said, wondering where he was going with it.

"There's a reason besides fashion that cowboys wear those gigantic belt buckles. They make a hell of a weapon. And they're perfectly legal to carry."

"And here I thought they were just to hold up pants or draw attention to small waists and curvy hips. I'll definitely keep the weapon potential of any belt in mind next time I'm in the market for one."

War smiled. "On to the next topic—every spy should learn one effective move and use it when necessary," he said after we'd practiced the body-parts-as-powerful-weapons drills. "I'm going to show you one that is potentially fatal. Use it only if you have to. But don't be afraid to use it if you must."

I kept up the bobble-head act.

"Listen and watch carefully as I demonstrate," War said. "Facing him, you grab the crown of the attacker's hair and pull his head back sharply. You have to do this quickly, catching him by surprise."

"Yes," I said.

"This unbalances the attacker and exposes his throat."

I winced.

"Hang with me, R."

"Right. I'm here."

"Good."

"What if the attacker has no hair?"

"Use a clawlike motion and grab at his nose and eyes, forcing his head back."

"Okay. What next?"

"You bring your fist up into his windpipe with one hard blow."

I nodded. "Okay," I said. "And it's best, and most lethal, if I have a fistful of coins, right?"

"You got it." War smiled. "You're a quick learner."

"That's what they tell me," I said.

"R, do you have a gun?"

"Yes."

"I mean your own."

"Yes."

"Where is it?"

"In the safe in my hotel room."

"Know how to use it?"

I nodded. "I do. I've got a membership to a gun club and I go shooting regularly. Plus I have a permit to carry concealed."

"When you go out of the hotel, carry it with you."

"Most definitely."

"R?"

"Yes."

"If you're going to carry a weapon, you have to be willing to use it. You have to be willing to shoot to kill."

I gave War a weak, but somewhat affectionate smile. "Now you're sounding like my grandpa Dutch."

"I'll take that as a compliment. One more thing," War said. "If Jim or any other legal beagle ever asks, I told you that members of the public should only use reasonable force in a self-defense situation and never take preemptive action."

I smiled. "Gotcha."

Chapter 10

After I finished my private session with War, I joined the others for the remainder of the reflexive, or instinctive, shooting session. We practiced it first at the range. Explained in the simplest terms, reflexive shooting is shooting with both eyes open, rather than one closed and one on the sight. This allows a larger range of peripheral vision for the shooter, absolutely imperative in a combat, especially close combat, situation.

The trick is to let your dominant eye take over and focus, allowing the other eye to process the situation and surroundings. Like most things, it's easier said than done. The other thing is to turn control over to the subconscious mind.

We practiced at the range, doing exercises and receiving individual coaching for well over an hour before we took a break in an actual break room. With tables and chairs and a pop machine and everything.

Van pulled up a chair beside me. "Soda?" He offered me a cola.

When I hesitated, he said, "The caffeine buzz will keep you going through the afternoon."

"Like I'm likely to fall asleep," I said. "Ever."

When Van smiled, he had lovely, sexy dimples. He popped open the top of the can and handed the soda to me. "So," he said. "I know my timing's bad. I know I'm crazy for asking again and a date is the last thing on your mind. But I only have a few days to get to know you. So dinner . . ."

"Dinner?"

"Dinner." He popped open his can.

"Dinner is a closed topic." I took a sip of pop.

"Is it?"

"I think I was pretty clear with my 'no.'"

"Were you?"

"I think so. I did everything but say, 'no, no, never, never, nah, nah, nah.'" I gave him a smile tinged with regret.

"But since you didn't, there's still room for negotiation."

"V," I said, pausing. "Did I ever tell you what a cool code name you have? You've got a hand signal and everything." I made a V with the first two fingers of each hand.

"Very Nixonian," he said, unimpressed. "Don't change the subject—"

"R, well," I said, ignoring his pleas to stay on track and crooking my first finger to make a little r, sort of. "It doesn't really have a great hand gesture. I could signal to you across the room and—"

He grabbed my hand, covering my r. "Dinner. You. Me. The two of us. Tonight."

"No."

"R—"

"Nyet."

He crooked a brow, daring me to come up with no in another language or use the nah-nah-nah chant.

"You know, there aren't enough creative ways to say no. Have you ever noticed that no is pretty much no in most languages?" I said, mellowing.

"R, dinner. Unless you're going to do the never-never thing."

"Is that a dare?"

"It is."

I couldn't. I could not do it. I wanted dinner with that man. Actually, I wanted a lot more than dinner. "I suppose you can guarantee reservations in Fort Knox. Do they have a café there, do you think?"

"How about someplace closer to the hotel? Like in Seattle?" he suggested.

I shook my head. "Not unless you plan on wearing full body armor and hiring an armed guard escort."

"Three's a crowd," he said.

"Van . . . in a world where Ket did not exist, I'd love to have dinner with you. But . . ." I paused, unsure how to phrase my thoughts without offending him and insulting his manhood. "You don't understand how jealous Ket is, how irrational and dangerous. He's not just jealous of other men. He's jealous of activities that take too much of my time and attention. He's jealous of babies and kittens and coffee and chocolate and anything else that's cute and cuddly and might make me take notice.

"I appreciate your bravery, I do. I'm so totally flattered that you want to dine with me at the risk of personal peril. But I can't let you do it."

"I can take care of myself," he said. And then he grinned. "Wipe that look off your face."

"What look?"

"The one that says you don't think so. The one that's dying to say, 'math skills are not enough. You can't add him to death.'"

I couldn't help it. I laughed. "Mind reader."

"Just call me Van the Magnificent." He paused. "So dinner."

"This isn't who's on first with Abbott and Costello," I countered.

"No, but wouldn't that be fun?" He studied me. "You think Ket would go postal if you went out with the entire FSC gang at once? He wouldn't object to a group dinner, would he?"

"He can object to anything. But I think it would be a little less threatening to him and a lot less dangerous to us. You know, as long as you didn't sit next to me. Or make eyes at me. Or play footsie with me under the table—"

"Stop, you're getting me excited."

"You're easily thrilled."

"Just around you." He was grinning as if he'd won. "So what I'm hearing is that if we all agreed to go out to dinner as a group . . ."

I nodded. "Then I just might agree to go along. As long as no one pays me any special attention."

"Understood."

The other CTs were sitting around at various tables, relaxing before the next high adrenaline exercise.

"Hey, guys, how about dinner tonight?" Van called out to them.

After break, we met in the warehouse at the end of Mock Main Street.

"Listen up, CTs." War stood in front of the group, in charge again. "Tomorrow, we'll get to play with the hostage simulator equipment, virtual reality stuff. Like a flight simulator, only better because you get to shoot bad guys and dodge bullets instead of flying a plane. Today we're going to play a live-action game to reinforce the reflexive skills you learned earlier. You will be both the hunter and the hunted." He grinned as if he liked the thought way too much. "I call this game 'Mafia with a Twist.'"

At the mention of Mafia, Peewee made a twin grin to War's. "Sign me up."

Kyle and Ace issued each of us a two-way radio to report our kills, a top-of-the-line Airsoft rifle so real-looking it scared me to hold it, and a bag of ammo pellets. While I held my gun gingerly, Peewee stroked his lovingly. Van inspected his. Cliff, Jim, and Steve loaded theirs like eager puppies.

War explained the rules. "I will be giving each of you the name of another CT. This is your mark. You will hunt, and shoot to kill your mark with your Air-soft rifle. No shooting at the head. Shots to the chest. Once your mark is 'dead,' you will radio in your kill and assume your mark's mark. Last CT standing wins."

"Sounds like a typical Mafia game," Van said. "What's the twist?"

"Pop-up characters. Dummies, cardboard cutouts, mannequins. Innocent victims that can pop up out of anywhere. Like in a real hostage rescue situation. Shoot one of them, you're out of the game. Shoot someone not your mark, you're out of the game." War grinned slowly. "And for your further entertainment pleasure, you'll be playing in the dark. Or the light. Our discretion when to mix things up. Any questions?"

I raised my hand. "If someone is trying to kill us, can we return fire?"

"Yes."

"Fatal fire?"

"Yes."

"What about their mark?" Peewee asked. "Do we get two then?"

"You do indeed."

Peewee's grin grew two sizes.

War put our code names into a hat. He handed the hat to Peewee first. "Draw your mark."

I had two sets of fingers crossed that he didn't draw me. Peewee pulled a name out, read it silently, and grinned that nasty, evil-faced grin that wouldn't die again. Then Cliff drew. Steve. Jim. Van. They all looked at their names. I watched them all for their "tell." The new Bond claims everyone has a tell. As far as I could tell, no one gave their mark away.

My turn. I put on my game face and did a silent chant. *Not V. Not V. Not V.*

I didn't want to kill that man. Hunt him, yes. But once I had him, killing him wasn't the first thing I had in mind.

I knew myself. I couldn't look at my mark's name

and not give myself away. Not if I'd gotten Van. I stuffed the name in my pocket.

War gave me a smile, shook his head, and proceeded to give each of us a starting position, aloud for everyone to hear. I cursed under my breath, trying to remember everyone's starting position. Maybe I should just peek at my name.

"You have five to get in place," War said. "If things get slow, we'll randomly announce clues to where CTs currently are to get the game moving. Now go get 'em."

And then it was off for a view to the kill.

Just out of sight of the others, I pulled the paper from my pocket and read who my mark was. *Jim.* I blew out a sigh of relief and headed for my second-story apartment mid Mock Main Street, mumbling Jim's location, the apartment below mine, over and over to myself.

My apartment was sparse. Not many places to hide. I slid into a closet like a child playing hide-and-seek. It'd be the first place anyone would look, and I'd be cornered, but so be it. My mind frantically tried to work out a plan. Would I be Bond-like and go on a badass body hunt? Or stay in the closet and ride out the body count?

"Boom, boom, out go the lights," War announced over a loudspeaker, and the slit of light filtering underneath the closet door went out.

This was just a game, but my heart was pounding like there was no tomorrow. I felt jumpy and edgy and, surprisingly, ready to go, fight, win! Badass, body hunt won. I was here, on vacation being scared spitless, to learn how to go down fighting.

There was a stairwell just outside the apartment. I made up my mind to charge down it and burst into Jim's apartment like Rambo, taking him by surprise with a shower of pellets. Finesse be damned. I was going with brute force.

I loaded my gun and slid out of the closet, pumping myself up by silently murmuring, "I love my gun. I love my gun. My gun is my friend. I am Rambo-ette."

I have excellent night vision and sharp hearing. I made it to the hall and down the stairs without incident. The dark, eerily quiet warehouse creeped me out. A door with a window led from the street into the first floor landing. I caught a glimpse of movement outside, and a chill ran up my spine. I looked back and it was gone. Everything was still. I fought off a wave of fear. I was in the clear. Ket could not be in the building. No one was taking me down.

I headed for Jim's apartment. Boots can be lethal weapons, so War claimed. For sneaking, they weren't ideal. I positioned myself in front of Jim's apartment door just as the loudspeaker came on, startling me so badly I almost gave my position away.

"C is out of the game." War's voice boomed and echoed off the walls like the voice of God.

I took a deep breath and tried the door. Unlocked. Fool! I threw it open and burst in, gun at ready. My eyes had adjusted to the dark. The room was clear. The apartment was identical to the one above it. I tried the closet. Clear. I stormed into the kitchen.

Jim sat at the table, drinking a cup of coffee. I raised my gun to shower him with pellets just as he pulled a child-size mannequin in front of him. I pulled my gun up. My shot went high.

"Close call." Jim took another sip of coffee. "Want some? There's a fresh pot."

I narrowed my eyes at him. "Hospitality and using a child as a shield, that's your strategy?" I kept my gun on him.

"Nearly got you."

"Close only counts in horseshoes and hand grenades," I retorted, wishing I had a grenade and wondering what to do next. "How do I know I'm not your mark?"

"You don't." Jim patted a chair next to him. "Sit. I've been wanting to talk to you. In private."

"In the middle of a game in the pitch-black darkness?"

"Yes."

"I see," I said, not seeing anything at all. "You're going for the confessional atmosphere." I cocked my gun.

"There's another child dummy sitting against the wall," he said, taking yet another sip of coffee. All he needed was the newspaper and he could have been my dad on a typical weekday morning, he was so calm. "Take it. Use it as a shield if it makes you more comfortable."

"No, thanks. I'm not a coward." I had the gun still on him. "Now talk so we can get on with the rat killing."

Jim laughed. "You think I'm a rat? I like you, R."

"That's touching," I said. "What do you want?"

"Huff has something that belongs to me. And I think you may know something about it."

I frowned. "I don't get it. He stole something of yours?"

"You could say that." Jim sounded deadly serious, not game serious, either. Real serious. So serious, the hairs stood up on the back of my neck.

"I don't know anything. Huff and I just met."

Jim ignored me. "I want it back and to do that, I need to find him."

"I can't help you there," I said. "I'm as surprised as anyone that he took off."

"What makes you think he just took off?"

"War searched his hotel room. Everything's gone."

Jim swore.

"S is dead," War announced, once again playing god-voice.

I jumped. Jim didn't. Cool bastard. There were just four of us left. Two of us were right here. Two lethal ones still on the hunt out there. I felt myself panicking to get moving.

"Let's say you could help me." A single streetlight popped on, shining through the window and illuminating Jim's face. I didn't like the glint in his eye. "I'd like to propose a working relationship. Help me and your legal problems with Ket are over. I can make sure he's locked up for a good long time for what he did to you."

"That would be double jeopardy," I said. "He's already served his time."

"We can find something to get him on. Trust me." Jim smiled and sipped. "I know people."

"Unfortunately, I don't know anything."

We both heard a movement in the hall, and jumped. Jim turned to look, dropping his child shield just enough for me to get a shot off.

"Ouch!" He rubbed his chest.

"Gotcha." I glanced around wildly, looking for another CT on the make, and not seeing any.

"Think it over. We'll talk later."

I ignored his comment and trained my rifle back on Jim. "Who's your mark?"

"P."

I spun out of the room, feeling like a shadow was on my heels. "I took out J," I said into my two-way and headed for the street. "I'm now after P."

"P's out," War replied over the radio. "Took out an innocent bystander. You have V. Good luck."

V! Damn. Instinctively, I scanned the street for him. All was silent. No sign of him. I slunk through the shadows, gun at the ready, looking for him in the stone stark silent dark. Eerie movement crowded around me. Van on the move? I couldn't catch it outright.

A flutter. A wisp of air movement. A footfall. My heart beat so fast I thought it was going to burst right out of my body. The gun trembled in my hands. I had to get off the street and compose myself.

Something moved overhead. I swung, shot, and screamed like a horror movie extra when a flutter erupted. A pigeon squealed. A bird! A stupid bird. In the FSC building. A stool pigeon!

I ran without thinking. Someone ran right along with me. Why didn't he just shoot me? I stopped. The stalker stopped.

"V?"

No answer.

"V, come out, come out, wherever you are, and let's have this out right here." I looked around the gloom, panicking. "Shootout in the FSC corral, how does that sound to you?" I whispered into the manic dark.

No one answered. I heard breathing. I swung my Airsoft around, ready to shoot. "Come out, you coward, and face me like a man."

More movement. Someone was circling me. I looked around frantically and ran. Ran for all I was worth with my heart racing.

At the end of the street, I tucked into the corner grocery without first scanning the perimeter. Heart-beat banging in my ears, I stopped just for a second to catch my breath and get my bearings.

Without warning, I felt the barrel of an Airsoft pressed against my back.

Chapter 11

The store windows were papered over haphazardly, letting small, dim slivers of light in between the seams. Inside was dark. I could barely see feet in front of me. Van's delicious aftershave gave him away.

I took a deep breath, some of my fear melting away, but not my competitive spirit. "You wouldn't shoot me at point-blank range."

"Wouldn't I?"

"No."

"Drop your weapon."

"Gladly." I tossed it away and spun around. I pushed his rifle away, put my hands on either side of his face, pulled him to me, and kissed him right there in front of the checkout stand, the front display window, and the godlike voice if War cared to use it. Open-mouthed. Full tongue. Full throttle. With complete abandon.

"R . . . baby."

I kissed his words away.

He clasped me tightly to him, his package hard

against me, his Airsoft pressed into my back, his free hand cupping my butt. This was better than basketball flirting.

"Gotta love a man with a gun," I whispered, running my fingers through his hair. I kissed him again.

We kissed each other until our breaths came in ragged gasps. I stroked his face, his hair, his shoulders, his chest. I slid my hands beneath his camo jacket and ran my hands up his back.

When we reached the part where it was time to start ripping clothes off for real, he pulled away and stared at me. "What was that about?"

I ignored his meaning. "Disarming you."

"Am I missing something?" he said, looking over my shoulder with an exaggerated gesture. "I still have a gun at your back. You may be disarming, but I'm not disarmed."

"I stopped you from shooting me. You can't pull the trigger from this angle."

"Momentarily." In one dizzying move, he grabbed my arm, spun me from him, and pressed his gun against my chest.

"You wouldn't dare." I looked him right in the eye, stunned by how quickly he'd gotten the jump on me again.

"Your self-defense plan is to use your sex appeal?" His eyes were twinkling and lusty in the light reflected from the street. "Boy am I glad you ran into me."

I smiled, still breathing hard from his kiss. "Why not? Jim was using coffee. As War says, 'use what you've got at hand.'" I tried to shake my arm free. He tightened his grip.

He looked puzzled by the coffee bit. "Jim was throwing coffee at people?"

"No. Offering them a cup to drink. Come on. You were there watching me. You saw it."

"No, I wasn't. I didn't."

"Come on. Fess up." I stared back at him, dumbfounded he'd lie at this point. "You had to be. It couldn't have been anyone else."

He shook his head, no, unconcerned, and probably thinking I was flighty. "Back to the kissing. What if it doesn't work?"

"All the way to third base," I said with conviction, still puzzled.

"But not home?"

"Not home. Absolutely not home." Maybe I'd been wrong. Maybe nobody was watching. I raised a brow. "What kind of a girl do you think I am?"

"Given that show?" When he grinned, I gave his shoulder a playful shove.

"Not even if your life is really threatened?"

"Well . . ." I tried to look like I was giving it some thought.

"If I startled you and made threatening noises, could I get to third?"

Threatening was Ket's MO. I shivered and paled, the moment ruined. Sudden Ket-inspired panic attacks inexplicably struck at odd times. I hated them. And him. "No, never threaten. Never." My voice came out shaky and uneven.

"R, I'm sorry." Van looked stricken. "That went too far. I'm a jerk."

"Don't apologize. I knew you were teasing. It's just . . ." I took a deep breath and stroked his arm.

"It's me, not you." I changed the subject. "How did you get into the store so fast?"

"What do you mean?"

"I thought you were circling me out there. Stalking. Someone was. Why didn't you shoot me? Or come out when I called?"

"Circling you?" He frowned. "I was down the street from you the whole time. Watching you make your way here. When I saw you running this way, I ducked in here."

"No, you were out there." I pointed to the street. "You had to be! Someone was following me. The whole way." I started shaking again.

"Probably that pigeon that flushed you out earlier. Revenge of the killer pigeon." He laughed.

I didn't. "I'm serious. Someone, probably foul, but definitely not fowl, was following me."

"R," he said, clearly not liking the implication in my voice. "Ket's not here."

"I hope to God you're right," I said, trying to buck up, but not able to shake the feeling of being watched and quietly stalked.

"You're worried he saw that kiss?" he said playfully. "Don't be. Even if he were here, which he isn't, he'd have to be a bat to have seen."

"Don't put it past him. Ket has many batlike qualities—he's dark, he's creepy, he gets in everywhere, and he's been known to swoop down on me out of nowhere." I paused. "You're right. Armed as we are with our high-powered Airsofts, we're perfectly safe. If he comes at us, we'll pellet him to death. We can always hope he has a plastic allergy I'm not aware of." I tried to sound light.

"That's the spirit," Van said.

"Just watch your backside," I said. "He doesn't fight fair."

"Why do I suddenly feel like Van Helsing?" he asked. "On guard against a sinister bat-type villain."

"I have no idea," I said, teasing him. "Vivid imagination?" I looked him over in the dark. "I like Van Helsing. He's hot."

"Van Helsing's hot?"

"The way Hugh Jackman plays him, yes."

"I could play him that way."

I smiled, feeling better at the thought of Van as a superhuman monster killer. "I'd like that."

"You like me," Van said. I could feel him smile.

"Maybe, math man."

We were interrupted by War making an announcement. "The remaining two CTs are in the store. Make a move one of you and get it done!"

"I'm all for getting it done." Van gave me a suggestive look.

I blushed and ignored his innuendo. "Okay, what do we do now?"

"About what?"

"About us killing each other."

Van shrugged.

"I already have one 'I've been spied' shirt. You want one?" I struck a dramatic pose and spread out my arms. "Take me, I'm yours."

He raised a brow and grinned at me. "Gladly, but not with a gun." He motioned to my rifle on the floor. "Get your weapon. I'll give you to the count of ten and the game is on. Full bore. No holds barred."

I nodded. "You're on."

"One . . ."

The mock corner grocery store was complete with shelves stocked with goods. I grabbed my rifle and headed down the diaper, feminine protection aisle. It took a brave man to venture into that territory. Pelt Van with a few packs of sanitary pads and I'd have him on the ropes. I glanced back over my shoulder.

He was at the front of the store. The first thing he'd do was scan down the aisles for me. I had to hide at the back of the store between aisles. Halfway down the aisle, I picked up on an odor. The store smelled vaguely like a meat counter gone bad. Or blood. But that was crazy. I kept going, trying to keep my boots silent on the vinyl floor.

I spotted a cardboard display near the end of the aisle. I decided it would make a good blind. If I hid behind it, I could surprise Van as he came around the corner looking for me, and maybe get a decent shot off.

But the farther I walked down the row, the more obnoxious the odor became, morphing from meat to bad body odor, like a stale gym after the big game. I gagged and considered turning back.

". . . nine, ten! Ready or not, here I come," Van called out.

No time! I swung around the display, misjudged the distance, and caught my toe on the corner of it. As I stumbled, I slid on something slick on the floor.

I grabbed the display in an attempt to right myself, bumping the goods. A can of something, probably baby formula, rattled and toppled off. I dodged it and cringed as I waited for the clatter that would give me away.

Only the clatter never came. The can landed with a dull thud, followed by the mildest clink as it rolled off whatever had cushioned its blow and hit the vinyl floor. I froze as it rolled almost silently toward me, coming to rest against the toe of my boot.

Instinctively, I knelt and grabbed it, dropping it again almost the moment my hand closed around it, shaking. The can was covered in something sticky.

I rubbed my fingers together, trying to figure out what I had on me. The odor was stronger here. I gave my hand a cautious sniff and gagged. No, it *couldn't* be.

Trembling, I reached out and felt around for whatever had broken the can's fall, carefully avoiding direct contact with the floor.

My hand made contact first with the upturned toe of a sneaker, a large sneaker, size ten or better, then a sock, athletic variety, and then . . . with a cold, hairy ankle.

I screamed.

Van was beside me in an instant. "R? R, what is it?"

I was trembling violently, barely able to speak. Van took me in his arms.

I clutched at the collar of his jacket, looking for anything solid and safe. And alive.

"He's dead. He's dead." I pointed to the ankle and the rest of the dead guy attached to it.

Van followed my line of sight and cursed under his breath. "Hit the lights!" Van screamed into his two-way radio. "Damn it! Someone hit the lights. We need help. There's a man down."

We heard feet shuffling, and then running. And then, of all things, laughter. The door burst open, letting in a shower of light and silhouetting War, Ace, and Kyle in the door like action heroes in a comic book.

"I see you found Fred." War's boisterous voice filled the room. "He gets the CTs every time."

"Hit the lights," Van said. "This isn't Fred."

War was still shaking with laughter as he flipped the light switch to reveal Van and me crouched in a puddle of blood at the feet of a very real, very dead, man.

I took one look at the dead man. "Jay? OhmyGod, Jay!"

I broke loose from Van and ran.

Chapter 12

Van found me in the ladies' room, huddled in the corner between the sinks and the hand dryers, rocking with my knees pulled close, shaking like warmth was a forgotten notion. He burst through the door, calling my name, and froze at the sight of me.

So much for my strong, athletic, femme fatale image. I was a mess. The fright queen. A horror movie reject. A girl having a bad day on Elm Street.

My clothes were blotchy and wet, soaked in spots where I'd tried to scrub the blood out. Damp wisps escaped from my ponytail. My jacket sat limp and splattered on the sink counter. I'd pulled my boots off. They lay toppled a few feet from me. Toilet paper, wadded and wet and ineffectual, lay in sad clumps where I'd tried to wipe away my trail of bloody footprints. A wet, white tail of paper led to a stall.

I couldn't remember opening the stall. Or getting the paper. Or scrubbing. I couldn't remember any of it.

"Reilly?" He spoke my name softly, somehow ignoring the dishevel around him, the white tornado gone bad.

He sounded like he was speaking through fog. I didn't answer.

He started toward me.

I panicked and pointed.

He paused and looked at his feet. "What?" He looked around and understanding dawned. "This?"

I nodded, worried, irrationally, irreverently, that he'd get toilet paper stuck on his shoe and I'd laugh. Inappropriately. And that would make me evil and unfeeling.

He picked his way to me, stripping off his jacket and sat down beside me on the floor laced with puddles. "Pulling a Lady MacBeth on us?"

I kept rocking, silently.

"No comeback?"

I put my head on my knees.

"Out, out, damn spot would be appropriate," he said. "Or pass the Oxi-Clean."

He reached to put his jacket around my shoulders. I shrunk away, pointing to the collar and my perfect, bloody handprint on it.

"Sorry," he said, understanding. He tossed his camo into the sink, where I'd left the water running, and put his arm around me. "You're shivering."

I cuddled into him. He scooted us over a few feet, and reached up and hit the button on the hand dryer. The warm, dry air ruffled the loose strands of my hair.

"Better?"

"Marginally." My teeth were chattering. I shrank closer against him.

"The blower will warm up soon." He paused. "The uniforms arrived. They cordoned off the crime scene and called the detectives and the ME. The detectives will want to talk to you."

I nodded.

"I asked the cops to give you a few minutes."

Neither of us said anything more for some time. The hand dryer shut off. I was still shaking. Van reached up and hit the button again.

He covered my hands with his. They were warm. Safe. Perspiration beaded on his forehead. The dryer was scalding him. He didn't move. Neither did I. I was still freezing.

"The cops will want to know exactly what happened. What you saw. What you heard. They'll take your prints." He tucked a wild lock of hair behind my ear.

We sat.

The dryer stopped. He hit the button. Bit by bit, I dried out. Bit by bit, the fog lifted. Bit by bit, the shakes receded.

"I knew him," I blurted out to my own surprise.

"The man out there?"

"Yes. Jay Woods." I closed my eyes, trying to shut out the image of Jay with his neck slashed end to end, his blood spread across the aisle, his eyes glassy and unseeing like the deer my grandpa used to gut.

"Jay Woods," Van repeated.

"He is . . . he was . . . a regular at the gym. Ket's gym."

Van nodded.

"I contaminated the crime scene?" I was amazed at my own sloppiness and stupidity. How could I? "*I* did, *didn't* I?"

He nodded. "It happens. Even on *CSI*."

The dryer stopped. I was still cold with fear, and denial, and regret, but no longer shaking. The relative quiet of the room without the white noise of the dryer made me feel vulnerable. Seeing my discomfort, Van hit the button again.

Water ran across the counter and dripped onto the floor near us. Van's camo had clogged the sink. Van ignored it. So did I.

"I'm responsible," I said.

"For what?"

I looked up into Van's eyes. "Jay. His death."

"If that's a confession, I'd keep it to myself." Van gave me a squeeze. "Personally, I didn't see you with a knife."

"Don't make light. I . . . I had a date with him. Two dates, actually."

"Was one of them early this morning?"

"No."

"Then you have nothing to worry about. You're not the killer."

"V," I said, "I had two dates with him. In public. While Ket was in jail." I pushed away from Van and stood up.

He rose with me and put his arms around me, turning me toward him. "What makes you think Ket did this?" Van took my face in his hands and forced me to look at him. "R, look at me. Ket would have had to sneak past security. Lure Jay up here from LA. Kill him in cold blood. Because you had dinner with the guy?"

"I know. It sounds crazy. Upside down. Vain of me, even." I took a deep breath. "I'm confused. I'm upset. But you don't understand Ket. He's diabolical. Obsessed. Narcissistic."

I paused, trying to order my thoughts. "Jay was a PI. The man was good with a gun." I forced a weak smile. "He could take care of himself. That's why I dated him. And that's why I stopped." I paused, trying to think of a rational reason for Jay to be in Seattle.

"What if Ket hired Jay to follow me? Someone's been watching me." I pointed toward the door. "Someone was watching me out there!" I put my head in my hands and took a minute to compose myself. "Someone's been watching me all along. How else would Ket know where I am and what I'm doing all the time?"

Van nodded his agreement. "But why Jay? And why kill him? Why kill him here?"

I shook my head. "I don't have the answers. I just don't like the alternatives." I paused. "If Ket didn't kill Jay, then who did? One of us?" My voice went very soft.

Van leaned his forehead against mine. "R—"

There was a knock on the door. "Ms. Peterson. Detective White. I'd like to speak with you if you're up to it."

The interruption shook me back to my senses. I pulled free of Van. "I'll be right there," I called to the detective.

I turned back to Van. "Stay away from me. Far, far

away. For your own good." I turned on my heel and fled, pausing at the door to look back at him leaning on the counter. He turned off the tap, head bowed. Then he grabbed his soaking camo and hurled it at the wall.

I told Detective White everything I knew, including my suspicions about Ket. I went over every tiny detail I could remember. I even apologized about the crime scene.

The cops had locked down the building and were reviewing the security tapes. They hadn't found anything or anyone.

CSI came. They took my fingerprints. And my clothes. Including my boots and my 3D moisture-wicking tee. War found me a replacement set of BDUs and promised to send Kyle out to buy me some new boots and have them delivered to the hotel. I was forced into wearing a pair of oversized flip-flops and a boxy, men's tee, sans bra. I was out there but not loving it. My girls were like the proverbial cats fighting in a bag.

A uniform escorted me to the break room where the rest of the CTs awaited interrogation. Van was missing. I assumed he was being grilled. Peewee's gaze landed on my bouncing bazoombas and refused to leave. I stalked off to the corner away from the others, took a seat, and crossed my arms over my chest, giving Peewee a defiant look. "Show's over."

He laughed and lowered his gaze to a magazine he was flipping through.

Cliff approached me. "Tough day." He handed me

a can of cola. "We could all use something stronger." He nodded toward the soda. "But this is what we get."

I popped open the soda without comment.

Cliff dropped into a chair next to me. "If it's any consolation, I knew him, too."

I looked over at him. "Too?"

"I have good ears. I heard one of the cops mention you knew the vic."

The vic. I shuddered.

"He was a PI from LA." Cliff stared at me.

I nodded. "I know."

"You had a few dates?"

"Yeah."

"I'm sorry. Jay was an okay guy." Cliff snorted, erasing any notion he liked Jay at all.

I arched a brow.

"I'm not questioning your taste in men. Jay was my nemesis's guy. Did a lot of work for him."

"You have a nemesis?" I played with the condensation on my can, not looking at Cliff.

"We all do."

I looked up at him. "Yours have a name?"

"It's not important." Cliff's smile was ironic and halfheartedly limp. "Nem and I collaborated on a movie a few years back. We had our creative differences."

"Your creative differences turned personal?"

"You could say," Cliff said. "The movie was a flop."

"Sorry to hear that."

"It happens." Cliff shrugged. "And so I ask you, is it just coincidence that Jay turns up here, right when I'm about to launch another big project with blockbuster written all over it?"

"You think he was following *you*?" I asked, stunned that Cliff would think it was him who was being watched.

"Why not? Nem used Jay to acquire a little extra legal help in resolving our differences, if you get my drift."

I frowned. I didn't.

Cliff laughed again. "You're a naive babe, but I like you. Woods was a wiretapper. He 'overheard' a few nasty remarks I made in private about some very powerful people. Comments I didn't want to get out." He shrugged again. "What can I say? I caved to protect my career."

"Oh."

"Yeah."

"And you think he was here spying on you, trying to get the inside scoop on your new movie?"

Cliff smiled. "Trying to get any dirt he could."

"But why would Nem do that?"

"To ruin me."

I gave Cliff a penetrating look. "Jay's dead."

He backed off with his hands up. "I had nothing to do with that."

I had the feeling that I wasn't getting the full story, but I didn't push it. I shifted the conversation. "Huff is a PI, too."

"Yeah, but he's my guy. Or so I thought." Cliff took a swig of his cola. "I just gave him a large retainer to do a little work for me."

"Don't tell me. Let me guess—collecting dirt on your competitors?"

Cliff's smile was rueful. He gave my arm a pat. "Cynic. One of my ex-wives has gotten greedy."

"You have more than one?" My tone indicated that was no surprise.

Cliff grinned, ruefully, ignoring my jibe. "Too many. I gave Huff money to get me something legal that will stand up in court. Something to stave off her demands.

"When he didn't show up this morning, I figured he was out blowing my deposit. Now I'm beginning to think he's blown town. With my cash."

Given what War had told me, I was inclined to think Cliff could be right. "Maybe he's off to do a rush job," I said, hoping he wasn't dead like Jay.

"He's not that eager. And neither am I." He gave me a sly smile. "If you know anything, have any idea where Huff might have gone . . ."

I didn't respond.

Cliff's gaze slid over me.

I shivered. Cliff's gaze had salacious and leer written all over it.

"You're a pretty girl." He reached over and covered my hand on the table. "Photogenic. Athletic. Well spoken. I could make a star out of a girl like you." His tone added, "and a mistress."

I thought of the flash drive I'd hidden for Huff and wondered. I tried to pull my hand free, but Cliff held it firmly in place. "I barely know Huff. I just met him at camp."

"I understand." He released my hand. "But if anything comes up . . ."

I nodded my agreement just as Van came into the room.

Chapter 13

After a brief consultation with the police, the FSC staff announced that camp would resume the next day for those who were interested. I was just cynical enough to think that shutting down would make FSC look like sissies and do major bottom-line damage. Excitement and danger were, after all, their business.

As it turned out, all of us were interested in continuing our camp experience. More out of morbid curiosity than anything else, I thought. And possibly out of a desire to learn a few extra self-defense techniques in case the killer came calling again.

War and staff were fully cooperating with the cops. They turned over all their security tapes, etc. And War promised that he was consulting with the police and his security experts to beef up security so that this could *not* happen again. Although he kept a surface cool, it was easy enough for the casual observer to discern that the fact that murder most foul had happened on his watch at his camp infuriated and puzzled him. He didn't like being made a fool. My take—though exciting and adding a touch of realism, a dead body was basically bad for business.

But, as Van said with a touch of rhyme and the logic of Garp, "We're probably the safest we can be at FSC. What are the odds of another dead body turning up at camp?"

I wondered. I also wondered if one of us was a murderer.

One good thing *had* resulted—the cops put out a missing person bulletin on Huff. Although whether they viewed him as a person of interest or another vic, I couldn't say.

The bus ride back to the hotel was quiet. Speculation and gossip had been wrung to death in the break room. Now people were exhausted. I know I was. We each retreated to our own thoughts. Mine ran toward retrieving that flash drive I'd hidden for Huff. With his disappearance, and Jay's murder . . . well, I don't know, it just seemed like the drive might mean something, give some clue. Did that mean I'd told the cops about it? No.

Why?

Because they hadn't asked. Childlike and obtuse, maybe. But there you had my logic.

I wasn't sure the drive meant anything anyway. Once I had it back in my possession, if I got it back, then I'd decide.

Steve pushed past Van as we got off the bus and took up residence next to me. I had nothing against Steve. But I had nothing for him, either. I definitely preferred Van to him.

Steve began chattering in my ear as we entered the hotel lobby.

I nodded along to his drivel as we strode into the lobby, wondering how I could ditch him. "Holy cow!" I said on seeing the lobby.

The Cindy Lous had completely taken over. Banners, posters, pictures of jewelry, information desks, and tons of jewelry displays and flowers everywhere. Not to mention more bedazzled, bejeweled women wearing more costume jewelry than I'd seen in a lifetime. The Cindy Lous covered the sofas, the chairs, the ottomans, and filled the lobby with the buzz of female-pitched voices.

"It's an explosion of glass beads and rhinestones in here," I said.

Beside me Steve scowled. "I hate Cindy Lous."

"You know them?" I asked, feeling afresh like a piece of meat as dozens of pairs of customer-calculating eyes spotted a completely unjeweled me.

"My ex is a self-centered bitch in every form of the word," Steve said with all of the passion of love gone bad. "Even in entertaining. She *loves* to throw a party. But only if she's the center of attention and walks away with free goodies and half-priced hostess gifts—candles, makeup, jewelry . . ." He trailed off, looking dazed. "She drove me crazy and bled me dry."

"You could always sue for half," I said helpfully.

Steve rolled his eyes.

Having had the pleasure of a Cindy Lou encounter earlier, Van avoided any eye contact with them. He stopped next to me and grabbed my arm. "Stick with me and I'll get you to safety."

Which sounded like a good plan to me.

Not to be outdone, Steve grabbed my other arm.

"After a day like this, I could use a drink. Stiff one."
He smiled at me, ignoring Van on my left. "You
look like you could use one, too. Buy you one?"

Steve's tone sounded suspiciously friendly, like a
drink was a prelude to a flirt or an ask-out for
dinner and a date, or a quick screw if he could get
it. He was a lonely, bitter divorced guy. The kind of
man I wanted nothing to do with. But I'd been plot-
ting on the entire bus ride home how to get to the
ladies' room in the bar without drawing attention
to myself. And Steve had just handed me a golden
opportunity.

Van's hand scorched on my left arm. He was one
hot man. Life would have been perfect if he'd been
the one to ask. "Can you match him? One drink or
best offer?" I whispered to him.

He leaned in and whispered into my ear, "I
thought it was too dangerous to be alone with you?"

"That's why I'm asking. Let's make it a group encounter."

Van arched a brow and glanced over at Steve,
who still had a death grip on my arm. "Three would
be a crowd. I'll pass."

"You have a death wish for Steve?" I whispered
back to him.

Van smiled and dropped my arm. "I'll join you
with the rest of the gang for dinner. See you both
in the restaurant later."

Steve nodded to Van. "Later."

I turned back to Steve. "Let's ask the others to
join us. We're safer in groups."

"No worries. The hotel's completely safe. War
notified security." He looked smug.

I was not so confident in security's ability to keep me safe and secure.

Van was still standing beside as he waited for the others to catch up. "Good luck," he whispered, looking amused, then headed for the elevators and safety.

Peewee, Cliff, and Jim followed on his heels, diving through the crowd with scowls on their faces to ward off any brave jewelry ladies.

Steve smiled and, taking my arm, led me to the bar.

"What would you like?" he asked me as we settled in at a small table.

"Anything with rum, except rum and Coke," I said, for once not in the mood for a drink that doubled as dessert. Rum was my poison of choice, but Coke ruined the flavor.

A cocktail waitress appeared, left the little napkins, and took our order.

I eyed the ladies' room. Curses, foiled again! There was a RESTROOM CLOSED FOR CLEANING sign in the doorway. I was forced to listen to Steve complain about his ex.

"Ever been married?" he asked.

"No."

"Smart woman. Don't do it." Steve scooted his chair around close to mine.

Oh, shoot, I thought. I didn't have the strength to fend off an advance. I glanced back at the ladies' room, hoping for an out. No such luck.

"I'll take that under advisement if I'm ever tempted," I said. "In the meantime I'm happily single."

We made small talk. Our drinks arrived. I had to resist the temptation to down mine in a single gulp. Personally, I was in the mood to drown out my life.

I had the feeling Steve was working up to something, probably asking me out. I tried to steer the conversation, far away from that topic.

"Jim and Cliff seemed upset by Huff's disappearance," Steve said.

At last, a safe topic. "We all are."

Steve leaned into me and spoke with a conspiratorial tone. "But Jim and Cliff particularly." He looked around the room like he was scanning to see if we were being watched. Considering lunch, probably a good move. "Huff has something they want. Cliff and Jim approached me, asking me if I knew anything about it."

I tried to look bored and nonchalant. "Do you?"

Steve laughed. "Why would I?" He paused. "They're offering a reward. I could use a reward."

I didn't speak.

"I assume they approached you, too?"

"Maybe," I said.

"You and me"—he pointed between us—"would make a good team, I think. I'd like to propose—"

"A toast, I hope," I said, glancing again at the restroom and that damned cleaning sign. What in the world was taking the janitor so long? "'Cause I think I just mentioned I'm happily single and it's a little early in our acquaintance for anything else."

Steve smiled. "Funny lady. A partnership."

I just stared at him.

"I say you and me team up, find Huff, claim that prize, and split it. Fifty-fifty."

I couldn't take it anymore. I had to get into that bathroom. I looked at Steve. "Excuse me," I said. "I have to visit the ladies' room."

"It's closed," he said.

"Too damn bad." I smiled at him. "I'll be right back."

I strode past the sign and right into the bathroom and . . . chaos in the process of being cleaned up. The room had been trashed. Tossed absolutely upside down.

A female janitor stood with her back to me. Her bucket of cleaning supplies sat on the counter by the sink.

"This place doesn't need a janitor," I said, absolutely stunned. "It needs a repairman. Have you called security?"

She turned around and scowled at me. "They sent me. This bathroom is closed. Don't you read?" She picked up her broom and swooshed it at me.

I ignored her, taking in the scene with a sick feeling building in my stomach. What in the world had Huff turned over to me and asked me to hide?

The hand dryer had been pried from the wall, leaving a nice hole in its wake. Someone, probably Miss Janitor Lady, had propped the dryer up neatly against the wall by a stack of drywall bits and paint flecks of a color that matched said wall above. Toilet paper rolls had been torn apart and strewn about the room. She'd made a tidy pile of them.

"I read fine," I said. "But I need to go and the Cindy Lous are hogging all the other ladies' rooms."

She eyed me, taking in my men's clothing and disheveled appearance and the fact that I was far from being one of those pesky Cindy Lous. She softened toward me.

"Those Cindy Lous." She looked like she was going to spit. "They make a big mess."

I nodded, but I didn't think the Cindy Lous had done this. I was petrified that someone had been looking for that darn flash drive and gotten it ahead of me. The way my day had gone that wouldn't surprise me. I did a little dance to emphasize my need to go.

"Fine. Go." She nodded toward the stall where I'd hidden the drive. "But be quick. And tell nobody." She tossed me a roll of paper. "You're going to need this. Somebody stripped it all out of the stalls."

I caught the paper, nodded and dove into the stall, closing the door behind me. The paper seat cover fixture had been pried loose from the wall. There were scratch marks on the feminine protection disposal receptacle and the lid was wrenched open. Someone had more might than I did.

Mercifully, the ladysafe bag dispenser was untouched and still bolted to the stall wall. Even still, I felt sick. What if I was too late?

With trembling fingers and not much hope, I searched the inside lip of the dispenser. Much to my surprise, whoever had done the damage, had missed it. It was still stuck in place with a bandage. Either the destroyers had missed it in their frantic hurry or maybe our sweet janitor lady had interrupted them. I was just glad they hadn't slit her throat.

I tucked the drive in the pocket of my camo. I was

about to flush to keep my ruse up when the automatic toilet flushed on its own. Some things never change.

I left the stall. As I was washing my hands, I thanked the janitor lady.

"You see those Cindy Lous," she said. "You scowl at them for me."

"You got it."

At the table, another drink and Steve were waiting for me.

"So?" Steve said. "What do you think of my proposal?"

"I think I don't have anything to offer." The drive was practically burning a hole in my pocket, but I forced myself to sit.

"You have brains and beauty." His gaze rested on my braless chest.

But not the desire to team with him.

"You'll keep my offer in mind?" He lifted his gaze to mine.

I sighed and nodded. But I had my fingers crossed so it didn't count.

He grinned and his gaze slid back up to my chest, but he didn't have the budding effect on me that Van did. "Now. How about dinner? What do you say we ditch the rest of the group and have a nice, quiet dinner somewhere decent? Just you and me."

I slid my chair back. "No thanks. I'm beat."

He nodded. "I hear you. Another time?"

I stood.

He pushed his chair back, too. "I'll walk you back."

"Thanks, but I'm fine. Finish your drink." I

flashed him a smile and dashed for the elevators just outside the bar before he got out of his chair.

Mercifully, no Cindy Lous. Break must have been over.

The elevator pinged and the doors slid open. A tall, big-boned woman wearing a gaudy pants suit was the only occupant of the elevator. She was next to the control panel, looking down, thumbing through a brochure. She was covered in so much dangly Cindy Lou jewelry that she looked like a necklace tree. A stout necklace tree.

I hesitated for just a sec before entering. I did *not* want to be corralled with a sales-pitching Cindy Lou. But the safety of my room and a chance to check out the drive awaited. I slid in and pushed the button for my floor.

The elevator had barely begun to move when Miss Cindy Lou reached over and hit the manual override to stop the elevator. She had hairy knuckles and chipped, dirty nails.

I screamed and lunged for the buttons.

When she looked up, I realized she had stubble and an Adam's apple. And a horrible, evil glitter in her eyes.

Chapter 14

"Give me the dongle," the goon dressed like a woman said.

"Dongle, dingle, dangle," I said. "You're speaking gibberish." I ran my gaze over him. "You're horribly over-accessorized. If you're going to impersonate a woman, try to do it with a little class." Brave words, scared girl. I cowered in the far corner of the elevator.

Goon pulled a switchblade from his pocket and snapped it open. "Give me the dongle or I cut you."

Seeing that black, sleek, very sharp-looking blade, I felt sick in the "upchuck and pass out" way. At least the knife wasn't serrated. Serrated was supposed to hurt more. And leave a ragged scar, should one survive. Almost made me feel sorry for bread. Serrated or not, the thought of being cut made me nauseous and dizzy.

"Security will notice this elevator isn't working properly and respond any minute." Damn, I didn't have my gun. Why didn't I have my gun? I didn't even have my FSC-issued Airsoft on me.

Goon shrugged. "Any minute I could have you cut into ribbons that would make my mama's angel hair pasta look thick like fettuccini. Like lasagna, even." He was really getting into the analogy thing.

At the pasta reference, I looked him over more closely and decided beneath the blond wig, he could be Italian. The thick, dark brows, brown eyes, and Mafioso attitude gave him away. He belonged on a vendetta order on an episode of *The Sopranos*, not in my elevator.

He waved the black blade at me and I remembered Jay and his smiling slit throat and thought better of asking.

"Nice switchblade," I said, trying to quell my fear. If in doubt, compliment to win friends and buy time.

"Thank you. I like it myself. It's Italian made, like me." He laughed.

I smiled weakly.

"Just so you know, switchblade is a politically incorrect term. Automatic knife is the PC term. This is a tactical black bayonet automatic knife sharpened to shave the hair off my arm. I like using it. Why have a weapon you don't use?" Goon grinned evilly. "So, the dongle? You going to give it to me, or am I going to use this high-precision instrument on you?"

"A bayonet's overkill for little, old me," I said.

Goon waved the knife. I went spitless.

"Okay, okay. You have my full cooperation," I said through my thin, tight throat. It wasn't a sexy, or even a helpful, sound I made. More like a croak. "Just . . . just tell me what a dongle is."

I must have looked genuinely panicked and confused. Goon smiled. At my breasts. I was shaking. And so were they.

"It's a little piece of hardware. A flash drive or the like," he said.

"Any flash drive?"

"I'm looking for a specific one. Huff had you hide it in the ladies' john."

I was trying to keep my face impassive, but something must have given me away because the Cindy Lou goon smiled. "Yes, I know about that."

"What have you done with Huff?" Not that I really wanted to know. Not if it meant Huff was fish food. But I felt indignant and indignant was definitely better than panicky scared.

Goon shrugged.

I made thin eyes at him. "Huff better be all right."

Goon was unmoved. "I already searched the ladies' john and came up empty. I figure you know where the item in question is."

"*You're* the dastardly fiend who tore up the ladies' room!" I put my hands on my hips and tried to look stern. "You're giving Cindy Lous everywhere a bad rep."

"Too damn bad. Those broads deserve it."

"And yet you chose to impersonate one," I said. "Now. What have you done to Huff?" I had images of torture in my mind.

"That bastard's fine." He sounded annoyed. And sincere.

Which made it hard not to believe him. But given the circumstances . . .

Goon held out his hand. Huff's words echoed in my mind. *If anyone comes after the drive, let them have it.*

At this point, his wish was my definite command. I would have loved to let Goon have it. Only, sadly, I had no hairspray, no perfume, no rolled up magazines on me. And neither did the elevator. It was damningly bare.

"If I give it to you, you'll let me live?"

When he hesitated, I stumbled on. "I can't identify you. Look at you. You're an ugly woman with stubble and a bad manicure. And too much Cindy Lou jewelry, which describes over half the women downstairs. You aren't a consultant, are you? Sorry. Scratch that question. I don't want to know. I don't want to know anything."

"Lady, shut up," he said at last, grinning. "You give me the drive, you live. I don't get paid extra for killing. Just delivering the goods."

"I have your word? I can trust you," I asked.

"You ain't got much choice."

"True." I was stalling, wondering if I could get a hold of that wig of his, yank his head back and sucker punch his neck. Every CT needs one lethal move. Only War never said what to do if your target was wearing a wig. Somehow, I didn't think wigs had the adherence, or pain factor when pulled, of natural hair. I didn't even have a key on me. Nothing but a stupid key card. And that was hardly lethal.

I wondered if I could bluff. Tell him I didn't have it on me and then escape when we got off the elevator. I was quick on the start, and fast.

Goon motioned for me to hand the dongle over.

"The sooner you give it to me, the sooner we both can go. I'm not being paid by the hour here."

"I don't have it on me," I said.

He sighed like work was a bore and he was tired of the setbacks. "I saw you go in there and then rush off and leave your date."

"He wasn't my date."

"Whatever."

"Did it look like a date?" I was thinking of Ket's reaction if it looked like I was on a date with Steve and Ket found out. "'Cause I was definitely *not* flirting with him. You saw that, didn't you? There was no flirting. No eyeing. And absolutely no lust."

Goon took a menacing step toward me. "Don't make me search you."

Reluctantly, I reached into my pocket and held it out to him. "What's so important about this drive?"

He took the drive and shrugged. "Oh, what the hell. It's the key to some sophisticated encryption software. Without it, the software don't run."

"Whose software?"

He grinned again and grabbed me, putting the blade to my throat. He held me from behind and looked down at me over my shoulder. I nearly fainted from fear, and the thought of the blood to follow.

Goon laughed and hit a button on the control panel. The elevator jolted to a start. "Since we're swapping fashion advice, anyone ever tell you that a big-busted girl like you ought to wear a bra?"

He was watching my jiggle.

"Without one, you're courting trouble. Too bad I don't have more time."

Before I could reply, the doors opened. Goon shoved me forward onto my knees, then took off past me at a run, disappearing down the stairs at the end of the hall.

I was trembling so badly, I couldn't stand. Didn't even try. I collapsed to the floor, stunned to be alive.

Something trickled down my neck. When I brushed it away, my fingers came up bloody. The bastard had cut me. Static interrupted my usually clear vision. My ears rang. As I fought to stay conscious, I clawed at my throat, feeling for a huge, gaping slit.

The more I clawed and felt up my neck, the more I calmed down. My head was still attached to my body by my pretty much intact neck. I rested my head against the carpet in relief. I had nothing more than a surface scratch. A long, knife-length one. I'd live. In fact, I probably needed nothing more than a bandage.

I took a deep breath. The static began to clear. It's not curtains, I thought. I was not going to bleed out on the red and gold diamond-patterned, low pile carpet. Good thing, too. I hadn't even clawed a chunk of flesh from the bastard, or pulled loose any strands of his wig, or taken a souvenir necklace so CSI could track him down.

The elevator pinged and the door opened. I jumped, startled, and tried to get to my feet to run. Peewee stepped out. I relaxed.

"Peewee! What a relief." Words I never thought I'd speak. "I've been attacked. I need help. Call—"

He stared at me, but made no move to help. "Where's the dongle?" he interrupted.

"What?"

"The dongle."

He was a big, ugly thug. Cliff and Jim didn't like him. At that moment, I despised him.

I was cold and shaking from the shock of the last few minutes. Peewee wore a sports coat, a warm-looking one. He didn't offer it to me. Or drag out his cell phone to call for help. Or even offer me a hand up. I wiped my bloody fingers off on my pants leg. Another camo outfit headed to the cleaners.

"The dongle?" He sounded frustrated and angry.

"Selfish brute." I pushed to a stand. "Why should I help you?"

He reached into his jeans pocket and tossed me a packet of tissues. "Do something to your neck."

I pulled a tissue from the pack and dabbed at my wound.

"You're a smart chick. You don't want to get involved here," he said. "Give me the dongle and I take care of you."

"I don't particularly like your way of taking care of me," I said, with a flash of anger. "You haven't shown great proficiency at it so far." I dabbed some more, buying time to think. "Anyway, I don't have it."

"Then who does?"

Goon was dangerous. There was a good chance he was behind Huff's disappearance. And that he'd killed Jay. For being such a callous prick, Peewee deserved Goon. The two deserved each other. And I wanted out of whatever I'd stepped in.

"A big, ugly woman, who was really a man." I did my best to describe him and pointed to the stairs. "He went that way."

Without a backward glance at me, Peewee took off after him.

Should have. Would have. Could have. Story of my life. I rushed to my room. I should have called the cops, only there was no way I was going to. I've seen *The Godfather*—you don't rat out the family. Melodramatic? Maybe. But if *I* called the cops, and they caught Cindy Lou Goon, they'd make me testify. Then I'd have to go into protective custody or risk a horse head in my bed. Protective custody and a complete identity change might be a good way to escape Ket, but that wasn't the plan I had for my life.

I was on my third attempt at sliding my key card into the lock of my door when Van came down the hall, carrying an ice bucket.

He smiled at my feeble attempt to connect card with reader. "Steve really liquored you up. You should have insisted he buy you some potato skins. Mojos take the edge off alcohol."

"Shut up. I'm not drunk." I hadn't realized I was so pathetic. Someday the shakes would stop. Hopefully that wasn't just another empty promise like someday my prince would come.

"Really? Prove it—walk a straight line. Or close your eyes and touch your nose."

"Forget it."

"Too bad. I could use the entertainment. It's a slow TV night."

"Getting the card in is harder than removing the

funny bone in Operation. Why do they have to make these slots so narrow?" I went for a fourth failed attempt and banged the door with my fist, resisting the urge to kick it.

"To frustrate the terminally unsteady of hand. And invite lawsuits from drunks. Allow me." Van pulled the card from my hand and slid it into the slot without a problem. There was a click. He pushed the door open.

I caught the door with my foot.

"Okay," I said. "Maybe some of us weren't cut out to be surgeons."

"Or Hasbro board game champion of the world," Van said, eyeing my neck. "What happened to you? You're bleeding."

"Still?" I wiped at my neck. Sure enough, blood.

Van was staring at me, looking worried, and waiting for an answer.

"Cut myself shaving."

"Good. For a minute there I thought you were doing a Jay imitation. Have you considered going electric?" he said. "It cuts down on those nasty nicks. Not to mention ingrown hairs. I hear electrolysis is good, too."

"That's not funny about Jay. And this hall is not a safe place to loiter around in," I said. In truth, I felt vulnerable and exposed out in the open. Like Cindy Lou Goon or Peewee would appear at any second to machine gun me down, execution style. I've seen the endings of all *The Godfather* movies—like Shakespearean tragedies, too much death for my taste.

"Paranoid now, are we? Next you'll tell me the

FBI is after you and the U.S. government assassinated President Kennedy."

"Shhh," I said, "don't talk so loudly. Big brother might hear you."

"All right then, invite me in. Let me take a look at that. I'm good at playing doctor." Van was leaning against the doorjamb, giving me one of his fabulous, charmingly sexy smiles. His invite-me-in had an "in like Flynn" tone to it.

Under ordinary circumstances, my knees would have nearly buckled and I would have grabbed him by the collar and dragged him in like my prize. Which is to say that I would have smiled at him demurely and we would have had a fine time. But I was simply too scared to tango. Or even make out.

"I think you promised me dinner first," I said, totally without guile or innuendo.

"Oh, yeah, the safe group dinner," he said, lacking enthusiasm. He leaned into me and my heart went into overdrive. Great. Now I was scared and lusty. "Let's be nontraditional. Mix things up a bit. Why don't I come in, you tell me what happened to your neck, and we can do dinner later?"

I stared back at him, wondering if that killer smile was merely a cover. Could he be a crazed, dongle-chasing maniac like the rest of the guys at camp? Was seduction his ticket to the dongle?

"With an offer like that, how can I resist?" I said.

He moved to brush past me into the room. I stopped him with my arm. "You can't brazenly breeze into my room. Someone might be watching."

"Oh, right. I forgot," he said with enough sarcasm to take most people back. But not me.

I leaned in to whisper to him. "Pretend nothing has happened. Go into your room. Meet me at our adjoining door."

He shook his head in that "she's a crazy dame" way, but pulled out his key card.

"After you," I said, waiting for him to enter his room. "Sucker," I whispered to myself as I slid into my room and closed the door behind me.

My jubilation in my keen intellect and guile lasted for less than five seconds, just until I spotted the gold jewelry-size box tied with a pink satin ribbon sitting squarely in the middle of my bed like the gem of the ocean.

Then I screamed.

Chapter 15

I ran for the adjoining door, fumbled with the lock, and finally flung it open to find Van waiting for me on his side.

"What happened? Are you all right?" he asked.

I pointed to the package on my bed.

His gaze bounced from me to it and back to me. "Someone left you a present? And this has you freaked out, why? You have low self-esteem issues? You don't feel worthy of a gift?" There was a tease in his voice.

I gave him an exasperated look. "Someone was here! In my room, my sanctuary."

He walked directly to the bed to get a closer look at the offending package.

I was right on his heels. I grabbed his arm. "Be careful. It could be a bomb."

"You are way too paranoid," he said.

"You would be, too, if you'd just been held at knifepoint in an elevator by a cross-dressing mafia goon."

"Is *that* what happened to your neck?" he asked

deadpan. "You were attacked by an inept mafia goon?"

"Inept!" I pointed to my neck. "He wounded me!"

"He barely scratched you. An ept goon would have done the job right." Van stepped into the bathroom and ran some water. He came out with a warm, wet washcloth and gently dabbed at my neck. "Just like I said," he said, inspecting my neck. "A surface scratch. What really happened? Old Steve go Dracula on you when he went in for a little love bite?"

I felt myself flush at Van's gentle touch, and rolled my eyes to cover. "FYI, I would *not* let Steve anywhere near my neck."

I frowned to emphasize my point and returned to my story. "The Cindy Lou Goon did this *after* he promised not to hurt me if I gave him what he wanted, the big, fat liar."

"And did you?" Van stepped back and tossed the washcloth into the bathroom.

"What?"

"Give him what he wanted?"

"Of course I did!"

When Van raised an eyebrow, I shot him a withering look. "Not that."

"Okay, so why is he a Cindy Lou Goon?"

"I already said he was a cross-dresser. He was literally dripping in Cindy Lou jewelry, way over-accessorized."

"Got it. Good cover. At least the goon has a few smarts. Did he try to sell you any of his finery?"

"Please! He was too busy holding that damn knife

at my neck. My guess is he got a little too zealous with his knife sharpener last time he polished up the switchblade—"

"He had a switchblade?" Van finally looked serious.

"A black one. It looked like a stiletto, but he said it was a bayonet."

"He took time to brag about his knife?"

I shrugged. "You know men, they like to brag about their toys."

"Do the words 'vivid imagination' mean anything to you?" He paused, studying me. "Or post-traumatic shock. I think this Jay thing—"

"I am not making this up!"

"Good," he said. "Because your story-making skills suck. If you're going to be a spy, you're going to have to get better at making up excuses, false explanations, tales, fabrications—"

"Can we get back to the knife? It was a sharp, big-ass one."

"Got it. Big-ass knife."

"And if you're one of the crew who wants the dongle just like Peewee, Steve, Cliff, and Jim, then you're going to have to go after Cindy Lou Goon, too." For some reason, I stared at Van defiantly.

"Slow down, bubalouey, what dongle?"

"The one I hid in the bathroom for Huff. The one the goon wanted."

We stood in front of the bed, leaving the package untouched, as I spilled the rest of the story to Van.

"That is some tale," he said when I finished.

"You don't believe me?" I asked.

"Crazily enough, though we got off to a bad beginning with the Cindy Lou Goon bit, I do. I'm just not sure who else will."

I sighed. "Yeah, it sounds too much like an FSC setup." I pierced Van with my really tough, truth serum glare. "There isn't a murder mystery dinner thing going on here that I don't know about, is there? This Cindy Lou Mafia Goon thing is so out there."

"An FSC gag with real knives?" Van said. "It's a little sporty for them. Though there was the realism of that dead body today." He was grinning, though how he could under the circumstances was beyond me.

"Show some respect."

"Oh, I forgot. You dated the guy. Sorry."

I ignored him, thinking. "Maybe Jay was after that dongle, too?" I plunked on the bed. "Why is it so valuable? If we could figure that out—"

"Hey! Careful," Van shouted. "The bomb. Remember?" He had a look of exaggerated horror on his face.

I gave the gold box a cursory glance over my shoulder. "Sorry. Forgot it was there."

"This goon really got your goat," Van said sympathetically. "The good news is the bomb doesn't appear to be motion sensitive."

"Poser!" I shot back. "You don't believe it's a bomb at all."

He shrugged. "I'm a cute poser though."

"Adorable." Which I totally meant, but I tried to sound sarcastic. "Now for the six million dollar question—do I go to the police about Cindy Lou Goon?"

"Do you want to?"

"Goon implied he was Mafia!"

"Do you want to?" he repeated.

"You mean, do I want to live on the lam for the rest of my life?" I shook my head.

Van looked thoughtful. "I say we only owe our fellow citizens so much civic behavior. Putting our life on the line for a dongle of questionable nature goes too far."

"You know what a dongle is?" I asked him.

He rolled his eyes.

Dumb question.

"Please. I am a math professor. I have some technological savvy. Do you know what's so special about this one?"

I told him what Cindy Lou Goon told me. "It's the key to some encryption software. I have no idea whose or what's encrypted. If we knew that . . ."

"That's a dangerous sparkle you've got in your eye. To quote a cliché, 'let sleeping dogs lie.'"

"But if we knew who the enemy is . . ."

He shook his head. "Do we really want to?"

"You're not curious?"

"I'm cautious."

"We're surrounded by people who want that thing. Desperately. If we could figure out the connection between them, we'd have a good idea of the who and why of the situation. With a little research . . ." I gave him a meaningful look.

"All right. I'm in, I guess."

I smiled. "Know anything about decryption algorithms?"

"Plenty."

"Damn," I said. "I wish we still had that dongle."

"If we did, you'd still be in danger."

I gave him a nudge. "That's your cue to run out of the room after it. Hope you're fast. Goon has a good fifteen minutes on you."

"No, thanks. I think I'll stay," he said. "But be my guest." He gestured toward the door.

"I just had a run-in with the goon. That's why I'm here in the relative safety of my room." I gave a questioning glance at that dumb gift again.

"And that's why I'm staying—to look after you." He had that tease in his voice again.

"Aren't you sweet?" I shifted on the bed.

"Don't look at me like that."

"Like what?"

"With that doubtful look that says you don't think stunning someone with theories about near and far infinity is going to keep you safe. You saw my prowess at the range. I'm good. I can protect with the best of them. Trust me."

Personally, I wouldn't have minded seeing his prowess in other areas, but I simply smiled like I believed his boasts and changed the subject. "So you don't think I'm—we're—in any more danger?"

"You don't know any more than you told me?"

"Nope."

"They have what they want. I think you're fine."

I nodded reluctantly. I still wasn't feeling safe. Or guilt-free. We Petersons are big on guilt complexes. Not telling the police what I knew was already bugging me.

"But what if Goon and the dongle *are* related to Jay's murder? What if by not telling the police what I know, they never solve the case? And Jay's murderer goes free?" I was also big on justice, especially since the injustice of Ket's short sentence for nearly annihilating me.

"Anonymous tip," Van said without missing a beat. "We call in an anonymous tip."

I nodded my head in agreement. "Good plan." I hesitated. "Only we leave me out of it," I said. "We don't mention my involvement at all."

"Yeah, I agree. So what's the new story? How do we extract you from the scene and still relate the pertinent details—goon dressed as a woman steals dongle?"

We concocted a story about someone seeing Goon running from the ladies' room with the dongle dangling by a cord from his fingers. It wasn't the most credible thing I'd ever heard, but it would have to do.

"I'll take care of it. I'll be right back," Van said and ran out to find a pay phone.

Less than five minutes later, he was back, looking excited and only slightly out of breath. "Call went great," he said before I could ask. "So, now that danger's reared its ugly head and passed you by, are you going to open your package?" He nodded toward it.

"Eager beaver. It's not from you, is it, you sly dog?" Hey, I could tease and flirt, too.

"No." He grinned again, giving me a hot flash.

I had to stop making him grin. "Then, no. I'm not. It's not my birthday, Christmas, or Valentine's. No one other than that sicko Ket would be sending me something. And him just to scare me." I shuddered involuntarily, imagining him in the room, touching my things. "Besides, Mom taught me never to open packages of unknown origin. This one has no return address."

"It doesn't have a 'to' address, either," Van pointed out.

"Good point. Maybe it's not even for me."

He snorted and laughed. "It's on your bed."

"Mistaken delivery."

"Only one way to find out. Open it."

"Mom wouldn't like it."

"Mom really taught you that? It sounds more like a post office/government warning. Anthrax, Unabomber, the like."

"You caught me. No, she didn't, but it sounds good. Next time I'll make up some postal experience." I flashed him a returning grin. "She did teach me not to talk to strangers. This is practically the same thing." I paused again. "We could call the front desk and ask who made the delivery and why they didn't just leave it at the front desk like a floral delivery? What in the world were they thinking invading my space? Maybe I can sue." I was all talk. I hate frivolous lawsuits.

"Somehow, I doubt they have a record of this," Van said. "My guess is he bribed someone to deliver it for him."

"Or came in himself," I said. That Ket had not personally been in my room, just some bribable minimum wage maid doing his bidding was only a marginally comforting thought.

"Did you notice any other signs that Ket made a personal appearance?" Van asked.

"You mean like fingerprints, stray hairs to check

for DNA, that kind of thing? I was so upset, I didn't think to check." Dumb mistake really. I was supposed to be keeping a victim's diary and collecting damning evidence against him.

"Well, he didn't pop out of the closet at you while I was gone. That's something. If he *was* here, he's not now."

"Yeah. But now you've scared me." I made Van search the room, including looking under the bed. "And remember my policy about under the bed—"

"Strictly a need-to-know basis. I know," he said.

His search came up Ket-clean.

"The coast is clear. Aren't you the least bit curious what's in there?" He nodded to the box again.

"It's a horse head."

"In a Cindy Lou box?"

"Cindy Lou box?"

"Yeah," he said. "Don't tell me you didn't notice their signature gold boxes everywhere downstairs?"

"Can't say as I did." I'd been too busy trying to avoid the Cindy Lous. I have a weakness when it comes to jewelry.

"If you're going to be a spy, you need to perk up the observation skills."

"I'm not going to be a spy."

"For your own safety then." He picked up the box and shook it. "Kaboom!"

I jumped.

He grinned and held out the box to me. "Sorry."

"I bet." As I took it from him, I grazed his fingers. "Your hands are warm." Which meant he wasn't cold with panic and fear like I was. I admired his strength as much as I longed to crawl into his arms.

He shrugged.

"Warm hands, cold heart?"

"That's just an old wives' tale." He nodded toward the box again. "Go ahead. Open it. Let's see what kind of a horse head it is, Vito."

"You rumpled the bow," I said. It had been a nice bow, the only festive thing about the stupid present.

"Open. Open. Open." Van made an open and close motion with his hands.

I untied the ribbon and slid off the gold lid. A gift card sat on top. I pulled it out and opened it, reading aloud, "I'd love to see this looped around your pretty neck. Yours always, K." I began trembling uncontrollably.

Van mumbled something about a bastard and put his arm around me. I curled into him, wanting to melt away with him, completely forget the horror that was Ket. Van's embrace was warm and soothing, not to mention sexy.

"It's Ket's handwriting." I shuddered. "His meaning is clear—he'd love to see this roped around my neck until my eyes bulge out. He has a nice way with words, doesn't he?"

Van ignored me for the moment, and with his arm still around me, pulled a long necklace from the box. "Crystals. Black beads. This thing looks like it would hang to your waist." He whistled. "Very elegant. Take heart, the guy spent a few bucks on this. Probably top-of-the-line Cindy Lou."

I stared at it a minute before looking away. "Spare no expense to torment me. He's mine always, whether I want him or not." I paused, trying not to think of Ket, and failing.

This was just another show of his nasty sense of humor. Ket loved bangles. Anything shiny. This style of necklace particularly got him hot.

"Put this on and nothing else, baby," he'd say. "Turn me on. Give it to your boy." His eyes would gleam with a dark, possessive emotion that had nothing to do with love.

And how many times had I complied, worn the necklace to please or placate him? Watched as he watched the bounce of the beads against my breasts, and the sparkle and play of light off the crystals while having sex. He loved to shift his weight against me until the beads cut into my skin, and his, and I cried out in pain that he seemed impervious to. He loved the power the necklace gave him. It was his choke chain over me.

"Once," I was barely aware of speaking aloud, "in a sudden fit of jealousy, Ket knotted a necklace I was wearing around his fist, cinching it around my neck until I choked and nearly passed out." While he accused me of fantasizing about another man. I kept that part to myself. "I can't stop hating him." Or worse, fearing him.

I turned to stare directly into Van's eyes, wishing there had never been a Ket. "He knows where I am. He got a package into my room, through bribery or intimidation. Either way, he'll be back. I can't stay here." I stood suddenly and headed to the in-room safe for my keys and gun.

Van dropped the necklace back into the box. "Where do you plan on running?"

"Home. My parents' house. Call me a mama's

girl, but Grandpa Dutch lives with my parents. He knows how to handle a gun."

"You live with your parents?"

"No." I stared at him. "Don't you ever refer to your parents' house as home?"

"Nope."

"Huh." I shrugged and opened the closet.

"This hotel is the safest place for you." He laughed at the irony of his own statement.

"Stop quoting FSC." I pointed to the bed and the open box. "Mafia goons. That hideous piece of jewelry. Top-notch security my foot."

"Isn't your parents' house an obvious place for Ket to look for you?"

"Yeah, but Ket's afraid of Grandpa Dutch." I punched in my self-generated safe combination. When the safe pinged open, I reached in and pulled out my camera, snapping a picture of the jewelry for posterity and Ket's trial of the century that some way, someday was going to happen and put him away for life. And I might have clicked a photo of Van, too. For myself, of course.

I went to the bed and scooped up the jewelry, grimacing as I did. "We've contaminated this with our fingerprints. I'd never make it on *CSI*." I sighed and went back to the safe and tossed the black necklace of death in.

I pulled out my Beretta. "There you are, girl," I said, as if purring to a cat. I held it up for Van to see. "I have a gun."

"I see that. He's a nice one."

"She."

"Guns are male."

"So says you," I said.

"You only have to look at one to see that," he said. "Where do you think the term ramrod stiff came from?"

I sighed and rolled my eyes as I tossed *her* into my purse. I grabbed my keys. "Okay, I'm off." I hesitated, not really wanting to walk to my car by myself.

Van remained on the bed, watching me.

"Well?" I said.

"Well what?"

"Aren't you going to walk me to my car?"

He raised a brow.

"Or insist on going with me?" I said in exasperation.

"I thought you'd never ask. Now that you're showing some faith in my protection abilities, I insist."

"Thank goodness," I said.

Van grinned. "Do you have a picture of Ket on you?"

I nodded. "Are you kidding? My picture of Ket is like my credit cards—I don't leave home without one."

"Good. Take it with you. We have some Cindy Lous to talk to. In fact, I think we should see if Cayla Smith is around."

"You're good with names," I said.

"Gotta be." He grinned again. I had to stop making him grin.

Chapter 16

I changed out of my spattered camos and baggy, braless T-shirt into jeans and a bra and a women's tee that fit. Then I called Mom and let her know to expect two for dinner.

We rapped on Cayla's door on the way out. Her room was just across the hall, but she wasn't home.

"Well," I said stoically, "at least I don't have to worry any more about Ket getting the wrong room and killing Cayla in my place. He's smarter than I gave him credit for."

"Comforting thought," Van said. "I prefer my thugs dumb. Cayla's probably downstairs in the exhibition hall, hawking her wares. I say we find her. I have a feeling she has a mouth on her. She'd make a great watchdog."

I agreed. We hit the lobby and found a copy center in the hotel where we made several dozen color copies of Ket's picture with instructions to contact hotel security if anyone saw him. We headed into the exhibition hall armed and determined.

An hour later, we'd distributed our flyers and

stoked up the indignation and protective instincts of hundreds of women to the towering inferno level. Van had been ogled and propositioned. He was desperate enough to escape the smoldering estrogen center that had it been a real blaze situation, he would have jumped.

Ket had spent $54.95 on his chosen instrument of torment, a high-end piece of jewelry in the Cindy Lou line. But no one fessed up to selling it to him. We also came up empty-handed as far as making a Ket sighting, but I was weighed down with jewelry bags.

"Let me take those." Van relieved me of my purchases. "I thought you hated the Cindy Lou ladies. Did you have to buy out their stock?"

"Asking them to keep an eye out for Ket was an 'I'll scratch yours, you scratch mine' moment. I had to buy something to seal the deal. I wanted them to remember me as the nice one, the one who bought, because believe me, Ket can lay on the charm. I'm still half afraid he'll charm them into silence. It's just a good thing we talked to so many."

Van sighed and shook his head. "I don't give a rat's ass about back-scratching. You should have let me do all the talking."

I gave him an amused look. "Mathman, they nearly had you for breakfast, lunch, and dinner. A few more minutes in there and you would have been lucky to escape with your shirt. They treated you like a rock god. They were getting ready to mob." I smiled at him. "Anyway, no hardship. I love jewelry. I think I may have an addiction."

"No kidding."

"Blame sports. Too many years of the no-jewelry-at-games policy. I grew up feeling jewelry deprived. I had to wait until I was in the seventh grade to get my ears pierced."

Van's look said he didn't understand the travesty.

"Aren't you going to ask why?"

"I give. Why?"

"Gymnastics. I was too tall for gymnastics. It was the first time I had an open sports season since third grade. Finally, six weeks to get my ears pierced."

Van still looked confused.

"You can't take your earrings out for six weeks after you get your ears pierced or the holes close over."

"Ahh," he said, in that way men have of answering, but you can tell their minds are millions of miles away. "Where's the car? I feel silly carrying these Cindy Lou bags."

We made a brief, furtive stop back by our rooms to pick up an overnight bag.

"This is why I never unpack and settle in," I told Van as I zipped up my bag and wheeled it out of the room. He had ostensibly thrown a spare pair of briefs and his toothbrush into a duffel bag. He carried that and my jewelry purchases to the car.

My car was parked in the lot smack-dab under a light and in direct line of sight of the hotel restaurant. If Ket was going to abduct me, he was going to have witnesses.

I popped the trunk and we stashed the bags. I beeped the locks and headed for the driver's side.

Van stood rooted in place behind the car.

I looked back at him. "Hurry. Get in. We're out in the open here."

"I'll drive," he said.

"Chauvinist, are you?"

"I know some evasive driving techniques. I went to the Bondurant Driving School." He shot me a challenging look.

"I have no idea who Bondurant is."

"Figures. Bondurant is the king of driving schools. If we're followed, our odds of escape are better if I'm driving. Besides, I know how to check for car bombs."

I sighed and tossed him my keys. "Who's paranoid now?"

"Hey, you're the one who implied Ket has explosive skills. It's as easy to rig a car as a package." He pulled a wand thingy out of his pocket. He waved it at me. "I come prepared."

"Thanks, Q. Got any other gizmos up your sleeve?"

"Maybe."

"Who made you an explosives expert, Mr. Math Professor? Afraid of unhappy students?"

"I've taken a few classes."

"They're teaching Bomb Making 101 in our universities now? Just proves what they say about our tax dollars going to waste." I gave him a skeptical look.

He grinned. "Bomb detection. Didn't take them at the university, either. Let's just say I'm into extreme adventures."

I pierced him with a look and waited for him to elaborate. He didn't. "Fine, keep the mystery in our relationship."

I watched as Van did a visual and wanded the car,

making wisecracks and admiring his butt as he bent over to inspect my car's underside. "We need one of those mirrors on a stick like they use in spy movies. I could lend you my compact."

"Very funny," he said. "We're clear. Hop in."

My parents' house was a thirty-minute drive from the airport strip. I punched their address into my GPS and let it do the directing. I was too distracted by Van and thoughts of being followed to pay attention. I wasn't the best at giving directions under ideal circumstances.

"I hope you checked for bugs and tracking devices while you were checking out the car," I said.

"I did my best."

Both of us kept glancing in the rearview mirror, and I took a gander over my shoulder at regular intervals, but I didn't see any tails. As it was, I wasn't thrilled with heading to my parents' place. I generally avoided putting them in danger. But at the moment, I was out of options.

"So you have your own place?" Van asked.

"Yep."

"If Ket's afraid of Grandpa Dutch, who I assume lives with your parents—"

"Since Grandma died. He lives in the guesthouse," I said. "Don't get any ideas about wealth and fancy places. The guesthouse is a converted root cellar and storage shed. Well, it's actually better than that sounds. It suits Grandpa."

"Why don't you live with your parents full-time?"

"'Cause one, we'd drive each other crazy. Two, I

love them and don't like putting them in harm's way. And three, there's that independence fetish of mine." I gave Van a direct stare.

The GPS told him to turn left. He signaled and made the turn. "Just what's so scary about Grandpa Dutch?"

"Worried?"

"I like to know what I'm facing."

"Where to begin? Grandpa's six six, three hundred. I can almost wear his ring as a bracelet. He's what you'd call big built in a Paul Bunyan sort of way."

"Sounds intimidating."

"Yeah, and that's not the half of it." I smiled. "Dutch is legendary. He can find fish in any lake anywhere any time without sonar. He's hunted and killed nearly every North American animal there is and, much to Mom's chagrin, has the antlers and stuffed fish to prove it hanging on the walls of the guesthouse."

I paused, smiling at Grandpa's antics. "Bigfoot's the only beast who's gotten away. Not that he'd consider killing one. But he'd like a good snapshot of an actual creature. So far all he's got is a picture of a footprint. Word of warning, don't so much as insinuate Bigfoot doesn't exist, not if you want to live."

"So Dutch is an outdoor sportsman."

"You got it. If Dutch tosses his hook out it comes back with a fish. If he aims his gun, he comes back with a buck. If he went after Ket . . ."

"I get the point."

"Good. Further point of interest, he's fluent in

both Dutch and English. Don't let him scare you with that 'me hoon it, me boon it' mangled English-sounding Dutch stuff he can lapse into when he wants to be intimidating. And"—I held up a finger—"Grandpa doesn't swear. He grew up in a strict, religious Dutch community and has never completely shaken their strictures. Which means he's confined to switching to a foreign language and yelling loudly to express his displeasure. Since Grandma died, he's been more frustrated than usual. She was the only one of us who spoke Dutch. None of us understand his rantings beyond the passion of his tone.

"One last thing, you don't want to swear in front of him, either. I'm still in trouble for using the word 'crap' in seventh grade."

"Seems mild."

"Not to Dutch."

"Warning taken."

"Good."

When we arrived, I instructed Van to park in the garage. Since the trouble with Ket, my parents insisted I park inside for protection.

Mom and Dad lived in an old converted farmhouse that had seen too many rambling additions to be considered either beautiful or a study in efficient space planning. The once rural countryside around them had gone suburban, raising their property value and threatening their clear view of Mount Rainier with ten-to-an-acre homes.

I selected a pair of pink crystal and bead earrings with a matching choker as a spontaneous present for Mom and we headed toward the house.

Dutch saw us pull in. He, and the pleasant smell of homemade chicken pot pie, greeted us at the door as we came around the front walk.

"What goes on here?" Grandpa pulled me into a bear hug. Up close, he smelled reassuringly of fish and cigarette smoke. Not your best combination, but steady.

He let me go and looked at Van through his startlingly blue eyes with an expression that said this new boy I was bringing home better be better than the last one.

Guess I hadn't made it clear to Mom that Van was just a fellow camper. Not that it was really possible to make something like that clear to Mom. She saw husband potential when I mentioned the paperboy.

"Hey, Gramps. This is Van. Van, Dutch."

The two men shook hands and Grandpa stepped back to let us in. "Come in. Come in."

I was only too happy to comply.

Grandpa's brow was creased in consternation and study as he stared Van down. I recognized the expression. I'd say Dutch didn't like the sex appeal that oozed from Van. Or maybe it was the way I had a hard time *not* looking at Van. I sensed a horn-locking coming on. Grandpa would try to save my virtue by scaring Van off. Just what I needed.

Grandpa had been trying to foist off studious, nervous, timid, nerdy types on me my whole dating life. Anyone I had zero chance of lusting after. Too bad he hadn't been in California with me when I met Ket.

I took Grandpa's arm and tried not to look at Van. "Where is everybody?"

"Your dad is away in Portland. He'll be home at the end of the week. Your mother's in the kitchen," Dutch said. "So what's all this about coming home for dinner in the middle of your spy vacation? Are you out on a covert mission? Are we your safe house now?"

So Mom hadn't told Grandpa about Ket. Grandpa was still staring at Van, who looked at me and shrugged.

"Sort of. Ket's out," I blurted.

My mother came around the corner from the kitchen with a smile on her face. Mom was average height, slightly built, and thin for her age with blond hair highlighted to hide the encroaching gray. She was a micro version of Dutch. We looked absolutely nothing alike. I wasn't surprised to see Van do a double take when he saw her.

Mom hugged me. "Glad you got here safely. I want the full scoop on Ket."

"I'll tell everything. Later." I stepped back from her hug. "This is for you." I handed her the gold Cindy Lou box. "And this is Van."

I made the introductions. Mom had to juggle the box as she shook his hand. In contrast to Dutch's disapproval, Mom's eyes lit up when she saw Van.

"Dinner will be in half an hour. May I take your jacket, Van?"

The house was warm. Van was dressed in jeans, a T-shirt, and a lightweight jacket. In other words, overdressed for the heat. Yet he declined Mom's offer. He was either catching something or overly fond of the jacket. I shot him a quizzical look and he shrugged.

Mom ushered us into the living room. "Sit, everyone. Can I get you something to drink, Van?"

Van wanted a beer. I wanted water. Once we were all beveraged, Mom opened her gift.

"Cindy Lou jewelry," she said. "I just went to a party last month. Becky next door. She's *always* having some kind of party. Twenty years I've lived here I've never given a single party where my *guests* have to buy something. But that Becky! Always having a sales party. Name me something I haven't bought from that woman."

"Well, take comfort, Mom," I said. "I didn't buy this one from Becky."

Van leaned into me and whispered, "Why doesn't she just decline the invitation?"

"You can't hide from Becky." Mom had good ears. "She'll rout you out. It's easier just to endure and buy." Mom rolled her eyes and put the choker on. "Very nice, though I was expecting something more spylike."

"Sorry to disappoint. There's a Cindy Lou convention in the hotel. Picture hundreds of Beckys running around selling, selling, selling!"

Mom and I shuddered in unison.

"Next time I'll bring you a magnifying glass and matching trench coat. Promise."

"I'll hold you to it." Mom excused herself to put the finishing touches on dinner.

"I'll just go help her," I said to the boys.

"You leaving me to entertain your friend all by myself?" Grandpa asked, clearly uncertain how to go about it.

"I trust you not to scare him away. Show him your

Bigfoot footprint picture, Grandpa," I called to Dutch over my shoulder as I followed Mom to the kitchen. "Van is a skeptic."

I winked at Van, whose eyes went wide before he mouthed an expletive back at me. "Live on the edge," I mouthed back and turned away.

I was dying to get to the guest room and use the computer. Van might not be curious about the dongle and its connection to the other campers, but my curiosity was threatening to take me down. Mom would never let me help in the kitchen. But Van had no way of knowing that. I intended to wander off to do my dirty work.

As anticipated, once I was in the kitchen, Mom rejected my help. However, she'd interpreted my presence as code for "grill me about Ket."

"How? When?" she asked as she tore up a salad.

"Legal technicality. This morning." I answered her questions to the best of my abilities. "Do you mind if I go freshen up before we eat?"

Mom arched a brow, bombarded me with a few more Ket questions and let me go. "I left you some goodies in your room. The local bath and body shop had their new line of fall scents out last week. I picked you up a few of those three-in-one body washes you love."

She had indeed. Pumpkin Pie Pleasures and Cinnamon Bun Bliss. I gave them each a quick sniff. Nice. I had a momentary fantasy of a double shower with Van and me, Van covered in luscious Cinnamon Bun Bliss lather and some bump and grind going on. They say that cinnamon is good for the health. In my fantasy, it was definitely very good for me. I smiled to myself and then I was off to the guest room to log on to Mom's computer.

Ten minutes later I'd Googled Cliff and found him and his movies on IMDb. I couldn't find anything more damning on him than that he'd made more than a few bombs. Nothing I'd ever rent, for sure. I turned my attention to Peewee and his big shot, rumored-to-be-Mafia uncle. Jackpot!

Mom called us to dinner just as I finished reading a fascinating article on one of those crime file websites about Sil Canarino, with a brief mention of his lowlife nephew Peewee. Sil was a Mafia boss and infamous wiretapper to the stars with more dirt on the Hollywood rich and famous than an excavation site. He was currently in the can awaiting trial and refusing to talk about how to decrypt his impressive encrypted library of audio files that housed all that lovely, rich sandy loam. The key to the encryption was a dongle. Everybody wanted it—the tabloids, the FBI, the guys Sil had the dirt on. And guess what? The dongle was missing.

"Shit!" I said, hoping Grandpa didn't hear. Shit had to be way worse than crap. And I was deep in it.

Chapter 17

The table was set for four with Mom's best every-day dishes and a floral arrangement in fall colors. A large bowl of tossed salad sat off to one side surrounded by an assortment of salad dressings. I sat next to Van and across from Grandpa. My mind was bouncing around *Godfather* endings and *Sopranos* episodes. I'd gotten rid of that damn dongle, if it indeed was *the* dongle. Everybody knew I'd given it up. I was safe in my childhood home, the one I hoped didn't turn into Massacre on 185th Street. I just needed to relax. Van had to be right. We were safe now.

Mom brought out the pot pie, apologizing for the simple meal.

"Never apologize for pot pie, Mom." I turned to Van. "It's her signature dish for a reason."

Mom smiled and I tried to relax. Everything was all better now. Grandpa said a Dutch blessing, which sounded mostly like butchered English, and we all dug in.

Mom couldn't keep her mind off Ket. She'd thought

of a few more questions. "Has Ket contacted you? Have you, or anyone up here, actually seen him since he's been out?"

Even though she was a champion worrier, my mother wasn't the kind of woman you could keep things from. I told her about the necklace in my room.

"Those wretched Cindy Lous!" Mom scowled. "Anything for a sale. I wonder how much extra Ket paid for delivery. Have you called the police?"

"I've talked to them," I said obtusely. Well, I had talked to the cops, though not about Ket. "There's not much they can do."

"Until he murders you in your sleep." Mom had that "I'd like to protect my kid by murdering Ket" tone in her voice that I'd grown to know and love over the past few years.

"I'm keeping up my victim's diary and storing all evidence." I gave Mom a look that asked her to drop it.

"Dutch showed me his Bigfoot collection," Van said, trying to arrange peace by switching topics. To my amazement, he and Dutch seemed to have bonded. "That footprint picture from 1998 is amazing. The print is huge, too large to be human, yet human-looking. Very ingenious putting that gum wrapper next to it to show the size," he said to Dutch, who did his own shrug.

"It was all I had on me," Grandpa said and launched into another one of his Bigfoot tales.

I knew the picture and the gum wrapper—Double Mint, Dutch's signature chew, especially when he was trying to quit smoking.

"I saw that print," I said to Van, since he seemed so impressed by the thing. "A week after Grandpa found it, he took me up in the North Idaho countryside to see it. It was still there in the packed dirt. The hair on the back of my neck stood up just seeing it." Kind of like it had been doing for the past twenty-four hours or so.

Mom wasn't into the Bigfoot discussion. She was more into the big jerk train of thought. "Reilly, you have your gun with you, right?"

"Always."

"Gun, that's a good idea." While we'd been discussing Bigfoot, Dutch had been coming to a slow Dutch simmer. I was amazed he hadn't thought of getting the gun before. Usually he wasn't so slow on the uptake. He pushed his chair back from the table. "I'll just go get the shotgun. In case. Keep eating. I'll be right back."

Mom watched Grandpa go. "I wish Ket weren't out. I liked it better when you kids were babies. I had so much more control over your world and safety back then. If there was a bully in playgroup, I simply talked to his mother. And if that didn't work, I pulled you out."

I nodded in response. "You could try Ket's mom. But she's firmly on her little darling's side and almost as much of a jerk as he is."

Mom sighed. "Come to think of it, the talking-to-the-mom thing didn't work much better back then. But sometimes I wish I still had the pulling-you-out-of-the-group option. Are you going back to camp tomorrow?"

I looked at Van who looked at me. "Yeah, I think so."

Mom frowned. "Are you sure that's a good idea? I heard a story on the news today. A man was found murdered in a warehouse run by your spy camp people. The police weren't releasing any details." Mom gave me another piercing look that conveyed the question, when were you planning on telling me about that one?

I withered just a bit in my chair.

Mom was a news junkie—talk radio, twenty-four-hour TV news shows, the Internet, she took them all in. Her addiction had gotten worse since my ordeal with Ket. I don't know if she was trying to comfort herself, prepare herself, or scare herself crazy. I should have known better than to try to keep something like a murder in a warehouse from her.

"Sorry. I got caught up in the Ket stuff and forgot."

"Forgot? You forgot about a murder?"

"Okay, delayed. I was going to tell you about it, but I thought you had enough to worry about."

Mom was still frowning.

"Really," I said. "Look how long it took you to get around to asking." I put a note of triumph in my voice.

"I didn't want to upset your grandfather by bringing it up in front of him."

"He doesn't know?"

"Do you really think he'd let you go back if he did?"

Fortunately, Van saved me by taking up the story, telling it in a confidential tone. Like he was letting

Mom in on the top secret scoop. The man had a gift. He made our discovery sound like an Abbott and Costello caper. Mom was actually smiling as he talked. She even giggled once or twice.

The way Van told the story, we discovered the body all right, although more like from afar, almost as if we'd spotted Jay in the bottom of a ravine from the top of the hill with our binoculars. Very safe and sanitary.

"I can't believe you two discovered the body. Danger certainly follows Reilly around." Mom looked directly at me.

I stared down at my plate to keep from giving the real story away. "Remind me to ask you to recount *Hamlet* and *The Silence of the Lambs*. Those two stories have always bothered me. If only I'd known they were comedies," I whispered to Van.

"I thought you'd be thanking me," he whispered back, reaching around me and giving my shoulders a squeeze. I noticed a bead of sweat forming on his forehead, but he didn't move to take his jacket off. "Reilly has a hard time talking about it," he said to Mom.

"Buck up, baby." Mom reached across and patted my hand. "They're sure there's no danger?"

Van answered. "They don't think the murder has anything to do with camp. He was probably just dumped there. They've added additional security. The place has never been safer."

"Well, if there's extra security," Mom said, giving me one last sympathetic look before letting the subject drop.

Neither Van nor I mentioned that I'd dated the

murdered man. Nor did we mention Goon or the dongle. If Mom didn't have enough of an inkling about them to drag the details out of us, she didn't need to know. Only a fool tells her mother everything.

"Where's your grandfather?" Mom asked, noticing Dutch had been gone longer than expected. "What in the world is taking him so long?"

"Maybe he had to reload some ammo?" I said.

"He doesn't reload shot." Mom pushed her chair back just as a loud crash came from the vicinity of the garage.

The crash was followed by scuffling and loud male voices, one of which was Grandpa's.

"Damn it!" Mom said, seemingly unafraid of Grandpa's wrath for cursing. In the next instant, she hit the outdoor security lights, flooding the lawn in brilliance that would have put the midday sun to shame.

Van reached beneath his jacket and ran out the door before I could stop him. "Stay here," he called after himself.

I ran for my purse, which Mom had stored in the coat closet in the front hall. Why did I never have my gun on me?

A door slammed. I jumped. My purse clattered to the floor as I pulled the Beretta out. By the time I got back to the kitchen with gun in hand, Mom had her pistol and stood at the ready, aiming toward the back door.

"What do we do now?" I asked. I really did not want to use the gun.

"You cover the front door. I'm taking the back."

"What is this?" I asked. "I feel like I'm in an episode of *Cops*."

"Just don't get trigger happy," Mom said, her eyes steely with that "protect the cub" look. "We don't need anyone shooting Van or your grandfather."

"Speaking of cops, maybe we should call the cops," I said, my voice rising in panic. "Has anyone called the cops?"

Mom's response was cut off by the squeal of peeling tires and flying gravel.

Grandpa came charging into the house. "Them sons of guns broke into the garage!"

Van was right behind him, panting. "They got away."

"Those high school kids again?" At first Mom sounded merely annoyed. "This is not a house to mess with. We have guns in this house. We have a creepy, scary, stalking maniac skulking about. We don't need any dumb high school kids dropping by to get shot." Her voice rose in pitch with each word. Looking spent, she dropped her gun and turned to me.

"They broke in last month and stole an old pair of pruning shears, of all things. Cut themselves in the process and bled all over the hood of the car. Very disturbing. Those shears were rusty. I can't imagine what they wanted with them. I hope they didn't get lockjaw. I can just imagine being sued by a trespassing delinquent."

"It wasn't kids," Van said quietly. That's when I noticed that he had a gun, too, and was quietly re-holstering it beneath his jacket.

I set my Beretta on the table. "You have a gun,

too? Is that what you've been hiding all evening?" I didn't even try to take the accusation out of my tone. "Aren't we a highly un-PC crowd? We'd make a good ad for the NRA." I put my hands on my hips. "You can take your jacket off and stop sweltering now."

Van grinned. "You aren't the only one with a permit to carry concealed."

"I bet," I said.

"If they weren't kids, who were they?" Mom asked. She slid her gun back in a kitchen drawer. For just a moment I hated Ket that much more for making my little mother a gun-toting mama.

"Adults. Looking for something in the garage. Dutch scared them off." Van slid off his jacket.

"Ket?" I asked.

Van shook his head. "Could be his henchmen, though. Maybe some PIs he hired. There were two of them." He shot me a look that said maybe they weren't even Ket's guys. I didn't like the possibilities. Fortunately Mom and Dutch missed the look. Van glanced around the room and then strained like he was listening for something. "Should we be expecting the cops?"

"I don't think anyone called them," Mom said.

"Nor should we," Grandpa said. "They won't do a bit of good. Haven't so far, anyway. Never kept Ket away and still haven't said boo about catching them high school hooligans."

Van didn't give an opinion.

I didn't notice until that minute that Grandpa had changed into his hunting camo and had a high-powered rifle in hand.

"I thought you went for the shotgun," I said.

He shook his head. "I meant to. But then I noticed a suspicious car parked on the road." He pointed in the general direction of the road. "That's when I realized this was no duck job. I needed my high-powered, night vision sight."

"Dad," Mom said, pointing to his gun and the muddy footprints on the wood floor.

"Sorry." He leaned the rifle against the wall and went to the mat to wipe his feet. "The sprinklers were on earlier today."

During all the domestic chatter, Van had gone to the window and was peering covertly through the blinds.

"Do you see anything?" I whispered. Why I whispered, I'll never know. It's one of those things. When you're sneaking around, hush seems required. "Is anyone out there?"

"Not now."

"I'd better arm the security system. Everyone stay away from the doors and windows." Mom headed for the security system control panel and I headed for Van, coming up behind him at the window and maybe standing a little too close for propriety's sake.

"What's up?" Van asked as soon as she was gone. He was still staring out the window.

"You tell me." I paused. "We can't stay here. We're putting Mom and Grandpa in danger." I blew out a breath. "Grandpa is going to be tempted to use that gun."

Van nodded. "What's your plan?"

"I have to go back to the hotel." And then I said the part I'd really been dreading. "And I'll have to make it obvious I'm leaving. I want them to follow me. I want them as far away from my family as possible." I drew in a deep breath. "You can stay here. Grandpa can drive you to camp tomorrow."

Van shook his head and started laughing.

Chapter 18

"What's so funny?" I asked.

"Do you really think I'm going to let you go off by yourself?" Van was still laughing and shaking his head in amusement. "Nice try, Miss Chivalrous, but no way. And don't give me that math professor nerd stuff. I'm a trained marksman and driver."

"Listen, Mr. Extreme Sport—"

Grandpa walked back into the room, interrupting my defense. "Of course he's going with you," he said. "That's what a gentleman does. You think I'd let my granddaughter go alone with that nasty son of a gun out there after her?"

"Outmoded thinking," I said, feeling some relief that I wouldn't have to go it alone. In truth, I felt safer with Van by my side even if he was a math professor.

"I'd go with you two if I didn't have to stay and look out for your mother," Grandpa said. And he was dead serious.

Mom walked back into the room. "Where are you two going?"

"Back to the hotel." Van explained the situation to her, and although she didn't like it, she agreed with our plan to head out.

Mom had the same "we can't have Grandpa shooting someone" look in her eye that I'd had earlier. "I made gingerbread and lemon sauce for dessert. Can you at least stay for that?"

Van and I both felt antsy to be gone so Mom packed up a dessert care package for us while Van checked out the car again.

Ten minutes later, we'd said our good-byes and were on the road.

"That was a bust," I said as Van backed the car out of the garage. "All I did was get Mom worked up and put her and Grandpa in danger."

Van turned the car around and pointed it down the driveway. I pulled the Beretta out of my purse and set it in my lap.

"What's that for?" Van asked.

"Guess."

"I'll do any shooting that needs to be done," he said.

"No way. You can't shoot. You're driving. You have to keep your eyes on the road, buster."

"I can shoot and drive."

"Not left-handed. For that maneuver to work, you'd have to shoot left-handed. Are you left-handed? Huh, buddy, huh?"

"I'm ambidextrous."

"Nice to know," I said, though he was probably bluffing. We drove in silence for a minute. But the silence made me feel like crying. And big girls don't cry. I mean, little petite girls cry and they get sympathy. Girls my size just look silly. To divert myself from my pity party, I spilled about my research at Mom's.

"I found a connection between Steve, Cliff, Peewee, the dongle, and Peewee's Mafia mobster uncle, Sil Canarino. I read all about them on a crime website after I Googled Peewee Canarino."

Van sat impassive while I told him all I knew, but his gaze kept flicking to the rearview mirror.

"In Hollywood, Sil Canarino's been the wiretapper to the stars since the mid-seventies. He's worked for just about everyone who's anyone in the biz.

"Plus Sil's not only an expert wiretapper, but a world-class encoder. He got his encrypting experience while he served in Vietnam, which is where he also apparently got his skills with weaponry and explosive devices.

"The FBI took him, his computers, tapping equipment, and encrypted tape library into custody months ago. But the Feds haven't been able to decode the files. If they don't succeed by this Friday, they'll have to drop the case and let Canarino go. Goon said the dongle was the key to decoding some software. I think it's Sil's key."

"Nice family Peewee has." Van paused. "How was Sil caught? Did someone rat him out?"

I didn't know if he was really curious, or just keeping me talking to keep my mind off those pesky garage raiders. Though talking about mobsters wasn't really the equivalent of a peaceful bedtime story.

"Sort of. Though it's a fishy story." I paused, smiling

at my own cleverness. "I'm actually a little hazy on the details. I was reading fast, trying to finish before Mom caught me or called me to dinner. Something about a fish on the windshield of a reporter's car, some kind of intimidation to get him to back off a story."

"A horse's head?"

"Exactly. And that led the cops to the lowlife Canarino used for the job, who fingered him. So the cops went to Canarino's office and found an arsenal. They arrested him on weapons charges, and later went back with a warrant to search for wiretapping equipment and discovered the files."

I kept glancing in the mirror, too. If anyone was following us, they weren't being obvious. But the feeling of being chased made me feel rushed and flustered.

"Where do the rest of our fellow campers come in?"

I spoke fast, as if there was barely time to get the story out. "Cliff allegedly hired Canarino to illegally bug other directors' and producers' homes and offices. He'll do anything to give himself the creative upper hand. He has what he thinks is a huge blockbuster in the making. A flick that will make his reputation and secure his financial future. If Canarino's tapes are released, he'll lose everything. That makes him an extremely dangerous man.

"And Jim. Odds are he used Canarino to illegally obtain information that he used for his clients' benefit. He'll be disbarred and possibly jailed."

"None of this has been proven?"

"Not yet. Not without the tapes," I said. "But everything points to it being true." I took a deep breath.

"Van, whoever has the dongle has tremendous power."

Van nodded his agreement. "Or is in tremendous danger. We can assume Canarino doesn't want it to surface. Not before Friday."

"True," I said. "Nor does anyone else. But after Friday, it's a blackmailer's gold mine. Whoever has it can cut a deal with Canarino for just about anything they want. He'll have the tapes and they'll have his key. The crime files said that there is only one dongle, and Canarino destroyed the blueprint for safekeeping. Unless he has a hell of a memory . . ."

"Huff?"

"I think Huff was Sil's man charged with safekeeping the thing. Then Huff got me to make the drop in the ladies' room. Something went wrong and whoever was supposed to pick it up didn't. Then word got out that I had the dongle. And here we are with goons after me. If I ever get my hands on Huff, I'm going to kill him." I slumped in the seat. I felt defeated. Anyway, slumping had the added benefit of making me less of a target.

Van shot me a deadpan look. "I wouldn't go making idle threats. Not in this climate. Take heart. With any luck, someone's beat you to it."

"Not funny."

"It wasn't supposed to be. And Jay?"

I sighed and blinked back an unexpected tear. "Okay, maybe Ket didn't get him. He was a PI to Cliff's nemesis. Could be he got too close and someone took him out." I paused. "Could have been anyone who wants the dongle." Which didn't leave me feeling very secure.

"What do you propose we do?" Van swerved to avoid a pothole.

I started, gasped, and almost screamed.

I put my hand to my heart. "Don't scare me like that."

"Just trying to preserve your suspension," he said, grinning. "So? The plan?"

"We've already made the anonymous tip," I said, thinking aloud. "Any police force worth its salt is going to find the same connection I did in a matter of minutes. Our problem seems to be information dissemination. Ooooh, I like the rhyme of that—information dissemination."

"Okay, big word girl, continue the thought."

"Oh, right. We need to get the word out that I no longer have the dongle. Those guys back at the garage might not have gotten the word. Either that or they were Ket's men. But breaking into garages isn't really Ket's MO. That's why I decided to leave. I don't think it's him."

"I agree about Ket." He paused. "You mean we advertise that you don't have the dongle?"

"You got it."

Van shook his head, but he was smiling like he found me amusing. Which was what I was going for. I chatted on about silly things all the time, but it was just my warped sense of humor. Ninety percent of it wasn't serious but merely meant to prevent silence.

"Okay, when we get back to the hotel, we'll post flyers for all mobsters and potential dongle stealers." Van signaled his intention to turn.

"With an artist's sketch of the goon so the bad guys will know who to go after. Can you draw?"

Van laughed. "Not well. Can you?"

"I thought with your mathematical prowess you'd be able to draw. Drawing's all about proportions and numbers. How disappointing."

"I have prowess in other areas."

My heart burst into overdrive. "Okay, no drawing talent. And here I love men who can draw, but never mind. We'll have to go to Plan B—call all the camp gang and tell them about the dongle theft. We'll simply have to describe Cindy Lou Goon."

"You serious?"

"But of course! Those guys will get the word out. They're all after the dongle, too. Then the bad dudes will leave us alone." My turn to wink, hoping his heart went into warp speed. I pulled out my cell phone and began dialing. "Did I mention I get benefits with this option?"

Van rolled his eyes and asked the inevitable question. "What benefits?"

"Jim's promised me free legal help if I help him out. He was looking for Huff, ostensibly for the dongle. He's promised to get rid of my little Ket problem. He's a legal exterminator of sorts." I grinned. "Oh, and Cliff has promised me a movie roll. A big one. Don't worry. I'll invite you to the premier. And Steve claims there's a reward out that he'll split with me. I'll cut you in on that, too."

"Aligning ourselves with the mob. That sounds like a great plan."

"Oh, it's ringing. Hey, Steve . . ."

Chapter 19

Twenty-five minutes later, we pulled into the same parking spot we'd left hours earlier. I snapped my phone shut, calls complete. "This parking spot gives me déjà vu, that feeling you get that you've already experienced something. Déjà vu—"

"All right, Miss Python, get out of the car."

"This lot is creepy in the dark." I did a quick perusal of the perimeter in unison with Van and then we both stepped out of the car. "Do you think we drew the creeps off Mom and Dutch? I didn't see anyone following us."

"I think we did. A good surveillance guy isn't going to be seen."

"You're just saying that to make me feel better, Dudley." I batted my eyes at him.

"Right, Nell." He laughed.

"Those guys weren't that good or Dutch wouldn't have surprised them," I said, trying for a moment of seriousness.

"Maybe Dutch is just good."

I shrugged. "Yeah, that must be it. Gramps is

good. And he had the element of surprise. They probably didn't expect a camouflaged, rifle-toting deer hunter to come after them. Although they should have thought about that. I mean, deer are almost in season."

Van was grinning as he pulled our bags from the car, and looking at me like I was a delectable, mouth-watering morsel. Well, that's what I liked to think anyway, because that's how I was looking at him.

"No one expects the Dutch Inquisition," Van said in a Monty Python tone as he handed me my car keys back.

"I thought that was the Spanish Inquisition?"

"Your grandpa out to protect you is way scarier."

"Just keep that in mind," I said.

We made our way back to our rooms without incident. Van rolled my suitcase in front of my door.

I paused, fending off a panic attack. "I can't sleep in there. Not even with Old Slugger and my girl gun for protection."

"All right," Van tried to sound resigned, but there was a flirtatious tease to his tone. "You can stay with me. If you have to." He pulled out his key card and opened his door, making a sweeping gesture with his arm. "After you."

I grabbed his arm and pulled it down. "Are you crazy?" I whispered into his ear. "Someone, for example Ket, might see me going into your room. I'll go into my room." Brave words. "And meet you at the connecting door. In the meantime, we'd better look like we're fighting, that we don't even like each other."

"Right. Good plan," he said. "It keeps with the whole spy camp theme we have going on. Everything must be surreptitious."

"Exactly."

The door across the hall opened and Cayla stepped out. "I thought I heard voices out here. Have you heard the news?"

We both stared at her expectantly.

She waved us closer. "Some jerk dressed as a Cindy Lou sales associate trashed the women's room in the bar and then accosted a patron as she came out. Then he held her in an elevator before releasing her. Everyone is very concerned and frightened. No one wants to use the public restrooms. The hotel has posted extra security, but still! I thought I should warn you."

"Thanks," I said.

"Perverts in the bathroom. And blaming the Cindy Lous. Can you believe the nerve!" She shook her head in total disgust. "At first, the hotel wanted to bill our organization for the damage we supposedly caused and ban us from returning. Fortunately, the police were on it. The outrage. One imposter could ruin our whole brand reputation!" She barely took a breath. "Hang on a sec."

Cayla ducked into her room and reappeared with a composite drawing of the goon, both in Cindy Lou drag and without. She handed it to me.

I stared at it and shuddered. Van peered at it over my shoulder and whispered into my ear, "What do you think?"

"Good likeness," I whispered back.

"The police artist drew that," Cayla said. "They came around asking about a man who might have bought a lot of jewelry earlier today. Well, several of us had made big sales to a man who fit the general description the police gave. We were only too happy to help out. And we came up with that!" Cayla was inordinately pleased, almost as if she were the artist herself.

"Fantastic." I nodded like I appreciated their co-operation.

"We're always glad to help. Though it's a shame, just a shame that a man would use Cindy Lou products for evil. If only we'd known his background and his evil intent!"

"Yeah, what's next? Background checks and waiting periods to buy costume jewelry?" I said. Van gave me a gentle elbow, but he was trying hard not to laugh.

"Exactly," Cayla said. "So now we have to be on the lookout for that creep *and* that handsome man you told us about earlier. What is the world coming to?"

"What indeed."

"Well." Cayla sighed.

I reluctantly held the flyer out to Cayla to take back.

"Oh, keep it," she said. "I have more. And if you see that creep, call the number listed."

I thanked her and she popped back into her room.

"Nice to know we have a block watch thing going

on our hotel floor," Van said in his dry sense of humor.

"Yeah. I wonder if there's a CrimeStoppers award for this guy. I could use some extra cash. And they take anonymous tips. I wonder if I can retroactively claim mine?"

"May I?" He held his hand out for the flyer.

I handed it to him. He pulled a pen out of his pocket and scrawled. "FYI, this guy has the dongle. If you want it, go after him." He showed me his handiwork. "Advertising."

"Very nice. I like a man who can write."

"Stay here. I'm going to get some tape." He disappeared into his room. A second later, he was back with the tape and posted the flyer on my door.

"That'll do, pig," I said.

"Okay, babe, I'll meet you at our adjoining door."

With that, we both darted into our rooms and closed our doors.

My heart was racing, from double excitement— fear and anticipation of spending the night with Van. How was I going to control myself?

The was a gentle rap on the adjoining door. Van called softly through it, "Everything okay in there? Any more untoward gifts? Costume jewelry? Flowers? Chocolates? Idle threats? Unidle threats? Bombs?"

I threw open my side of the door. "Nothing obvious. Want to check it out?"

"I thought you'd never ask." He did a quick search of the room and bathroom, and hefted my suitcase back onto the suitcase rack. "Sorry to disappoint you—no boogeymen at this time."

I flashed him a smile. "There's always next time."

Van glanced at his watch. "We have an early morning tomorrow. I say we hit the sack."

I was hoping for "hit the sheets." Hit the sheets had more innuendo attached. "Sure. Fine. I just need to change."

I thought his eyes went wide. Just for a second. Then he motioned toward his room. "I'll do the same. I'll just close the door and when you're ready, knock."

I nodded my agreement. As soon as he was gone, I sifted through my suitcase for my PJs. I was a single girl. I was supposed to be better dressed at night than the married gals. I was supposed to be ready for all romantic emergencies by traveling with the sexiest of lingerie. Only I wasn't.

I slept in camis and boxer shorts because I figured if I had to make a quick escape from Ket in the middle of the night, I wouldn't be thoroughly embarrassed to be seen running through the neighborhood in a cami and boxers. Partially embarrassed, maybe. The PJs were the right blend of sleeping comfort and respectability. I comforted myself by thinking that a cami and shorts wouldn't blink like a beacon to Van, "I'm expecting some hot sex tonight." They gave both of us an out.

I sighed. At least I had a matched set.

I changed and reluctantly took off my makeup. I wore the kind that was powdered minerals. You were supposed to be able to sleep in it, wear it for days, and it was actually good for your skin. It had the obvious advantage that if Ket ever kidnapped me and stuck me away somewhere, I'd look fresh for my rescue, possibly days later. However, I wasn't currently being held hostage. I scrubbed it off, brushed my teeth, and applied a fresh squirt of perfume. I wasn't a saint. I wanted Van to know he was sleeping with a woman.

I threw a zip-front hoody over my cami and tapped on our door with Mom's gingerbread in one hand and Old Slugger in the other. When he opened the door, I held the bag with the gingerbread out to him. "I come bearing food to this pajama party."

"Thank goodness. You look vicious with that bat." His eyes weren't on the food. His gaze was actually focused in the exact area of my double Ds. I wasn't wearing a bra. I budded right up for him so hard I was certain he saw the budding through the hoody.

He took the bag from me. He was wearing a T-shirt and knit boxers that left practically nothing to the imagination. I looked around the room to keep from staring at his package, which was nice by the way. We were practically a matched set. I tried hard to keep from drooling.

I know. Call me a hard woman. Jay was dead, and I was upset by that. But, really, I wasn't close to him. I'd spent the last several years in a constant state of fear. Life was short. And during the last day and a half, I'd realized it could be much shorter than anticipated. For the moment, I was feeling relieved and out of immediate danger.

The minute I was in Van's room, I realized something was wrong. Well, different about it than mine. "You only have one bed!" Which led to all sorts of inner speculation on my part.

"Yep." He opened Mom's goody bag and spread

it out on a round table by the window. Good old Mom had put it all in disposable containers and included plastic forks and paper plates.

"My room has two."

"I know. How did you get so lucky?" He was slicing gingerbread and putting it on plates. "Go ahead and put Old Slugger on whichever side you prefer. I'm easy."

I bet he was. When I didn't answer, he looked up. "You want me to sleep in your room tonight?"

"No, that's silly. That would defeat our purpose of mutual safety," I said, meaning it, but still puzzling over whether this night would involve sex or not. "I don't want you to get killed in your sleep."

"Then you don't mind sharing?"

"Not if you don't." I paused. "I assume the bundling board's in the closet?"

He grinned. "Come eat cake." He placed a piece in front of the empty chair across from him.

I put Old Slugger on the right side of the bed, noting Van's gun on the nightstand on the other side, and took the empty seat and pulled the dessert toward me.

"Looks like we'll be safe tonight," Van observed. "Where's your gun?"

"In the in-room safe with my purse and keys."

He arched a brow in question.

"Hey, you've got a boy gun. I've got a girl gun. The last thing we need is a bunch of little baby guns in the morning."

"Do guns reproduce that quickly?" he teased.

"They do on the mean streets of the city. Cops will tell you that." I rolled my eyes and shook my head to mock him. "Please! They're worse than rabbits."

Van had never had gingerbread with lemon sauce before. "My mom serves gingerbread warm with whipped cream," he said.

I made a face. "But the whipped cream would melt and soak into the gingerbread. Soggy, milky gingerbread." I shuddered.

"Yeah," he said. "It's great."

"Oh, no! Irreconcilable differences! I may just have to sleep in my room and take my chances with the boogeyman there. I don't think I can share a bed with a whipped cream man."

Van grinned again. "Just hang on there, Quitter. We may be able to come to a meeting of the minds. Convince me of the merits of lemon sauce."

"Well, for starters, usually the lemon sauce is hot. If Mom were here it would be hot."

"But other things would not," he said. "I'm glad she's not."

I grinned back at him, ignoring his slight to my mother. "When it's hot, the sauce is thinner and oozes over the cake—"

"Does it soak into the gingerbread?"

"A little, but not like melted cream. Is that a problem for you?"

"Doesn't have to be."

"Good. Cooled, it congeals. Tastes the same, just different texture." I spread some over my cake like jam.

He did the same.

I took a bite and lemon sauce oozed out onto my lip. When I licked it off, Van said, "Now *that* I like."

When we were finished, we still had half a ginger-bread left. We dumped the paper plates in the wastebasket.

"I don't suppose you have any games? Like maybe Twister," I asked, suddenly delaying the inevitable bedtime thing. What was the protocol here?

"No games."

"Sleepovers always have games."

He was standing directly in front of me, staring at my lip.

"How about a movie?"

"You have lemon sauce on your lip again." He leaned over me. I liked a tall man with a big presence. And Van's presence was definitely growing on me.

"I don't suppose you have a napkin on you?"

He didn't answer, just pulled me into him, bent over and licked the sauce off my lip. "Lemon sauce is good on girls, too."

"Better than whipped cream?"

"Could be."

The lick turned into a kiss. Gentle. Tentative. A whisper of lip on lip. Then deeper. Fuller. Harder. At his insistence. At my insistence. Full mouth on mouth. Open mouth. Thrusting tongues. He tasted of my mother's gingerbread and lemon. I kissed him with the full force of my being. I could not get enough.

I ran my hands through his hair, pulling his face to mine. He tangled his hands in my hair. Put his hand on the back of my neck to keep me tipping toward him. He cupped my butt with a hot, scorching touch. His hands were big and confident. I cupped his ass. It was feel and feel alike, taste. and taste alike.

"V?" I threw my head back and arched my neck.

"Yes?"

"I think I dripped sauce here." I gently pushed his head lower, deep into my perky, standing-at-attention, begging-to-be-noticed double Ds.

"Here?"

"There. Lower. Everywhere."

I could feel him grin against me, feel his hot breath. Then his tongue flicked my nipple through my cami and I shuddered with pleasure.

"You're a slob."

"I am."

"Good. I like messy girls. And I concede the lemon sauce point. Lemon sauce is heaven."

I kissed the top of his head while he kissed my breasts. My feet left the floor and my legs wound their way around his waist. I wanted to ride him hard and good and he knew it. We arched and tangled until we tumbled onto the bed with him on top.

My cami came off. His shirt fell away.

I was so turned on, I ached. Ached with yearning. Ached for fulfillment. Ached to have him.

And then, in the heat of the moment, a panic began to build. A rapid heartbeat that had nothing to do with lust or desire or love. I tried to ignore it, but it grew, spreading to my stomach, throwing my heart's rhythm out of sync until I feared I'd hyperventilate. I heard Ket's voice in the back of my mind threatening to kill any man he caught me with. I saw Van morph into a madman like Ket.

"Reilly?" Van stopped and was staring at me. "Are you okay?"

I was trembling. "He said he'd kill anyone who . . ."

Van held me. "He won't kill me."

I looked up at him, hoping he was right. "He'd kill over a look, over sitting next to me at lunch."

"Then I'm too far gone already."

I clutched his arm. "Don't say that."

"I mean, in his sick mind, I've crossed the line." He smoothed the hair back out of my face. "This isn't going to change anything."

"I'm not the kind of girl who falls into the sack with just anyone. I can't be."

He looked me in the eye and tried to lighten the mood. "You want me to respect you in the morning?"

I spoke in a rush, my words tumbling over themselves. "I don't want him to kill you. I don't want you to go all psycho, stalker committed to me. I don't . . ." I tried not to cry. "I wish I were different. I'm sorry. I'm not accusing you." I paused. When I spoke, my voice was very tiny. "I'm scared."

He rolled off me and ran his hands through his hair, fighting for control. Van's look clouded and he did that swearing under his breath thing. He was frustrated. We both were. We both hated Ket.

"Would you like a background check? I could arrange it." He was still trying to cheer me up, make me feel less like a jerk and a tease.

"Yeah, maybe." I forced a nervous laugh and

clutched his arm. "I'm sorry. I really am. I like you, Van. I like you very much."

"Don't be. But FYI, the background check thing will take a few days." His tone was very gentle. He was giving me time. He was willing to wait.

He handed me my cami.

Chapter 20

I couldn't get comfortable. I could *not* sleep. Not with Van next to me. Not with frustration and guilt and sexual desire acting like a major dose of caffeine in my system. Just because I was a wacko and afraid of my own shadow didn't mean the need subsided.

Next door some deaf jerk was watching a movie on mega volume. I wanted to feel safe and secure next to Van, but there was a definite gulf between us. I was afraid he was mad. And I felt bad. I didn't like mad. I liked Van. I really liked Van.

Curled up behind me, facing away from me, Van wasn't sleeping, either. And it wasn't my tossing and turning that was necessarily keeping him up.

I rolled over, facing his back. "I can't sleep."

"What?" Van asked, first looking back over his shoulder, and finally rolling to face me.

"I can't sleep. You don't have an Excedrin PM on you, do you?"

"No. Sorry."

"Oh, well." I shrugged.

"I could run out to the all-night Rite Aid down the street?"

"No."

"No?"

There was a hideous silence. "The boogeyman."

"Oh, yeah. Him."

"And Cindy Lou Goon."

"Sure."

I tried to frame my thoughts. "Earlier, you stopped. You stopped when I wanted you to."

His look was a mixture of anger and pity. I didn't like it. He thought I was wounded, damaged goods. And I was. I expected him to say so. I didn't think I could stand hearing it. I tensed.

Seeing my look of apprehension, Van nodded toward the bat by my side of the bed. "Well, with Old Slugger there, what could I do?"

"You have a gun on your side."

"Yeah, but you're a former college fastpitch starter. I figure Old Slugger is equal force."

At that moment, I thought I could love a man like him. The earlier panic had disappeared, replaced by a sense of safety.

I slid into him and threw my leg over his hip so that we were locked together, his rod to my hot spot. "You're poking me," I whispered to him.

"Sorry. I have sharp elbows."

"It's not your elbows." We both knew what I was talking about.

He gave me a questioning look.

"I'm saying, I don't think a background check is really necessary."

"You don't?"

"No. We're basically in spy training."

"Yeah."

"And spies, like Mata Hari, have to be able to do it with complete strangers at the drop of a hat."

"True. Where are you going with this?"

"Well, you aren't a complete stranger."

"No. You've known me for a whole day and a half." His tone was cautiously optimistic.

"Yes, well. The more I thought about things, the more I realized how irrational I've been. I already have a steroid stalker, various unsavory types, and possibly the Mafia after me. On the off chance you are a psycho, how much more real danger could I be in?" I touched his cheek. "Besides, you're a man with restraint. And compassion. Restraint and compassion are excellent character references."

Van ran his hands through my hair. "Are you really ready?"

"Oh, I'm ready. Believe me. I'd like to try some bona fide spy sex right here, right now. A real Mata Hari act."

"Mata Hari was a renowned temptress." He grinned and bent over to kiss me.

"Yeah, I know."

The sex we had was phenomenal. So phenomenal we slept tangled together through a wake-up call and an alarm. We barely woke when Steve pounded on the door.

"Hey, buddy, you coming? You'd better drag your ass out of bed before you miss breakfast."

Van opened his eyes, glanced at the clock, and sprung up. "I'll be down in a few," he called out to Steve while I cowered under the covers, a demure little thing.

Steve's footsteps receded. Van turned to me. "If we hurry, we have time for a quick shower. I'll go check out your room and make sure it's clear so you can get cleaned up over there."

"You mean shower over there?" I said.

"Yeah."

"No."

"No, what?"

"No, I'm not showering over there. I've seen *Psycho*."

"Okay, I'll shower over there."

"Not safe, either."

"There's no time for two showers, one after the other. So, you're saying?" His eyes lit with anticipation.

I ran my fingers lightly down his arm until he shivered. "I need a shower buddy. Shower buddies would definitely be safer. No one is ever killed while showering with someone else." I grinned and put on my flirty look.

"Do shower buddies get benefits?"

"Shower buddies definitely get benefits." I leaned over and kissed him. "I have Cinnamon Bun Bliss three-in-one bath gel and a fluffy, white bath scrubby Mom gave me that I'm willing to share."

"Those aren't the benefits I was thinking of."

I kissed him again, deeper this time. "Think wet, naked bodies, water droplets, bubbles, lather . . ."

"Let's get in the shower, Mata."

* * *

Ten minutes later, we were out of the shower and I was French braiding my hair. There was no time for a blow-dry. We could have been faster in the shower, but there were those hot, steamy, hard, slick quickie benefits I'd promised. Sometimes, quick can be fantastic. We were both smiling like idiots as we put on our camo.

"That Cinnamon Bliss tingles the skin and smells great," Van said as he pulled on his black T-shirt, "but it tastes like soap. That's false advertising."

I smiled indulgently at him. "Of course it tastes like soap. It is soap. I can't believe you didn't know that."

"How would I know that? I'm a regular spring fresh, bar soap kind of guy." Then he grinned. "I'm not complaining. You tasted good." He grabbed his gun and holster.

I looked down and smiled. "You're taking your gun to camp?"

"Aren't you?"

"No," I said.

He shrugged. "What about Old Slugger?"

"I'm giving him the day off. He can stay here and lounge around the pool, picking up lady life rings."

"Lucky bastard. Make me proud, Old Slugger. Get a little ring for me." Van smiled at me and headed toward the door. "You coming?"

"I am, but I can't go out your door. What would people think?" Meaning Ket, of course.

"Sure. I forgot." He walked me to the adjoining

door, pushed it open and scanned the room for intruders. "All clear."

"Good." I put my hand on his arm. "V?"

"Yeah."

"About today—I'm worried. How can I act normally around the guys now that I know what I know? What will I say to Peewee?"

"Ignore him."

"You can't just ignore a mobster."

Van shrugged. "Try."

"He could off me."

"Why? He hasn't so far." Spoken like a true guy. "Concentrate on the other guys. Or, better yet, me." He flashed that grin that turned me on.

"You? I like that idea." I smiled at him. "You I can handle."

"Can you?"

"I can certainly give it my all." I lowered my voice to sultry. "Why are we even going back to camp today? Especially when we can stay back at the hotel and . . . enjoy each other."

Van looked tempted, but something changed his mind. He took my face in his hand. "Very tempting, but we've both spent thousands of dollars to attend this camp."

I stuck out my pouty lip. "Is money all that matters?"

"No," he said gently. "Spending time with you would be worth every penny I paid for camp. But you need to go and get your training. Especially now."

I sighed, resigned. He was right.

"I promise you more fun later."

"I'll hold you to it."

"Great. Let's go."

I tightened my grip on his arm. "What about Cliff? And Jim?"

"Hey, slow down." He put his finger on my lips to silence me. "None of those accusations against them have been proven. Give them the benefit of the doubt."

I pulled his finger away. I was turning into a first-class worrier. Well, why not? I'd been raised by one.

"Not yet," I said. "But everything points to them being true."

Van grabbed the hand that was holding his arm and squeezed it. "Don't think about it, R. Just forget it. Neither of us have the dongle. Neither of us want it. This isn't our game."

I stared up at him. I was still scared and my look must have conveyed it.

"I'll watch your backside," he said.

"You better."

"Believe me, it's no hardship."

We missed breakfast and had to settle for leftover gingerbread without sauce. We made the bus, flagging it down just as it started to pull away from the curb without us.

There were only five of us. Huff was still missing. I had conflicted feelings about that. On the one hand, I'd liked Huff. The man was a charmer. On the other, I wanted to kill him for involving me in the whole dongle mess.

Peewee was also absent. Either Cindy Lou Goon

wasn't so easy to track down or Peewee had lost a fight to the death with Goon. Other than loss of human life in general being a sad business, I wouldn't have been overly upset if they'd each offed the other and the dongle had fallen to the bottom of Puget Sound.

After some initial speculation about Peewee, no one spoke the remainder of the trip, which was fine with me. The morning was foggy, but the weatherman was promising another sunny, unseasonably warm day once the fog burned off at midday. I couldn't see the mountains in either direction. The trip seemed to exist in a time warp.

When we pulled up to the warehouse, the news crews were gone. But the horror remained. At least for me. Several trucks from a well-known security company were parked out front. I walked past them, trying not to think what they meant.

Inside the warehouse, the mock city was cordoned off with crime scene tape. FSC had hired two security guys to guard the scene. War led us past the mock city to a gymlike room out back. I walked past the guards without looking at them.

We spent the morning learning close quarter battle (CQB) techniques, and playing with the simulator. It may have been my imagination, but Steve kept staring at me. He approached me at the break in the hall as I headed to the ladies' room, grabbing me by the arm as I tried to walk off.

"You wouldn't be trying to cheat me out of half of the reward for the dongle, would you?"

I stared at him, rage building beneath the surface. I was already jumpy. I didn't need Steve on my case.

"I gave 'the dongle'"—I made quote marks in the air with my fingers—"if that's what it was, to the goon who jumped me and threatened to slice my neck end to end. While you sat sipping a drink totally oblivious to my peril, I might add." I shook his arm loose. "I'm not a fool. When a knife-wielding maniac says, 'the dongle or your life,' I choose life." I stalked off to the ladies' room.

Lunch was another quiet affair. MREs, this time eaten inside in the staff kitchen. I sat next to Van, admiring him and remembering bubbles and his slick, hard body. It was hard not to.

In the afternoon, we returned to the gym to practice what we'd learned in the morning session.

"Okay, folks, we're going to partner up and practice subduing and taking down an attacker." War paced in front of us. "Everyone line up against the wall."

"Firing squad style," Van whispered to me. "Nice."

War stopped pacing front and center of us. "Listen up, CTs, CQB is not a sport. It's not an art. It's science balanced with dirty tricks." War grinned. "Let's just review a few basics." His grin deepened. "A knife is always loaded. Boots are for combat; bare feet for bathing. Never drop your guard. Talk reduces your decision and reaction time. Never apply a hold or take down without a dirty trick or distraction. The best prisoner come-along techniques have the prisoner bent, either forward or backward, never upright. Speed and power equal velocity and require a stable platform. And, finally, the basics are only limited by your imagination." War scanned the group. "Any questions?"

Steve raised his hand. "Can I partner up with R?"

Van shot him a dirty look and Cliff murmured something about wanting me for a partner, too.

"No," War said. "Any other questions?"

Not to be shut down so easily, Steve hammed it up, waving his hand wildly to be noticed as War struggled to ignore him. Finally, War rolled his eyes. "Yes, S."

"Can R be my partner?"

War turned to me. "R, since you're the only female team member and seem to be in popular demand, you may be the first to choose your partner."

I didn't even hesitate. "I choose V."

War's gaze bounced between Van and me. "V it is."

Steve scowled. I ignored the twerp. As it turned out, no one wanted him for a partner. Jim chose Cliff. War had to assign Ace to partner with Steve.

Partnering complete, War continued the lesson. "First up, we'll practice H2H, hand to hand, for you civilians," War said. "No firearms or explosives allowed. Feel free to use whatever else gives you the advantage."

The gym floor was covered with mats and divided with masking tape into sparing squares. War assigned us each a square and then issued us all helmets, mouth guards, elbow pads, and kneepads.

"CTs, listen up. Face your partner," War said. "Look him over good."

Van's gaze skimmed my body like he was undressing me.

"Watch it," I whispered to him.

"He said get a good look."

"Uh-huh."

"He didn't say it couldn't be indecent."

War didn't notice us. He kept talking. "Your partner is the enemy. In this exercise, either you kill him, or he kills you. Each team is standing in a square marked on the floor. You will defend your territory. First one to either take down, or force the other from your square, wins.

"This is a single elimination exercise. The winners of each round will face off. Losers will watch and take note of victorious techniques. Get ready."

I grinned at Van and he at me.

"Oh, I'm going to take you, big guy," I whispered to him.

"Sounds good to me." He tried to disarm me with that charming grin of his.

"You better put up a fight." I put on my competition face. "I don't like quitters and I have no sympathy for those who surrender."

"Not even for those who surrender to their desires?"

"Shut up."

He laughed. "Don't worry. If anyone does any taking, it's going to be me taking you. I like it on top."

"I'd like to see you try."

"Get ready." War raised his arm in the air.

"Looks like you're going to get your chance," Van said.

"Go!" War shouted, dropping his arm like a starter.

Van and I rested on the balls of our feet, bent like wrestlers ready to grapple, staring each other down.

"I'm hearing the *Rocky* theme in my head," I said, slapping at Van's face.

"Yeah?" He fended off my blows.

"You know what that means, I'm psyched for battle." I slapped at him again and missed.

He whipped his head around like I'd clobbered him a good one. "Pow!"

I threw another missed blow. "Socko!" Pretty soon we were in the midst of a mock battle pretty much of the variety you learn in high school drama class with *Batman* sound effects thrown in for fun.

In the square next to us, Cliff and Jim sized each other up. Dancing around each other like they were playing ring-around-the-rosy.

"Come on, men!" War shouted. "You're all aggressive dogs. What did I teach you? You don't stare an aggressive dog in the eye. And you don't turn and run. Keep your eyes on the enemy and attack!"

That was all the encouragement Ace needed to quit donking around with Steve and take him down in a single move. There's only so much dancing with a pansy a man can take, I suppose.

War turned his gaze on Van and me. "You two, stop kidding around before I make you drop and give me five. Put your heart into the fight."

I nodded, thinking, not likely. One of the things that turned me on about Van—he made me feel dainty and feminine—was not a good thing when I was looking to overpower him with sheer physical force.

"Dirty tricks, people," War yelled. "Distractions! Haven't I taught you anything? Never apply a hold or a takedown without one."

Distraction is the better part of valor, or something like that. I could distract. And I was quick. I threw another mock blow at Van. When he reacted, I raced behind him and kicked the back of his knee. His leg buckled and he went down on the knee hard as I grabbed for his arm. Unfortunately, he was quick, too, and got his arms around front where I couldn't get them.

I cursed under my breath and reached around his leg, trying to get leverage to pull it out from under him and send him sprawling. I accidentally copped a good feel of his crotch in the process.

"I'll give you an hour to stop that," he whispered. "It hurts so good."

"Ah, the art of distraction. If this were a real situation, I'd have made a eunuch out of you by now," I whispered back.

"Tease." Without warning, he pulled free of my grip, grabbed my arm, stood, and swung me around, finally grabbing me around my breasts from behind. "Oops! Meant to grab lower. Heat of battle and all that," he said, copping his own feel of my double Ds.

"Liar!" My traitorous breasts liked his touch too much and budded right up. Mind of their own, those girls. Didn't they know he was the enemy?

Steve stared at us from the sideline. I caught a glimpse of his glare. "Why does V get all the fun?" he called out.

"Watch it. We're in public and we have spectators," I hissed to Van, struggling to free myself.

"Struggle all you want," Van said. "I'm loving the bounce."

"Creep."

"Creep? That's the best you can do?"

"Smart-ass. I tell you, I'm taking you down."

"I like a competitive woman."

I dropped, limp, floppy dead weight like a two-year-old who doesn't want to be carried. Smart creatures, two-year-olds. Van was so surprised, he dropped me and I wrenched free.

I'd wrestled with my brothers. I knew a few moves. I had to get his feet out from under him. While he was recovering from my surprise escape, I lunged and looped my leg around his knee, preparing to knock him off balance by pulling his leg out from under him with my leg.

Despite my determined effort, Van remained solidly planted and shaking his head. He grabbed my braid and gave it a tug, pulling my head back. "Doing a pole dance for me?"

"I hope you're not planning on using my top secret move on me." I was thinking of the punch to the neck that War had taught me.

"You have a top secret move?"

"Every good spy has a top secret move."

Van smiled and bent over me, moving his face close to mine like he was going to kiss me. "Wanna see mine?"

"Stop."

He kept giving me that slow, seductive smile of his. "Keeping your heart rate low? The higher the heart rate, the lower the skill level and less the reaction time."

"I'm doing just fine, thank you." I released his leg and twisted my braid free from his grasp, going in for a good boot-stomp of his arch, all in one fluid move.

My boot hit his boot and . . . nothing. Just more smiling.

"Talking reduces your focus," Van said, again quoting War. Then he grabbed my arm, twisted it, roughly and painfully, I might add, behind my waist while I struggled and clawed like a wildcat. He kicked the back of my knee, buckling my leg. I went down on the knee. Van had complete control of me. I felt like he could rip my arm off at any second. Despite this, I had the feeling he was holding back. Trying to be gentle and maintain his machismo at the same time.

Using my arm like a joystick, he maneuvered me into the doggy position, with him behind me, pressing his package into my butt.

"I win," he whispered in my ear, giving it a little lick.

My breasts were heaving like a heroine in a bodice ripper and my heart rate was through the roof. If only we'd been in the bedroom, I'd have shown him exactly what he'd won. "What are people going to think? Back off."

"Not until War declares me the winner."

Brave words, but from what I felt, Van was going to be in a world of hurt himself if he kept this position up long.

I heard footsteps and started to laugh. "You're hurting my arm."

"All's fair in love and combat, darling."

A shadow spread over me and I looked up to see War standing over us. "Let the lady up, soldier."

Van released me and gave me a hand up.

"R, rehydrate," War said to me. "V, match up with Ace. He beat Steve and Cliff in the time it took for you to beat a girl. Let's see if you're so cocky around a real competitor."

I ignored War's slight and headed to a table off to the side that the staff kept stocked with bottled water.

Steve met me there. He was dripping sweat from his two-second defeat by Ace. "You two did it." His tone was venomous as he handed me a bottle. I ignored his offer and grabbed my own from the table.

I stared at him. "Did what?"

"Boink, boink, boink!"

"You're a jerk," I said, and turned away from him.

"Just saying, it's obvious. A word to the wise, if your ex is watching, he'd have to be blind not to see it." He walked off to watch the fight, throwing me a smug look over his shoulder.

Chapter 21

I took a swig of water and headed back to the action center court. Van and Ace were deadlocked in heated combat. An athletic competition raises my adrenaline level, regardless. Seeing two buff, handsome guys grapple with each other was just icing with chocolate sprinkles.

As Dutch would say, they charged each other like two rutting bucks fighting for territory during mating season. Parry. Spin. Turn. Release.

"Go V! Get him!" I jumped up and down on the sidelines, watching the sweat fly. Surprisingly, especially given Ace's superior training and experience, the two appeared equally matched.

Cliff shared my surprise. "My money was on Ace. I thought he would have taken V by now."

I nodded, gaze glued to the action. "V's a man of many talents."

Beside me, Jim shook his head. "You're enjoying this. What kind of a woman are you?"

"Not the shrinking violet kind, if that's what you're

getting at." I was making my own jabbing, rock 'em, sock 'em robot motions from the sideline.

Jim was still shaking his head. I shot him a quick glance. "Hey, wipe that censure off your face, mister. You guys have your *Girls Gone Wild* videos, I have this."

Jim laughed.

I stared in awe at the look of concentration on Van and Ace's faces. They were both breathing hard. Sweat dripped down their foreheads and highlighted the muscles on their arms. Every once in a while one or the other had to wipe the drips out of their eyes. Yet, despite their intensity, both men looked like they were having the time of their lives. I was just the slightest bit jealous, wishing I could give Van the same level of competition that Ace could. Still, I had other assets that Van appreciated.

Finally, Ace made the smallest of mistakes. He turned his back on Van for less than a second, giving Van just the right angle to grab Ace's arm, twist it, kick his leg, and take him down. He fell with a thump.

I was a girl gone wild on the sideline, jumping, screaming. War pronounced Van the winner. "First time anyone has ever beat Ace."

I couldn't tell whether War sounded happy or upset by the fact. There was definitely some wonderment in his voice.

I met Van at the sideline with a cold bottle of water and a towel. "H2O? That's water to you civilians."

He grabbed it out of my hand, smiling.

"Nice fight."

He nodded. "Just showing off for my girl."

My turn to grin like an idiot.

"All right, everyone," War said. "Take fifteen."

I was ready for a break. Too much water in too short a time. Guess I'd overhydrated. On the way to the ladies' room, I walked past the crime scene, keeping my eyes averted. The two guards still sat there doing their thing. I barely glanced at them, preferring not to remember the reason for their presence—the scene of Jay's bloody death.

I freshened up, still high from the day's events. My reflection in the mirror was a woman I hadn't seen in a long time—she looked uncannily happy. I checked my cell. There was a message from Mom. Dutch had spent the night in the Lounge Boy by the window, his trusty rifle at ready, but there hadn't been any further incidents. I gave Mom a quick call to let her know I was fine, more than fine, actually.

"You're echoing," Mom said. "Where are you?"

"The women's bathroom."

I could picture Mom's grimace.

"By the mirror. It's the only private place."

We chatted for a few minutes until I'd reassured her all was as well with the world as we could expect given the current circumstances. Then I hung up with a promise to keep in touch and call if I had any trouble, any trouble at all, including a sniffle.

One last glance in the mirror and I headed back. I threw open the ladies' room door and came to an abrupt halt.

One of the security guards stood there with an

ugly grin on his face. Something about him looked familiar.

"We can't keep meeting like this, Goon," I said, my heart suddenly jumping speeds from content to fear.

Goon had something tucked in his hand. He reached out to grab me. I flung the door, trying to slam it shut in his face. Unfortunately, the door had a slow-close-slam-prevention spring on it. It floated closed like a butterfly rather than stinging like a bee.

Goon got not only a toe in the door, but a shoulder, his head, an arm, and a leg. I jumped back too late. He grabbed my arm. As I fought to shake it loose, he stun-gunned me. I did my limp two-year-old imitation again, only this time, against my will.

When I woke up, I was lying with my cheek pressed against the cold tile of the ladies' room floor, my hands bound behind my back. Disgusting. I tried to lift my head and the room spun. Spillage, splash, and a lax cleaning schedule were not my friends. I had to get up before I caught the plague or something worse.

As the fog of unconsciousness keeping me relatively calm burned off, my fight-or-flee response kicked in, highly in favor of flee. I shuddered, cold with fear and contact where bare skin met the floor. Bare skin? I was pretty sure I'd gotten dressed this morning, yet my midriff was bare. My midriff was bare? What the—?

I glanced down at my prone body. My tee was

hiked up over my double Ds. One of my girls had popped free of my bra. My pants were unzipped, revealing my new thong underwear. My pockets turned out. *Oh, my gosh! Oh, my gosh!*

I felt like I was going to throw up.

"Good morning, sunshine." Standing over me, dressed in security guard blue, smiling like he was perusing a copy of *Playboy*, was Goon.

I summoned the strength to look him in the eye. "How the hell did you get in here?" I wiggled, trying to get my tee down and think up a way to attack with my hands bound.

"I've been here all day. Walked right in the front door in broad daylight." He chuckled to himself. "Hell, they welcomed me in."

I felt sick as I weighed my options. I could scream, but I seriously doubted anyone would hear me. I hadn't heard any noises from the men's room next door since before I called Mom. The guys had all gone back to the gym.

I had to stall, keep Goon talking, hoping someone would miss me and come looking. "The perfect disguise. I have to hand it to you. No one ever really looks at security guards. They're expendable. That's why they always die when they go to the planet with the starship captain."

"Damn straight."

"Where's a starship captain when you need one?"

"Glad you have a sense of humor."

I lifted my head, still squelching that sick feeling of being about to regurgitate my bottled water. "I didn't think you got paid extra for raping and pillaging."

Goon shrugged. "A man should enjoy his work."

"Bastard."

"Hey, strong words. No raping, I promise. I'm a married man. If I copped a feel, fondled the goods as I searched for my property, who could blame me? It's all part of the job."

I managed to pull myself into a sit, but my breasts kept my tee hiked up. The perils of being buxom. I looked like Janet Jackson at the Super Bowl. "What property?"

"What property? That's a good one." Goon pulled out a knife, the same stiletto from before, and switched it open. "You cheated me, my luscious little double-crosser. Now you're going to give me the real dongle." He took a step toward me.

"I don't know what you're talking about. Put the knife away or I'll scream."

"Scream and I cut you." He sounded dead serious as he squatted beside me, just out of reach. "And this baby is sharp."

Visions of slit throats danced in my head. I swallowed hard. "I gave you the only dongle I had." I wiggled, still trying to get my double Ds covered. "And did you really think I had room to stuff something in my bra?"

"It was worth a look to see."

I cocked my legs, ready to kick him if I got the chance. I was afraid of that knife. War's words in training echoed through my mind—a knife is always loaded, treat it as such.

He had the stiletto in one hand and a stun gun in the other. He flashed his stun gun at me. "Don't make me use this again. There's debate over the safety of repeatedly stunning a person."

"I appreciate your concern. But I don't have any more dongles. What makes you think I do?" I looked him over, trying desperately to come up with an escape plan. I was scared, scared to the point of spitless and clammy cold, because I was telling the truth. And if he didn't believe me . . .

"My associates believe you do."

"You're associates are flat out wrong." I looked at him pleadingly. "Listen to me. I'm basically a reasonable person. I place a high premium on my life. No dongle is worth it. If I had it, I'd give it to you in a heartbeat."

"Reilly! Reilly!" Van's voice floated in from the hallway, growing louder as it moved toward us.

Goon started. His gaze flicked toward the door as he cursed under his breath.

It was now or never for me. I inched toward him, cocked my legs, and kicked his out from under him.

Goon's stun gun went flying as he fell. It clattered across the floor just out of reach.

"You little bitch." He lunged at me with the stiletto.

In the heat of battle, my thoughts came in short bursts. I remembered War saying that talking reduces reaction time. So I shut up, stifling a smart-ass comeback. I dodged Goon's lunge, rolling out of the way. I opened my mouth to scream for Van. And shut it again. I wasn't going to lead him into danger. Which didn't mean I wasn't hoping he'd retrieved his gun from his locker and would come riding to my rescue all on his own.

"He's armed," I hissed at Goon. "And he's a crack shot. He'll take you out."

Goon cursed full speed and looked at me wild-eyed, as if wondering whether to believe me or not.

We could hear Van's footsteps pounding down the hall toward us.

"Your choice. Believe me or not. I won't be the one with the bullet holes in my head." Fortunately, I'm an expert bluffer. I had no idea if Van had his gun or not. But I could vouch for him being a great shot.

"I'm getting too old for this. I got responsibilities. This job is getting too damned dangerous." Goon slid to his feet and ran for the door. "I'll be back."

"Spoken like a true Terminator." I scrambled to my feet and headed for the door to warn off Van. This time the slow-closing door worked in my favor. I caught it with my shoulder.

I stepped into the hall just as Van slid to a stop at the bathroom door.

"You okay?"

My boob was still partially showing. He was a hetero male. His gaze lingered on it a second longer than necessary as he took in my condition.

"I'm fine." I turned my back to him. "Untie me and call for help."

He ignored my plea for freedom and pulled my tee down, making me decent. "I'm going after him. Go back to the gym. Find the others and stay there."

He turned to follow Goon before I could stop him.

"Come back here! V! He's armed. He has a knife." He ignored me. "Knives are always loaded!"

Van had his back to me, but he held his gun over his head for me to see.

"Shoot!"

Goon had reached the end of the hall and the exit door into the alley. He hit the door's push bar and plowed out. Van was behind him and gaining. The man had speed.

Fortunately, so did I. No way was I heading back to safety and letting Van go it alone. We were a team.

I took off after both of them, losing some speed because I couldn't pump my arms. Bad running form. I hit the push bar with my hip and held the door open with my shoulder.

Call me gun shy, but I halted in the doorway. No way was I going to be a victim of friendly fire. The alley was narrow with just room enough for a single car to pass. The warehouse stood on the west side. On the east side of the alley there was a small drainage ditch, a chain-link fence with another drainage ditch and another warehouse on the other side.

Van stood in the shadow of the buildings maybe half a block to the south of me. South in Seattle is easy to find, just look for Mount Rainier and you've got it. Van was scanning, looking for Goon. He pulled out his cell phone and flipped it open.

A gentle south breeze was blowing, carrying his conversation in snatches to me.

"Lost visual." "Get chopper." "Hunt him down." "Can't be far."

I frowned. That didn't sound like your typical call to 911.

A movement caught my eye. Goon was hiding

behind a Dumpster maybe twenty feet in front of Van. I could see him from my angle, but Van couldn't from his. I screamed to Van, frustrated that I couldn't point. He didn't hear me. I stepped out into the alley and the door closed behind me. I screamed to Van again. Goon heard and made a dash for it.

Van saw him and took off after him, gaining on Goon and grabbing him by the shirt collar, ready to take him down.

Out of nowhere, the revving of an engine and the squeal of peeling tires drowned out the sounds of the chase. A silver four-door sedan pulled into the alley south of Van from the parking lot.

"Getaway car!" I screamed, bouncing and nodding wildly with my head toward the vehicle.

The sedan revved its engines again and aimed for Van.

"Van!"

Chapter 22

Van looked up at the car barreling toward him. I could practically see him weighing his options. There weren't many, and all of them involved letting Goon go.

Capitalizing on the distraction, Goon broke free of Van's grip, sucker punched him in the gut and ran for the fence.

For the fence? I was confused. Why wasn't Goon waiting for the car to pick him up?

Van doubled over. For a horrified instant, I thought he was going to collapse and become a speed bump for that maniac sedan.

I stepped out into the alley, terrified and unsure what to do. There was no way I could reach Van in time. And I couldn't get to my phone.

The American-made sedan picked up speed, closing the gap between it and Van.

Goon scaled the fence and took off.

Clutching his stomach, Van straightened and dove for the fence. He caught the chain link, and swung himself over with mere inches to spare before becoming road kill. He landed safely on the other side and gestured at me to get back, screaming and waving his arms.

I hunkered into the door well, scrambling blind to find the latch. I fumbled, finally found and grabbed the handle, but couldn't manage to hold down the thumb button and maneuver the door open. Damn, why didn't they put those push bars on the outside? Fighting against the rising sense of panic taking control of me, I tried to remember my training. This was it, do or die. I remembered War warning us to keep our heartbeat under control. Rapid heartbeat equals rampant problems.

I took a deep breath and flattened myself against the door, looking for another escape route as the car raced toward me. Could I scale the fence without using my hands? Did I have time to dive into the ditch?

The car was close enough now that I could see the driver. I froze. My heart fell into my stomach. *Ket!*

Oh, God, oh, God. No! I was a dead woman.

Ket saw my look of horror and smiled. I turned and began kicking the door, screaming in a banshee pitch to be let in.

Behind me, I heard the sedan screech to a stop. A car door opened. I kept kicking and screaming as if sheer effort was going to save me.

"Help me! Help! Fire! Rape!" Tears flowed down my cheeks.

Ket threw his weight against me so hard he knocked my breath from me. The door handle gouged into my hips. My head bounced off the door. I reeled, stunned, and fought the stars clouding my vision.

Ket jammed me against the building door. I hadn't seen him in months, hadn't felt him in longer. The body holding me hostage against the door was definitely beefier and more bulked up than I remembered. Solid, raging bull muscle. He'd been training, probably spending every spare minute in the prison gym. And no doubt double dosing on steroids. He pressed his package into my backside. He was hard. Violence and control turned him on.

I shuddered and fought an almost overwhelming sense of nausea. I wouldn't give him the satisfaction.

Ket grabbed me by the arm to keep me from slumping. He shook me and held me with a bruising grip, branding his handprint into my flesh. "Surprised to see me, baby?"

I didn't answer. He'd hurt me either way, answer or no.

He wrenched my bound arm tighter behind my back so far I thought he'd dislocate my shoulder. "I asked you a question."

I winced, trying to breathe through the searing pain. "I had no doubt . . . you'd . . . come."

"That's my girl." He eased up his grip and ground his groin against my butt. "Didn't you get my present? Why aren't you wearing it?" He spoke directly into my ear, his breath hot and disturbing against my neck.

"You mean the cheap jewelry? Way to impress a girl."

He shook me again. "Cheap gets as cheap deserves." He grabbed me by my French braid and jerked my head back so that I was looking up at him into his eyes glittering with jealousy and rage. "Did you screw him? Did you?"

I glared at him. "Screw who?"

He banged my head against the door and yanked it back again.

I was so dizzy, I could barely think.

"You know who, bitch. Lover boy. The one in the alley."

"That security guard assaulted me." My voice broke.

Ket stiffened and looked confused. "Security guard?"

Clearly not the guy he was thinking of. "Yeah, the one in blue."

"What the hell?" His already dark look clouded to thunderstorm level.

"In the ladies' bathroom."

It didn't take any effort to cry. Damn it all, I was going to get that Goon. Ket would kill him. All I had to do was sic Ket on him. Or he would kill Ket. Either way I won.

"He stunned me as I was coming out of the bathroom, then he shoved me in and tied me up and felt me up and now I have one breast hanging out of my bra." I broke down completely.

Ket had gone quiet and completely still. Maybe he still had an ounce of humanity and compassion in him.

I trembled, waiting for the thunderclap to hit. He reached up my shirt, felt the exposed breast, squeezed the nipple, hard, and tucked the breast back into my bra.

I gagged.

He yanked my braid so hard I thought my head was going to snap off and my tears trickled back toward my eyes. "What did you do to lead him on?"

"I showed up for camp! Honest. Honest, I didn't lead him on." I'd been reduced to begging. I hated myself for it. But I was stalling. Hoping the cops Van had called showed up soon. "He's a sick pervert."

"He's a dead man. I'll deal with him later." Ket shoved me toward the car as I struggled to get free.

The chain-link fence jingled. I glanced at it without thinking. Van was scaling the fence.

Ket heard and looked. "In the car, slut." Ket opened the back car door and shoved me in.

Van hit the ground and ran toward us, gun drawn, yelling for Ket to halt.

Ket ignored him and scurried into the front seat, sliding behind the wheel without securing me in. He reached for the automatic locks as Van wrenched the front passenger door open.

Ket slammed the car into gear and floored it. Van grabbed the door frame and struggled to pull himself inside while Ket tried to sideswipe him on the fence. Van's gun flew out of his hand while he struggled to hang on.

I kicked the back of Ket's seat, screaming for him to stop the car.

Somehow Van managed to get inside the car. He lunged at Ket, who swung back. The car veered dangerously toward the building as the two men fought for control of the vehicle.

The car lurched back and forth. Van threw a punch. Ket threw a punch. I bounced around the backseat like a kernel of Orville Redenbacher, unable to catch myself with my hands. "Stop it! Stop it, now, you two. You're going to kill us!"

At the far end of the warehouse, a small cement loading dock jutted into the alley. It popped up out of nowhere, surprising Ket. He misjudged the clearance in the alley and hit the brakes too late. The front left side of the sedan crashed into the dock, crumpling the driver's door, throwing me against the headrest. I was lucky not to be thrown through the windshield. The air bags deployed.

In the front, the two men sputtered and tried to swim their way free of the air bags. Ket tried his door. It was jammed. He smashed the window and crawled out before Van could get a firm grip on him.

In the next instant, I heard footsteps overhead on the car roof. From my window, I watched Ket take off and scale the fence. Van rushed out of the car and watched as Ket escaped on the far side. He made a move to follow Ket, then shook his head like it was a lost cause. He pulled a two-way radio from his pocket and began giving instructions.

"Bring the chopper around. Suspect number two. On foot. Fled to the south. White male. Early thirties. Six feet four . . ."

I leaned back against the seat and closed my eyes, trying to get my arms around the idea—Van was a cop. Not a math man, a mild-mannered professor. A cop. Cripes, to use one of Dutch's swear words.

Finally, Van put the radio away, climbed into the car, and fell next to me into the backseat.

"I really need to get in better shape." His nose was bleeding and he had a gash over one eye.

"You're going to have a shiner in the morning," I said.

He nodded. "Yeah. Are you okay? You have a big goose egg on your forehead."

"A goose egg is better than a concussion. Ket's losing his touch." I turned my back toward Van, motioning for him to untie me.

When he finished, I turned back to look at him.

Just as I reached to tenderly touch his wounds— what a sucker women are for wounded men—I heard the distinctive rush of a chopper. All my sympathy for him evaporated. I dropped my hand. "You bastard!"

The force of my words startled him. He reared back, hands in front of him for protection. "Hey, I just saved your life. I'm the good guy here. What does a guy have to do to please you?"

"You're a cop!" I rubbed my wrists and pointed a finger at him. "FBI if I'm not mistaken." I stared at him through thin, angry eyes. I opened the car door. "You're after the dongle just like everyone else."

"Reilly, wait!"

I put a foot out onto the pavement. "You used me. You're no different than Ket."

"Wait a minute!" He grabbed my arm where Ket had.

I winced and he backed off.

"I'm sorry." He wiped his bleeding nose on the back of his sleeve.

I wiped my runny nose on my sleeve. Stupid crying.

Van looked exhausted and so pitiful I almost wanted to comfort him. Almost.

"You're an agent. On the Canarino case."

"For God's sake, Reilly."

"Why didn't you tell me?"

"Lower your voice." He leaned into me. "I couldn't. I'm undercover."

"You were undercover, all right." Anger was the only thing keeping me going.

Van wiped his nose again. He was having trouble talking clearly through the blood. "This has been a hell of a day. Two bad guys get away. I blow my cover. *And* I lose the girl." He looked at me for confirmation of the last point.

I'm stubborn. I refused to commit.

"You're the only camper who knows. You won't give me away, will you?" His voice sounded like he was talking through sludge. I imagined he was swallowing blood.

"You need help."

"That's what they tell me."

"I meant medical attention." I heard sirens. Several cops and a paramedic unit pulled up at the far end of the alley.

I sighed. "Fine. I won't out you. What are we going to tell those guys?" I nodded toward the cops.

"They're in on it. We're working with local law enforcement on this case." He gently took my arm. "Cheer up. Running down and assaulting an FBI agent is a federal offense. When we catch Ket, he's going to jail for a long time."

My phone rang just as the paramedics finished looking me over. I had some bruises and abrasions, and goose egg aside, a mild concussion. The paramedics wanted to send me to the hospital for observation. I talked them out of it. A concussion was nothing I couldn't handle. This was a tiny baby concussion compared to some I'd had. I'd been hit in the head by softballs and bats enough times to know how to care for myself. They gave me a Tylenol and told me to take over-the-counter painkiller as necessary for the headache that was sure to follow and released me.

I flipped open my phone. "Hi, Mom."

"What's going on there? Who's dead now? I'm watching the news—there are police choppers circling the FSC warehouse."

Shoot! "No one's dead, Mom. How do the news crews have video? I don't see any news crews."

"There is no video. They're just reporting it. Some guy in a neighboring warehouse called it in," Mom said without missing a beat. "Two incidents in two days. Come home, Reilly. Come home now! That place is too dangerous—"

"I'm fine, Mom. And I can't." I paused, wondering how much to tell her. "It was Ket."

"Ket! Ohmygod."

"He tried to kidnap me—"

"How in the world did he get inside that building? I thought they put extra security on?"

"They did, Mom." I hesitated. "I stepped outside and he pulled up in a car and grabbed me."

"Outside . . . outside! What were you doing outside?"

"Having a smoke."

"Reilly! Be serious."

"Getting a breath of fresh air, Mom. That's it." I related the story to her, leaving out any mention of Goon and praying that the news never covered that part. It took me nearly fifteen minutes to calm her down. "I can't come home, Mom. I'll only be putting you, Dad, and Grandpa in danger. Arm the security system and tell Grandpa to keep his gun handy."

A policeman was waiting for me.

"I have to go, Mom. The police want to talk to me."

Chapter 23

The police took me to a conference room off War's office. Several Seattle PD detectives were there, along with Van, who had an emergency ice pack on his black eye, which was rapidly swelling shut. I had one pressed to my goose egg, paramedic's orders. We were two ice pack packing peas in a pod. Mine was giving me brain freeze, which wasn't helping my already cloudy thinking, but I had to keep it on for twenty minutes or risk being sent to the hospital. Plus I was vain. A goose egg didn't enhance my natural beauty any. Several people that Van introduced as his fellow FBI agents completed the fine-looking, but battered, ensemble. A uniform guarded the door.

We gathered around an oblong table.

I sat in a gray swiveling office chair opposite Van. "Did you check that uniform's ID, Cyclops? Did you make good and sure this time that he isn't our master-of-disguise Goon in yet another incarnation?"

I didn't sound friendly. But I had a good excuse. Mild concussions make a girl testy. That's a medical fact, and one I'd used to my advantage on the numerous times I'd been hit in the head during a fastpitch game. Being banged around by two big guys and nearly kidnapped by my ex didn't exactly elevate my mood any, either. Stir in being peeved at Van for being a cop and you have a major tempest in camo. Right now anger was the only thing preventing me from having a meltdown.

"You want to check him out? Feel free," Van said, picking up on the accusatory tone in my voice. "You're the one who's seen him up close and personal."

"Hey, black eyes aren't a medical excuse for sarcasm, buddy." As much as I wanted to glare at Van, I paled and started visibly shaking from a combination of shock, horror, ice pack, and an overactive air-conditioning vent overhead. Somewhere along the way I'd lost my jacket.

One of the agents swiveled out of his chair and returned with a space blanket from an emergency kit. As the agent tucked it around my shoulders, Van swore under his breath. He looked tired, and beat, and utterly frustrated.

"Sorry." Van dabbed at his eye with the ice pack. "That was uncalled for."

I shrugged and decided to cut him a miniscule amount of slack. We were both grumpy and on edge. And who wouldn't be in our situation? His job performance and reputation were on the line, as was my life. I snuggled into my astronaut-like silver blanket, crinkling all the way, and softened my tone. "It's all right. He was wearing an invisibility cloak in the form of a guard's uniform. No one really looks at security guards. They're always the first ones biffed."

Van gave me a weak smile out of half his mouth. The other side of his face was obviously in pain.

"What happened to the real security guard?" I asked, feeling a sudden cold shudder despite my warm blanket, as though someone had walked over the security guy's grave, which was probably either a back alley Dumpster or a shallow ditch near the Duwamish.

"We're looking into that now," one of the agents said in that official tone of voice that means we ain't giving nothing away and leaves the listener fearing the worst.

"Maybe there was no security guard to be biffed," I mused aloud, hoping for the best. "Maybe Goon was the real guard. Maybe he used a fake ID and somehow managed to get hired by the security company. He's wily enough. And you could get him for ID theft.

"Or maybe Goon bribed the real guy with a hefty wad of cash and security guy is on his way to Hawaii right now. I hope you're checking into that." Which was the scenario I was hoping for.

Van seemed to be in charge of the operation. He flashed me a sympathetic look. "That's not the information we have."

As I opened my mouth to ask another question about the guard, Van's radio crackled to life. He answered, looking relieved by the interruption. The rest of us listened in to his end of the conversation without any of the usual subterfuge eavesdroppers use. Unfortunately, Van's end consisted mostly of swearing and frowns. He signed off and set the radio down. "They got away." He looked at one of his fellow agents. "Rock, coordinate with Seattle PD. See what we can do to track them down."

Rock nodded and left the room.

"Both Ket and Goon?" I asked, anxiety creeping into my voice as the door closed shut behind Rock. I hadn't realized I'd been so optimistic the Feds would catch at least one of them.

Van nodded. "Both."

"Both," I muttered to myself. "Both. Both. Both. Both."

Van shot me a concerned look. "You're saying the same thing over and over."

Perseveration is a sign of concussion. I'm sure Van knew that. "Just digesting the news. I'm fine."

Van didn't look one hundred percent convinced, but he turned to the guy on his right anyway. "We've got news copters buzzing the site and reporters dogging us."

"Channel Five's been reporting police chopper action almost since the action began," I said. When Van gave me a questioning look, I said, "Mom called. Our little party's been on the news for the last half hour. Someone called a tip in."

Van sighed, looking like he hated news-tippers. "Probably somebody listening in on police band radio." He looked at the guy on his right again. "Ben, you have any ideas for damage control? For those of you who don't know," he looked at me, "Ben's our PR guy."

"'No comment' always works," Ben said.

Van's dislike of Ben's answer was obvious from

his expression. "We have to give them something. Something with a ring of truth to it. Something to throw them off the scent of our mission. Something to investigate." He set his ice pack down on the table in front of him. Ice on. Ice off. He knew the drill.

I glanced at my watch. Twenty minutes? Close enough. My head was numb. I set my ice pack on the table, too.

"The trial's coming up fast. We have just days left to get that dongle and nail Canarino or our case goes in the crapper. We don't need the media blowing our operation." He paused in thought. "We tell them about Ket." Van glanced at me for affirmation.

I had my impassive face on. I wasn't committing one way or the other until I knew where this was going.

"We don't mention the dongle. We tell the media that we believe the suspect I'll refer to as Goon is working for Ket. That he infiltrated FSC headquarters as part of a plot to help Ket kidnap Reilly. The plot went awry when Reilly fought back and I walked in on him.

"We'll tie Jay's murder in, saying we believe Ket murdered Jay because he was jealous that Reilly dated Jay for a brief time while Ket was in jail. If we're lucky, we'll get Ket to turn himself in."

I shook my head. "Ket will never turn himself in."

"How do you know?"

"Because I know Ket."

"He didn't hire Goon to kidnap you," Van pointed out. "We don't think he murdered Jay. Everything points to Jay's murder being tied to the dongle. If Ket thinks we'll make him a deal—"

"If you make him a deal, I will personally bean you with this ice pack," I said, grabbing my ice pack and holding it like a weapon. "And I throw hard and with extreme accuracy. Then I'll track Goon down and hire him to off you." I paused. "I mean it."

"Put the ice pack down," Van said dryly. "It's not nice to threaten an officer of the law—"

"Tell it to the judge." I cut Van off. "I've had enough of the criminal justice system letting Ket loose to torment me." I set the ice pack down and crossed my arms in front of me.

Van sighed and put his ice pack back on his eye, shooting me a challenging look and nodding toward my ice. Yeah, it was safer for him against my head than beaning his. I uncrossed my arms and picked up my pack to apply to my goose egg, staring Van down with a look as cold as my instant ice.

I rested my elbow on the table and pressed the ice pack against my head, wincing. "Ket's back on the steroids. I could tell. He's buffer than he's ever been. He's not rational. And he won't be. He's angry and he feels invincible. He's walked right past you guys since the beginning. He won't turn himself in." I paused and pinned Van with an angry look. The Tylenol was helping, but my head was still spinning and it was hard to think straight. "And I don't like your scenario. It makes me sound like a tramp in the midst of a torrid love triangle."

"It makes Ket look like a dangerous nutcase." Van stared back at me, daring me to challenge him.

All the others in the room were watching us, trying to hide their grins.

I let out a loud sigh. "Let's go with the assumption Ket doesn't turn himself in. What then?"

"We're tracking him down. Both him and Goon."

I had a lot less faith in Van now that he was a cop.

Though I didn't officially consent to the story, I didn't lodge a major protest, either. Van sent Ben out to talk to the press. Then he and his agents left me alone in the room while they made their battle plans.

Van pointed a finger at me as he left. "And don't fall asleep on me while I'm out." Then he instructed the uniform to check on me every few minutes and keep me awake.

How touching. On the other hand, a comatose me wouldn't look good on his job performance report.

"We need your help, Reilly," Van said when he returned. He took a seat opposite me at the table, all business.

"You don't have to use the FBI voice. It's just us."

He gave me his in pain half smile. His eye had swollen completely shut, but he was still giving the instant ice a go.

"You're the designated bearer of bad news," I said. His posture gave him away. "They could have sent someone prettier. Right now you are the sore eye, not the sight for it."

"Nice to see you have your sense of humor back."

"Yeah." I was still peeved.

"We have a plan to catch Goon and Ket and retrieve the dongle. And we need your help."

I didn't like the expectant way he was looking at me. Like I was bait he was ready to cast out and angle with. "Too desperate. Too calculating," I said, critiquing his approach. "Try that again and put some sympathetic Agent Jack Malone into it. Soft, firm voice. Sympathetic eyes, in your case, eye."

"Reilly . . ." He did his best Jack Malone imitation.

I couldn't help smiling. "I'll make this easy on you, Jack. If your plans involve me in the Cone of Silence, you got it. Mum's the word. Anything else, forget it. Can I go now?" I pushed my chair back, ready to stand.

Van stood and blocked the door. "Not so fast. You haven't even heard the plan yet."

"I don't have to. I take it that it involves more than silence." I sighed, but remained seated. "Does it involve danger?"

"Danger, duplicity, acting skills. Everything you've learned in camp. What do you say?" He put that rah-rah tone in his voice that people use when they're trying to rev you up about something as appealing as cold, canned spinach.

"You're a lousy salesman. I don't want danger and I've had more than enough of duplicity." Okay, that was a direct barb.

"Reilly, please?"

"Can you guarantee a happy ending?"

"Nothing in this life is guaranteed. I am authorized to offer you a limited warranty."

I stared him down. "Why do I have the feeling

'limited' refers to notifying my next of kin when the whole plan backfires?"

His answering grin wasn't as pretty as it used to be. The black eye and the wince of pain thrown in ruined the whole effect.

"No thanks."

"The odds are in our favor." He was still doing the grin/grimace of pain thing. Which played on my heartstrings, probably just as he'd planned. Even banged up, he was damned cute. And he had probably saved my life. "If we succeed, your problems with Ket are a thing of the past."

"The odds better be better than fifty-one to forty-nine. They'd better be a lot closer to ninety-nine to one."

"They are."

"Uh-huh. You're a big, black-eyed bluffer." I put my ice pack and my hands on the table. It was a whole lot better than having my hands trembling in my lap.

"So you're in?"

"Not so fast. I never sign a contract without reading the fine print. First, I want to know everything about Canarino and the dongle. Then, I'll want to hear the plan. Then we'll talk."

Van nodded. "Fair enough."

"I'm Reilly the spy, and I'm listening." I leaned back in the chair and wrapped myself back into the space blanket like I was waiting for a bedtime story.

"Thank you," Van said, looking amused despite the tense situation. "Where do you want me to start?"

"Canarino," I said. "I was reading fast at Mom's."

Van nodded again. "Like you said before, Canarino's a high profile investigator who's an expert in audio analysis. In the mid-nineties, he worked with a software guru named Wagner to develop a device that converted audio and spoken words into computer files. That doesn't sound like much today. You can buy cheap consumer products that do that. But back then, it was a big deal.

"It was pretty low-tech, a shielded box that attached directly to phone lines and drew the power it needed directly from those lines so that it wouldn't need a battery that would have to be replaced. The device could also capture the touch tones of the numbers the target dialed and read incoming numbers.

"Canarino claimed he was developing it for use for law enforcement. In reality, with the assistance of a phone company employee he bought off, he was using it for illegal wiretapping that he did on behalf of his clients.

"Canarino bought off several cops to break into DMV records and criminal history records that aren't available outside of law enforcement. His clients had the edge, which made him very popular. And very rich. Canarino got results."

I shuddered. "Dirty cops."

"Don't worry. We have them. They've been charged with racketeering, along with Canarino. We have them dead to rights on those charges."

I nodded. "You didn't miss any?"

"No."

"How old is Canarino?" I asked.

"Sixty-nine."

"What's the sentence for the racketeering charges?"

"Twenty years."

"You've got him for life then," I said. "Why do you need the audio files?"

"Canarino and his clients violated the privacy rights of dozens, maybe hundreds, of people. Those people have the right to justice, don't you think?"

"And you have many more fish to bring in and fry," I said. "This could be a career-making case. Am I right?"

He shrugged. "It could be."

Which meant it was.

"If we let one dirty PI get away with it, what happens to the system? Who's safe?"

My turn to shrug. "So Canarino has the encrypted audio files."

Van nodded. "When Canarino was arrested on weapons charges earlier, Wagner destroyed the wiretapping equipment and software. Only Canarino knows the key to decoding his files. We've spent nearly nine months trying to decode them without success. This is where your theory about the dongle comes in." Van's eyes lit up.

"In August, Canarino suffered a mild stroke in prison. While he was recuperating in the prison hospital, someone tried to kill him."

"Nice," I said.

"Canarino realized that someone was trying to guarantee his silence. If he dies, his secret dies with him. So he 'let it slip,'" Van made quotes with his fingers, "that before his arrest, he had made a dongle that contains the key to the decoding algorithm.

He'd entrusted an associate with it and should he die, his associate would turn it over to the cops. Now he's shifted the balance of power."

"But is he telling the truth?" I asked. "He could be bluffing. What if there is no *real* dongle? Only the fake one? You all could be searching for the Holy Grail. And I have no intention of swinging by my neck from the rafters with you for an imaginary item."

Van looked puzzled by my ramblings.

"Excalibur?" I said. "King Arthur. There's always a Mordred to mess up the plans and cause death and destruction."

"I get it now. Slow down. We have verification of the dongle from other sources."

"I hope you don't mean me."

He smiled. "More other sources."

"Huff was the associate," I said. "I was right."

"Yes. We've been following him. When he registered for camp, I did, too."

"So you're not a math man at all?" I couldn't hide the disappointment in my voice.

"I have a degree in mathematics and computer science. I was a lab rat for CRRU before I went into the field as a special agent. That's why I'm on this case. Does that make you feel any better?"

"It might if I knew what CRRU was?" I rolled my eyes and muttered about people using industry specific acronyms and jargon and expecting everyone else to understand.

"Cryptanalysis and Racketeering Records Unit."

"Good to know. Where is Huff now?"

"We don't know."

"I feel so safe," I mumbled under my breath. "On to the plan then."

Van swore me to secrecy. "This is where it gets fun." He went on to describe a plan where I was indeed bait. "You play out the final day of camp like nothing has happened. We don't think they'll try to take you here again. Too risky."

I nodded, but I didn't necessarily agree.

"After our last session, the instructors will suggest we all go out for a celebration dinner at a pre-arranged restaurant. We'll make it common knowledge that we're going out and where we're going. We'll have you wired. We'll have agents and law enforcement officers undercover everywhere. We'll put you out in the open and wait for Goon, and Ket, to make their moves."

I frowned. I didn't like this plan. "You get a career-making case. But what do I get out of all this?"

"Protection twenty-four seven until we find the dongle." He gave me a steely-eyed look as only a man with a black eye and an ice pack can. "Right or wrong, the bad guys believe you have the dongle. Until they either get it back or determine to their satisfaction you don't have it, you won't be safe."

"For cripes sake," I said, sounding more like Dutch by the minute. "But I don't have the dongle. If they manage to steal me away somehow"—I gave him a look that said I thought it was definitely possible, "they'll try to torture it out of me. And I'll have no recourse. Because *I don't have the dongle*! They'll think I'm just being brave when I'd give it up in a heartbeat."

"Drama queen. We won't let them torture you," he said.

I rolled my eyes and winced.

"We won't."

"Is that the same kind of 'won't' as in I was safest here at camp?"

"Trust me."

"I'm not overly trusting of cops," I said, giving him a steely look of my own. "And you've got a bad track record of lying to me since we met. Plus, if you guys were so sharp, why didn't you know about the dongle in the bathroom?"

Van looked sheepish again. "We knew about the dongle in the bathroom. We swapped it out and re-placed it with a fake—"

"You what? You . . . you . . ." Words and epithets failed me.

"We were guarding you."

I shot him a look that told him what I thought of their protection.

"I just got word from our cryptanalysists at CRRU this afternoon. The dongle Huff gave you was a so-phisticated fake," Van continued, unfazed. "What we don't know is why they think you still have the real one."

"Does it matter?" I asked.

"Not to me. Not if you go along with my plan."

I considered my options. I didn't have any, only bargaining chips. "Only if you promise me that you'll stick with my case until you catch Ket."

"Hey, the bastard tried to run me down. I want him, too."

"You'll put out an APB on him? You'll plaster his picture in post offices?"

"He isn't exactly one of the ten most wanted."

"He's my number one," I said.

"Goon's worse," Van said. "He should be your number one."

"He only wants the dongle and then he goes away," I countered.

"Goon's a hired killer. He has mafia connections behind him. You don't want to mess with the men paying him. You don't want to mess with him."

"Are you trying to scare me off?" I frowned at him.

Van held his hands up in a "no contest" kind of gesture. "Just saying."

"You can't get Ket on post office walls?"

"I don't have that kind of power. But I'll bring him in and do everything in my power to see he's locked up for the maximum the law allows. What do you say?"

I believed the resolve in his voice. "Do I have a choice?"

Van called several of his agents back to the room and made me repeat to them everything that had happened to me since arriving at camp.

"We'll need to go through your car and everything you have with you at camp again," he said.

"Again?"

Van had the decency to look sheepish a second time. "You can cooperate or we can get a warrant."

I waved him off. "Fine. Go ahead and look."

I hesitated. "Are you going to tell me what you find?"

"I'll tell you what I can."

"Cop-out." I gave Van's guys my key card and the password to the in-room safe. "You'll send someone right out to protect my family?" My voice broke and it took me a minute to get control back. "If Ket gets desperate enough, he'll go after them. And the bad guys . . ."

"We've got someone on it already."

Chapter 24

The team dispersed.

"FSC has arranged for an armed escort back to the hotel when we're ready for you," Van said.

"You mean when your team's finished pawing through my belongings."

"Yeah." He was packing up to leave.

"Tell them to paw gently and clean up after themselves. I've seen the cop shows. They manhandle the shoes and they're gone."

"Sure."

"Liar."

He smiled and turned to go.

I caught his arm. The startled, optimistic look he gave at my touch was almost enough to thaw my anger. Almost.

"I want to leave before the press does. Get me out to the car while the cameras are rolling."

"You don't want to avoid the press?"

Almost subconsciously, I rubbed my big, fat goose egg. "Not this time. I'm not Ket's girl anymore. And I'm not modeling, making my living on my looks. I

don't have a perfect professional image to protect."
I gave him a pleading look, begging him to understand. "I want people to see what he did. I want them to know who to blame. I don't want to be afraid."

He stared at me for a long minute. "Don't say anything that will compromise the case."

"Wouldn't dare."

"You didn't hear that from me."

"I never even talked to you."

When it was time to leave, Van came to get me in the "sick" room where I'd been resting. To preserve his cover, he was riding back with the rest of us.

"We're ready to go. The reporters are still out there waiting for fresh blood." He gave me a look that asked if I'd changed my mind about braving them.

"I'm ready."

His gaze flicked over me, and it wasn't exactly the most appreciative, lusty gaze I've ever received. "Do you want to freshen up first?"

"I want them to see me exactly as he left me."

"Preserve the evidence?"

"My VC is always nagging me to keep a victim's diary. Let them have a photo essay."

"Let's go then. War wants to meet with everyone in the lobby before we leave."

"What about?"

"Another discussion on whether we should continue to sally on with our camp." Van paused. "We need you to insist that you want to come back for the final day."

I nodded. I wasn't real keen on being on my own quite yet, anyway. Not with Ket and Goon on the loose.

"The new security guys are fresh from the security company and we've checked them out. No Goon."

I gave him a half smile. "Good."

"They'll be guarding our floor at the hotel all night."

"Good PR stunt," I said.

"My guys will be watching us, too." Van touched my arm. "Thought you'd want to know. We found the real security guy locked in the trunk of his parked car in a grocery store lot near his home."

"Is he?"

"Shaken up, but fine. Ready?"

Our meeting with War lasted only minutes. We all quickly agreed to come back.

War introduced our bodyguards. "This is Bob. And this is Bob."

Tall, sturdy, no necks. Sunglasses. Black tees and jeans. They looked like guys you'd hire from Bodyguards and Bouncers R Us, Hollywood office. Next time War could hire Pete and Re-Pete.

War turned the show over to the Bobs. Bob and Other Bob gave us instructions on how to safely get to the bus. We formed up and prepared to move out with Bob and Bob flanking us.

I took off my jacket. I'd been huddled in it ever since War had brought it to me in sickbay. I shivered.

"Put that back on. It's cool out there and you're still in shock." Van gave me a stern look.

I shook my head and glanced down at my bare right arm where a handsome set of welts in the shape of Ket's hand had formed, underlined by the distinctive purple of bruising. "When we go out, stand on my left. I want the reporters to see this arm. Ket's handprint is so clear, there's no way they could miss it."

It was hard to peg the look Van gave me. Kind of a mixture of sympathy and pride. "They'll be in our faces. They know who Ket is. And you. And Cliff and Jim. Everyone here but Steve and me are high-profile fodder for the story."

"You're high profile. You're the hero, the knight in shining armor of this tale." I don't know why I said that. I was still mad at him. I took a deep breath. "Anyway, I'm counting on the fodder. You can stop trying to talk me out of this now."

Bob and Bob got the group of us moving.

"Let them see your good side," I whispered to Van.

"My good side has a black eye."

"That's the side I mean."

Flanked by Bob and Other Bob, we stepped out into a crush of reporters, who let their questions fly rapid-fire. Some at me. Some at Cliff. Some at Jim. Some at Van. Steve, they pretty much ignored. And it may have been my imagination, but Steve seemed steamed by that.

Given a day or two, my cognitive powers would

have returned to normal, but at the current moment, I was still finding it hard to think straight and focus on the questions directed at me. Mostly, I just cued in on my name and took it from there. Ahead of me, Cliff was trying to steal the show, to the point of breaking with the pack and being herded back in by Bob and Other Bob. Cliff blatantly played the PR card for his upcoming film, answering questions that weren't even his with answers that extolled the virtue of his soon-to-be shooting movie.

"Ms. Peterson? Reilly?" A local female reporter I recognized from the five o'clock news stuck a mic in my face. "What happened in there?"

Bob, or maybe it was Other Bob, brushed her back.

I tucked my head down. "I can't comment on that."

"We heard your ex-boyfriend Ket Brooks tried to abduct you?" someone else shouted.

I neither denied nor verified.

"Did he hurt you?" Still another reporter.

I turned my full face to the bank of reporters long enough for the photographers to get a clear shot of it and my arm, and then looked down and away.

"What were you doing at Fantasy Spy Camps?" another reporter yelled.

"Vacationing."

"This session teaches participants self-defense, close quarter combat, and hostage rescue techniques. Do you find that ironic? Is that why you're here? Were you afraid of Brooks?"

I teared up a bit. "No comment."

"How did you escape?"

Van was walking next to me. I touched his arm, did a Nell looking at Dudley Do-right, and flashed him a "my hero" look. "No comment."

"Were you afraid for your life? Did you fight back?"

I reached the shuttle bus steps. "I used what I learned here at FSC."

It was rush hour. The radio news—traffic, news, and weather every fifteen minutes—repeated the day's top story. Ket Brooks, celebrity trainer to the stars, was wanted for the attempted kidnapping of his former girlfriend, former UW fastpitch star pitcher and sports model Reilly Peterson, and an attempted vehicular homicide for trying to run down her rescuer, math professor Van Keller.

By the time we got back to the hotel, the story was blaring all over the five o'clock news. Bob and Other Bob escorted us through another rabid pack of reporters and back to our rooms.

Van and I were the last to be dropped off. As we reached our side-by-side doors, Cayla popped her head out from her door across the hall.

"So it's true! Look at you two." Her gaze flicked over Van and she suppressed a wince, her thoughts written all over her face. He definitely wasn't as pretty as he used to be. She may as well have clucked her tongue.

Her gaze bounced to me and she flashed me her sympathetic look. When she shook her head, her myriad of beaded necklaces rustled. "At least you're all right." She smiled at Van. "You're being hailed a hero."

"Yeah, he's my hero."

Cayla looked taken aback by the obvious sarcasm in my voice. "Didn't he—"

"Yeah, he saved me."

Next to me, Van did his half-face grin.

"I didn't think you'd be coming back to the hotel tonight." Cayla looked uncertainly between us and then at Bob and Other Bob.

"We have protection." I nodded toward the two security guys. I'd memorized Bob and Other Bob's every facial detail on the bus ride back. No more switcheroo for me. Not that Goon could ever do a convincing impression of either of those two pieces of beefcake. "Meet our bodyguards." I introduced them.

"And as an added bonus, the hotel has beefed up security and the cops will be making extra rounds by here tonight. We'll all be safer than we've ever been." Where had I heard that before?

Van paused at his door, watching my conversation. We hadn't spoken on the ride back.

Cayla looked over my two hunky bodyguards, sizing them up as potential jewelry customers and one-night stands.

Bob and Other Bob were a little too buff for my personal tastes. And a little too strong-silent-type, heavy on the silent. Under normal circumstances, she was welcome to them. But tonight I needed them on duty and standing between me and the Grim Reaper dressed as Ket or Goon.

Cayla ogled the Bobs as she spoke to me, putting

out some strong come-hither vibes. Cayla was attractive in her own heavily bejeweled Sweet Gypsy Rose way, rings on her fingers and bells on her toes. She actually didn't have the bells on her toes . . . yet, anyway. Maybe one of the Bobs would go for her. Stranger things have happened.

"If there's anything I can do for you?" Cayla said.

"No. Thanks." I answered for all of us, even though the guys might have had other ideas.

Cayla bobbed her head up and down, but made no move to retreat into her room. Maybe she was still hoping for an opportunity to slip the Bobs her number.

There was an awkward pause while we all stood silently in the hall. I glanced at the Bobs. As soon as I was safely in my room, they were free to go about their business and protect life, liberty, and the American way, not to mention the hall. Kind of like the guards at Buckingham Palace, they weren't moving or smiling, simply standing and guarding. Maybe once I was inside my room they'd turn into total cut-ups. Maybe it was only in the presence of the guardee that they had to act like statues. They were probably eager to be on their way. I glanced at my door.

I really, really did not want to be alone in my room. Not with two very real boogeymen after me. I had the same creepy feeling I'd had as a kid when, against my parents' orders, I'd watched the old horror flick, *The Shining*. It's pretty scary when your dad goes psycho and tries to kill you. It's not so different when your boyfriend does the same and could show up with an ax at any minute.

Van stalled at his door, too, waiting for me to go into mine. Which only irritated me. I made a flicking motion, indicating that he should head on in. He ignored it.

I rubbed my red, raw wrists. Goon's binding hadn't been kind to them.

Cayla lingered, watching the action, or rather inaction, and looking like she wanted to say something more to me. Maybe like did I know the Bobs' numbers?

So there we were, standing in the hallway, staring at each other. Very boring. Someone had to say or do something.

Cayla spoke up first. "You poor thing. Your wrists look horrible. I have some nice lotion that might help. And some beautiful bracelets that would hide those wrists. Hypoallergenic. Just the thing. Want to come in and see?" She motioned me to her room.

If I hadn't been so desperate not to be alone, or so curious as to what Cayla had to say that she obviously couldn't in the hall, I might have declined. The sudden, ridiculous image of me emerging from her room wearing huge cuff bracelets like Wonderwoman almost scared me off.

I turned to my bodyguards, sounding a little overeager. "Thanks, boys. You can go now. I'll just be across the hall."

Van had been watching the whole exchange. He shook his head.

Cayla had my arm.

"We'll wait out here until you're finished," Bob said.

"I will, too." Van leaned against his door.

"You, go in your room. Get some rest." My words said one thing. My tone said go to hell.

Cayla's eyebrows shot up.

"I won't be long," I said to Bob and Other Bob, and followed Cayla in, leaving the door open.

Cayla got me the lotion. Pink, with a nice sweet pea scent. Reminded me of my mother's scented lotion obsession. As I put it on, Cayla dragged out one of her large cases of jewelry and laid it on the bed. "Van and you and a picture of your old boy-friend have been all over the news." Cayla picked up a bracelet she thought might work and handed it to me.

I nodded. The bracelet wasn't half bad. I tried it on and admired my wrist.

"All the Cindy Lous agree. They'd remember seeing a man as handsome as your ex."

I snorted. I hadn't thought of Ket as handsome for a long time. Now I mostly thought of him as the Source of All Evil. And evil, once exposed, isn't all that pretty. "You're telling me no one's seen Ket?"

She nodded. "No one. I don't know where he got that necklace, but it wasn't from us." She paused significantly.

"Yes?"

"Well, you know what *is* odd? I did a little sleuthing of my own, trying to find out who all had sold the black and crystal necklace you were asking about?"

I paused in my perusal of the jewelry and looked at her. Cayla was sharper and nosier than I'd given her credit for. "Uh-huh."

"Only one person has sold one all conference. Linda Small. She sold it to your friend Steve on

Monday." Cayla walked to her dresser and returned with a business card in hand. "Here's her card. In case you want to talk to her."

I took it, frowning. Wondering the same as Cayla at the coincidence. "Thank you."

"It's the least I could do."

"Don't mention this to anyone else. Please." I gave her a sharp look.

She got my message. "Never."

Ten minutes later, I walked out of Cayla's room humming "Hello, sweet pea, won't you dance with me," and wearing two cuff bracelets that weren't all that Wonderwoman-like and looking pretty decent. I carried two of Cayla's business cards and had Linda Small's in my pocket.

Back in the hall, Van had ignored my command and was chatting with Bob and Other Bob, who evidently weren't mutes after all. The three were all having a jolly time. I felt a twinge of jealousy. I wanted the Bobs to like me better. Like me better, guard me better. Or so my reasoning went. And I wanted Van to . . .

Well, I wanted Van. But I was still peeved at him.

Ignoring Van, I tucked Cayla's business card, one each, into Bob and Other Bob's pocket like a tip. "In case you need anything." I pointed at Cayla's room and winked. "Once you're off duty, of course."

I shot Van a defiant look and, unable to avoid the inevitable, cruised into my room to find . . .

Chapter 25

Nothing amiss.

Bob, or maybe it was Other Bob, I really had to get them straight, pushed past me and checked my room, including under the bed, for the big, bad wolf, and finding none, left.

"We'll be right outside," he said as he closed the door behind him.

"Yeah? Well beware handsome gym owners bearing gifts," I called after him. I think maybe he grinned.

I stood frozen by the door, weighing my alternatives for the evening.

Like any girl who's been violated in any way, my first instinct was to bathe, bathe, and bathe again. But add actual blood, grit from the alley, germs from lying on the bathroom floor, and perspiration from a strenuous workout to my "dirty, want to wash it all off" feeling and I really, really needed a good scrub. And a good soak. A good soak and a good scrub.

Maybe, if I hadn't felt like I was staying in the Stanley Hotel in the midst of an emporium of evil,

I would have acted on my urge. But the last thing I wanted was to be caught naked by either Ket or Goon.

It's not like I didn't trust the Bobs, the cops, and the FBI guys. But Ket and Goon loomed in my fears like a bad odor, able to float under doors.

I moved on to urge number two. Check out the room. See if the FBI guys had taken anything. Inquiring minds wanted to know. I would have asked Van, but . . . I had my pride.

I began my investigation with my suitcase. It sat on its rack with every fiber of my neatly folded clothes in place. I rummaged a bit, but everything looked pretty much present and accounted for.

I couldn't stand the silence in the room. I turned on the TV and flipped through the network channels, scanning the local news. The anchors had moved past the hard news and were on to weather and sports. The top of the hour when the national news came on would tell where we ranked in the national news scene. I flipped briefly to one of the all news channels and watched for a few minutes.

We made the news ticker, banner, whatever you call it, that scrolled across the bottom of the screen. I stifled an urge to call out to Van, switched back to network TV and headed for my closet. Next door, I heard Van's shower turn on.

Somebody didn't have a problem showering alone and without a guard posted immediately outside his bathroom door. Which only made me madder at him. Confident, arrogant . . .

I forced my attention back on my closet. The only things I kept in the closet were my sexy, strappy party shoes and the valuables in my safe. I picked up my silver sandals and cuddled them. "You look marvelous," I cooed to them. "Those mean, old FBI guys didn't manhandle you, did they?"

If only shoes could talk.

Next door, I swear Van pumped up the volume on his shower just to irritate me. I set my shoes down, scowled in the direction of Van's room and opened the in-room safe to take inventory. Purse. Good. I opened it—lipstick, wallet, tissues, spare change, sanitary protection . . .

My gaze slid to the adjoining door. I wondered if Van had locked his side. I wondered if I should just try it and see. Just to make sure he was safe in there. In his nice, steamy shower. Keep an eye on him while he was vulnerable . . . and naked.

Running, cleansing, beautiful water. Slithery, sudsy, smooth luscious lather. Bubbles trailing down Van's naked skin . . .

My hand actually tingled with the urge to try the adjoining door. The rest of me tingled, too. But not for the same reason. I forced myself to return to my inventory of the safe. Keys. Gun. Naked Van . . .

Thoughts of Van were like the Stay Puff Marshmallow Man. They just popped in there.

A teaser for one of the seven o'clock hour celebrity gossip shows caught my attention, temporarily diverting my thoughts from marshmallows, naked Vans, and other delectable treats. A photomontage of Ket's picture with various celebrities he'd trained flashed across the set, followed by an old modeling shot of me, and an old picture of us together, smiling, laughing, happy.

I shuddered. Was that how it was going to be? Were they going to focus on the what was, what's over, what's fake? Yeah, we looked good in that picture. But it was taken a week after Ket hit me the first time. In the picture, I was wearing the diamond teardrop earrings he'd given me during his conciliatory, apologetic, make it all up to me, he'll never do it again mood. Diamonds are forever teardrops. How bizarre. And ironic. I should have been so out of there.

Like the absolute lust for deep, dark sixty-three percent cacao chocolate during a PMS mood, there are some urges that are completely beyond my control. The need to wash off the stench of a goon and a creepy, murderous ex in complete safety, and possibly get a glimpse of Van's naked body sparkling with lather is evidently one of them.

I slammed the safe shut, raced across the room, threw open my side of the adjoining door, then his side of the door without stopping to knock. I was breathing hard and so worked up that I didn't register that he hadn't locked his side. I didn't even notice that the shower noise had stopped.

As I stood there panting, Van stepped out of his bathroom wearing a loose-fitting pair of lounge pants and nothing else. That I could see. He was sparkling, squeaky, lusciously clean. His hair was damp and tousled. His skin glistened with a freshly scrubbed glow. The swelling around his eye had gone down. He could open it some now. But there were deep, ugly bruises on his ribs and arms and the bottom of his jaw. And his lip looked a little puffy, and it wasn't from kissing.

"What took you so long?" He was trying the killer grin again, and doing only a slightly better job of it than a few hours before.

But I wasn't really concentrating on his face anyway. The tingly urge to touch was back in my fingers, along with a crazy desire to straddle him and bite that perfect shoulder of his. The unbruised one.

"Thief!" I pointed an accusing finger at him, trying to ward off the tingles with anger. "You stole my three-in-one Cinnamon Bliss body wash. How am I supposed to get clean without it?"

He opened his mouth to speak, but I cut him off. "Don't even try denying it, mister. I can smell the cinnamon on your skin from here. And I bet you used my bath scrubby, too. You have the glow."

He shrugged. "You left it here."

I glared at him. Tried anyway. I think there was some guilt that he'd been beat up on my account, and some lust and desire thrown in subconsciously.

"Hey, you could have stopped by to retrieve it at any time." He winked with his good eye. "I practically turned into a prune in there." He left the "waiting for you" part unsaid.

I sputtered, but nothing coherent came out. I wasn't sure what made me angrier. That I'd missed the opportunity of showering with him by being so damn stubborn. Or that he actually expected me to join him in the first place. After he lied to me, deceived me, let Goon almost kidnap me . . . and saved my life.

On second thought, maybe he wasn't *so* bad.

I changed the subject. "You left the door between our rooms unlocked! What were you thinking?"

He tried the grin again.

I ignored it and his obvious meaning. "Anyone could have walked in here and offed you. After they first killed me, of course."

"And hotel security. And the Bobs. And my guys."

"Don't interrupt me. My concussion is making it hard for me to concentrate." Well, that and his bare chest. "Those other guys are beside the point. I was your last line of defense. I would have tried to protect you. Which is why I wasn't showering in my own room. Because how could I while you were vulnerable?"

"How do you know I was vulnerable?"

"Were you naked?"

"I don't shower with my clothes on."

"Then you were vulnerable. Everyone's vulnerable when they're naked."

"That explains the rarity of nudist colonies," he said.

I scowled and gave him my reproving look, the one I learned from my mother.

He put his hands up in defense. "I had my gun."

"In the shower?"

"On the counter. I had a different kind of barrel in the shower."

I rolled my eyes.

He laughed and stepped toward me.

I stepped back, my eyes tearing up without warning. I hated these pendulum emotions I'd been having since the attack this afternoon. I felt like I was having the worst PMS day. If only a Midol would solve the problem.

"Don't. I . . . I feel dirty." And I meant from more than physical grit and grime.

He froze. The sympathetic, concerned look he gave me practically caused me to break into a floodgate of tears. I sniffed, trying to hold them back. "Sorry."

"It's all right." He sounded like he understood, yet there was a hard, angry undertone to his voice. Like he wanted to kill Goon and Ket.

I wiped my eyes with the back of my hand.

"You want to shower now? I left you plenty of Cinnamon Bliss." He nodded toward the bathroom. "I'll watch your backside."

"You're damned right you will." I took a deep breath. "I'll just get my things and be right back."

"Don't forget your gun. Two barrels are better than one."

I stifled a comeback about how he probably meant holsters. Barrels were my thing, and I was a one-barrel-at-a-time woman. "Order us some room service. I'm starving."

I came back with my gun, clothes, and toiletries, and Linda Small's card. I put the gun on the dresser. I handed the card to Van. "The only Cindy Lou at conference who's sold a black necklace like the one Ket gifted me in my room."

Van raised his one good brow. "To Ket?"

"To Steve."

Van's look clouded. "Cayla your source?"

"Yep."

"You warn her to be careful?"

"Of course."

"I'll get my men on it."

I nodded.

"Drop your clothes outside the door," Van said as I headed into his bathroom. "I'll bag them and send them out to be cleaned. You'll have them back by morning. Promise."

"Thanks, but don't bother," I said. "Just bag them and toss them out. I don't want to ever see them again."

He gave me another serious, slightly worried look. "Aren't you running a little short on camp uniforms?"

I turned to look over my shoulder at him. He looked like he was worried about more than my uniform shortage. "How would you know? Did your guys take inventory?"

"You ruined one yesterday."

"Oh, yeah," I said and started for the door again. I paused in the doorway. "Your guys didn't . . . did they find . . . anything?" I meant the dongle.

"No."

"Oh. Sorry." Damn. All this for nothing. I felt unaccountably let down.

"It's all right. We'll get them."

I nodded and closed the bathroom door. The mirror was still steamed from Van's shower. I avoided it anyway, turning my back to it as I stripped. Then I opened the door a crack, extended one arm out, and dropped the clothes. I don't know if I was trying to be provocative. I definitely wasn't trying not to be. I was so confused.

I felt dirty and abused. Scarred and betrayed.

Scared and in lust. Full of longing for Van and in need of comfort. Angry at Van and the world and ready for justice. Nothing reconciled.

So I jumped in the shower and used gobs of Cinnamon Bun Bliss on my bath scrubby and scrubbed until I'd practically loofaed off my top layer of skin.

While I showered I took inventory of my injuries. My breasts were bruised where Goon had felt them up, ostensibly looking for the dongle. I vowed that if I ever got the chance to feel him up, I'd give him more than bruises.

My arms were bruised where Ket had grabbed me. I had bruises on my legs and hips where Ket had thrown me against the door handle. I had a goose egg on my head. And a scrape on my knee. I'd been worse, and I'd been better. I looked a lot like I used to in high school after back-to-back basketball and select fastpitch practices. But I was alive and, if you don't count my psyche, nothing vital was damaged.

I finished showering and sunk into the tub for a soak to ease my sore muscles and mind. I stayed there until I heard a knock on the door to the room, followed by some murmuring, followed by a gentle rap on the bathroom door.

"Dinner's here," Van said.

"Be right there."

I towel dried my body and hair, dressed in my cami and sleep shorts, and gave my hair a quick hit with the built-in blow dryer. Five minutes and I was out, pink and flushed from the soak and the heat of the blow dryer. I've never learned how to take a lukewarm shower or bath. I always come out too hot and need a cooling off period. When I opened the bathroom door and found Van still shirtless, I really needed cooling off.

"How was your shower? Feeling better?" He stole a glance at my braless double Ds. Men have a hard time *not* staring at them. I forgave him his temporary lack of eye contact.

"Great and yes." My double Ds budded up for him and I didn't even have the excuse of being cold.

The TV was on. It was almost seven and time for the celebrity gossip show that I had seen a commercial for earlier.

Van led me across the room to the small round table. He'd set it with an assortment of covered dishes, a bottle of white wine, a carafe of what smelled like coffee, and a bud vase with a single red rose.

"Dinner, I presume?" I ignored the obvious romantic touches. I wasn't letting him off the hook so easily. One rose and a bottle of wine was not going to get me to forgive him.

"Come and get it." He held my chair out for me before removing the cover to a plate of oysters on the half shell resting on a bed of ice. "Appetizer?"

I raised a brow and he grinned his half killer, half battered face grin.

"I don't suppose you have any deep-fried mozzarella sticks?" I wasn't letting him get any ideas. If he'd known me better, he'd have realized how much more hot, gooey, breaded cheese turned me on than slimy oysters.

"Not an oyster girl?"

"Not unless there's a pearl in it."

"Noted."

"Feel free to indulge, though," I said, using my magnanimous, "it's not going to be that easy to seduce me" tone, even though I was having a hard time keeping my hands to myself and my eyes above his chest level. And my breasts refused to unbud, which was probably giving him ideas that I'd forgiven him. The budded nipples were a completely involuntary reaction. I was just about as mad at them as I was at Van.

"I never oyster alone." He gave me a sidelong look that begged the question, would he have to?

I clenched my hands in my lap. When I didn't otherwise respond, he proceeded.

"On to the entrée." He began removing dish covers. "Chicken kabobs with fennel. Figs. Asparagus spears with pine nuts. Baby carrots with slivered almonds and honey." He kept his tone perfectly serious, but I got the feeling he was trying not to crack up. I mean, he was being so blatant.

My gaze swept the table. "Looks like we're heavy on the aphrodisiac food group tonight," I said conversationally.

"Really?" He gave me his best nonchalant, incredulous, I hadn't noticed impersonation. "I didn't know there was an aphrodisiac group."

"Did you flunk nutrition? It's one of the four basic groups right along with sugar, fat, and salt. Guess the kitchen was out of bananas?"

"Bananas?" Van was having a hard time maintaining his composure.

"And avocados," I said. "You know what you get when you mix one banana and two avocados?"

"No idea."

Actually, I think Van had a pretty clear idea. He was trying very hard not to laugh.

"This is just your basic selection of chicken, fruit, and vegetables." He pulled a bottle of wine from the ice bucket. "A fine Washington Johannesburg Riesling. May I offer you a glass?"

"Offer me two. I've had a rough day."

"If you'd like something stronger, there's whiskey in the mini fridge? Or rum? Some vodka?"

"Wine's fine. Pour." I tried to keep my defenses up as he filled my glass. No way was I dallying into hard liquor territory. I still had a bone to pick with him and I wasn't relenting until it was picked clean and he was in a figurative skeletal heap on the floor. "I was expecting something more junk foody, like a burger and fries."

"I owed you a *real* dinner."

"I thought that was scheduled for tomorrow."

"Dinner at a pub with everyone? Agents watching our every move? That's business."

He gave me the opening. I couldn't help but take it and stab to the heart of the matter. "Hasn't this *all* been business?" My tone wasn't playful.

He held a glass out to me. When I crossed my arms and didn't reach for it, he set it on the table in front of me.

"No."

"None of it?"

"Not the part you're worried about." He gave me

a steely look. "I don't seduce women for the hell of it while I'm on assignment."

"Never?" I stared him down.

"Never."

We glared at each other. I felt my nostrils flare.

"Once—" he started.

"Ah ha!"

"Hang on." He knelt in front of me and grabbed me by my crossed arms. With two fingers, he tipped up my face to look at him. "Once, I really fell for someone and lost my professional perspective. Reilly . . ." He paused. "Are you going to forgive me?"

"Maybe." Okay, I was mellowing.

"I'll take maybe. Maybe's better than no. Maybe has possibility." He stood and headed for his chair. Evidently, he wasn't the begging kind. I admired that.

The theme song for the seven o'clock gossip show blared. I grabbed my plate and glass of wine and headed for the bed to watch the show. "I can't see from here," I said when he shot me an optimistic look and followed me onto the bed with a plate of his own.

"Don't look at me like you're hoping all these aphrodisiacs are going to do the trick. I just need sustenance." Brave words, but my breasts had been budded so tightly for so long that I was beginning to wonder if they were going for the Guinness World record.

His gaze flicked to them. "Uh-huh," he said deadpan.

I should have worn a thicker cami, like maybe something in plated armor.

I took a sip of my wine, and then another and another. I drank most of the glass before finally setting it on the nightstand and waiting for the relaxing glow to settle over me.

The hosts came on and gave a brief overview of the stories ahead. "Coming up later, the case of popular Hollywood gym owner Ket Brooks who's wanted by the FBI for attempted kidnapping, but first . . ."

I did a silent, sarcastic mimic of the host, popped a fig in my mouth, and took my frustration, sexual and otherwise, out with a little rigorous chewing. Fig. Chicken. Carrots. Fig. Fennel. Sip of wine.

At the first commercial, Van hopped up and refilled my glass. When he settled back on the bed, he was leg-to-leg, foot-to-bare-foot with me, staring straight ahead. When I didn't immediately move away, his foot began playfully rubbing mine. I had to fight hard to keep my toes from curling.

"How's the chicken?" he asked, like he wasn't up to a thing.

"Hotel rubber chicken is hotel rubber chicken." I turned to stare at him. "The rubberizing process negates any and all aphrodisiac properties."

Undaunted, he grinned and stepped up the foot rubbing action. I drank another half glass of wine and maybe my toes rubbed his foot back.

More silly, superficial stories of the stars blared on the TV. I grew impatient, and nervous. "We've been bumped by fashion faux pas and—"

I was interrupted by footage of Ket's gym. "There

we are," I said, feeling my heartbeat speed up. "Turn it up."

The perky female host was getting testimonials from Ket's most famous clients, all of whom protested that they'd never, ever have dreamed he'd do something like this. And maybe they couldn't. Ket was pretty good at hiding his evil underbelly.

"He's accused of assaulting and trying to kidnap his former girlfriend, Reilly Peterson, a former sports model and spokeswoman for the popular 3D Sportswear Company . . ."

They flashed a few shots from my magazine days, followed by the footage of us leaving FSC. "Ms. Peterson looked very different today as she left the Fantasy Spy Camp facility . . ."

I took a deep breath and looked away from the screen.

Beside me, Van tensed. "I'm going to get him, Reilly. Both of them. They won't hurt you again."

I turned to stare at him. His jaw was set and his eyes darkened with determination. I believed he'd try. I believed he'd give it everything he had. I believed he wasn't a man I should toss away lightly.

"I know," I said very softly.

He turned to look at me. "Reilly?"

"I think I forgive you."

"Think?"

"I'm fairly positive."

He cupped my face with his hands and leaned in to kiss me. Our lips met. Our kiss deepened. Our tongues tangoed. He kissed me harder. I kissed

him harder. But just when everything should have
been dancing tongues and wonder, he winced.

"V?"

We were both breathing hard, panting for each
other.

"Fat lip," he said, touching his mouth gingerly,
his eyes full of apology and frustration.

"Poor baby." I gently outlined his mouth with my
finger. "Have some more wine. Wine will make you
feel fine." I handed him my glass and he drank.

We tried the kiss again. Gently. He slid his
arms around me. I tangled my legs in his, running my bare toes along his foot, and up his leg
under his lounge pants. He ran his hands along
my ribs and up under my cami until he was cupping my breast. He squeezed my breast. And
I . . . winced.

He broke the kiss and looked at me. "R?"

"Bruises. Big ones."

"Let me see."

I pulled up my cami for him. "Here and here."

"Poor baby," he cooed back to me, pulling my
cami off, and tossing it away. He kissed the
bruises, rolling my nipple between his thumb and
forefinger. "Do you need some more wine," he
whispered into my breast, finding my nipple and
sucking on it. "Wine, wine, wine will make you
feel fine."

"I am fine," I murmured, in no mood for him to
let go. "But I have a bruise here, too." I pulled
down my sleep shorts, exposing my bruised hip.

He stroked my hip softly and examined the
wound. "That looks bad. I think you need whiskey."

"Whiskey?"

He grinned and moved his hand lower and to the middle, dead center between my hips right into the o-zone. "Whiskey, whiskey, whiskey, makes you feel frisky . . ."

I knew where he was going with this. "I already feel frisky." I pulled his pants down and off and did a little stroking of my own.

By the time the seven-thirty gossip shows came on and Ket's picture flashed across the screen in a teaser, neither one of us felt like taking a break in the action to look for the remote.

We were tangled in each other. Kissing each other. Stroking each other and heavily engaged in a competition to see who could wince less and get the other to the brink first.

When we were both breathing heavily and on the edge of control, Van pulled a condom out of thin air. I put it on him.

He braced over me. "Ice cold duck, ice cold duck, makes me want to . . ."

I arched up to meet him.

He plunged in. Over and over again, hitting just the right spot. He plunged until waves of pleasure radiated through me and the world melted away, and I didn't care if Ket was on the TV. I didn't care if he saw me with Van. Van plunged and I arched until a giant moan escaped my lips and he grunted and we collapsed against each other grinning like idiots.

"In a shocking stunner today, Ket Brooks, popular owner of . . . " the woman on TV was saying, accompanied by pictures of Ket.

I smiled, cuddled into Van and kissed him on the cheek. "He'll never be able to hurt me in the same way again," I whispered.

"Not if I can help it," Van said, running his fingers through my hair.

Chapter 26

Van and I cuddled under the covers through the rest of the program, making snide, irreverent comments about the seemingly soap-operatic problems of the Hollywood elite. Gotta love a man who knew how to poke fun. Ket was such a sycophant.

Van had his arm around me, his hand idly playing with my hair. I rested my head in the crook of his neck and traced circles on his chest as we both basked in afterglow heaven.

"No leaks on TV about Canarino or our dongle." Van kissed the top of my head, sounding satisfied with more than the lack of a dongle leak. He tipped up my face to look at him. "You're pretty damned photogenic, even with a goose egg on your head."

"Yeah? I didn't do a bad damsel in distress, did I?" I wrapped my arms around him and gave him a squeeze. "You don't look half bad on celluloid yourself. The black eye gives you badass appeal."

"Does it?" He kissed the tip of my nose.

"I like you without the black eye, too."

"Good. I plan on healing." He pulled me flat on my back on the bed, poised over me, and bent down for a kiss.

Things were just getting interesting when his cell phone rang. Van cursed under his breath. "I have to get that."

"The office?"

He nodded as he got out of bed, threw on his lounge pants, and picked up the cell phone. "Keller."

He moved to the windows and turned to face the curtains as he spoke. It was obvious he wanted privacy. But hoping for good news, I listened to his end of the conversation anyway until I grew bored with his cryptic responses and gave up. It didn't sound like the FBI had caught Ket or Goon yet.

I took the opportunity to put on my cami and shorts and headed to the bathroom to freshen up. Much as I liked lingering around naked with Van, naked, as I said, was a vulnerable state. If I had to beat a quick retreat, I wanted to do it semi-dressed.

Van was off the phone when I came out of the bathroom. He sat at the table, his brows knit in thought over a cup of coffee.

"Hey, big boy, I hope that look of deep concentration means you've caught Goon or Ket, or better yet, both, and are planning your case to throw them in the slammer for life." I joined him, taking a seat opposite him, pretty much certain I was hoping for the moon.

"No."

"Damn." I snapped my fingers to emphasize my point and put on my hangdog expression.

"Cheer up. We'll get them eventually. Coffee? Chocolate?" He pushed an assortment of chocolate truffles toward me.

"Eventually? I won't be appeased so easily. I want immediately. Or soon. I might settle for ASAP. But that's as low as I'm willing to go." I declined the coffee.

He rattled the chocolates at me. "Chocolate will take the edge off your disappointment."

"You mean my despair, gloom, abject fear for my life. That's a tall order. Even for chocolate." I picked one out and took a bite. "Mmmmm." I rolled my eyes in ecstasy. "Now this is an aphrodisiac. You should have led with this." I winked at him.

He shook his head and leered at me. "You're getting entirely too much pleasure out of that."

I grinned and rubbed his leg with my foot under the table. "Help this chocolate out. Tell me your agents have at least gotten a lead on our least favorite bad guys? Gotten a bead on them?" I pointed at Van with my truffle. "'Cause if they have I say take them out."

"No. No. And that would be, no. And either put that down or eat it. You're scaring me."

Or making him horny again. I grinned and took another bite, playing up my enjoyment of it. "Okay, man of one word answers that consist entirely of no, I'm tired of playing twenty questions. Give me some dirt."

"Sandy loam."

"Not what I meant."

He took another sip of his coffee as he watched me enjoy my truffle. "What do you want to know?"

"What is the ultimate answer to the great question of life, the universe, and everything?"

"Forty-two."

"Okay, that was way too easy."

"You should have thought of a better question."

"I'll try harder. How's this—what is Goon's real name?"

"Salvatore Rossini."

"A goon named Sal."

"A thug and hit man named Sal." He blew on his coffee and took a sip.

"Who's working for . . . ?" When he didn't reply, I rolled my eyes. "Geez, do I have to pull teeth?"

"Could be for any one of three or four suspects or a coalition of them all. That's all I can say." He watched me pop the rest of the second truffle in my mouth. "You want some water with that?" He hadn't touched the chocolate.

"And dilute my chocolate hit? Are you crazy?" I reached for a third truffle while he shook his head in disbelief. "Enough beating around the bush. Are you going to tell me what that call was about?"

Van set down his cup and stared at me, looking like he was having a mental wrestling match with himself and the side opposing me was winning.

"Come on, you can tell me." I used my best cooing voice. I gave him my big, trustworthy, Girl Friday smile and leaned across the table, exposing a pile of cleavage while I reached up and stroked his jaw.

He grabbed my hand, kissed it, and squeezing it in his, laid our clenched hands on the table. "Maybe."

"Please?" I begged, giving his hand a returning squeeze. "I promise not to tell anyone. Mum is the absolute word."

"I'm not worried about mum."

"What *are* you worried about?"

"You dissolving on me or going ballistic."

"Wow, two peg-the-meter responses." I was watching him. He was serious about the options, which worried me considerably. "I'm tough and thoroughly nonsoluble."

He pursed his lips and sighed deeply. "Yeah, you've shown that."

"Give me a break. I'm not usually weepy or fragile. Today was a tough day."

"You just made my point." He moved his cup closer to him. "On the other hand, you have a right to know."

I nodded encouragingly, my heart going a million beats a minute.

"My men ran a background on Steve. Steve isn't his real name." As he spoke, Van was watching me closely for my reaction. He moved the coffee carafe away from me. He was worried.

"The cheater! Taking a code name before camp is against the rules." I tsk-tsked and grew serious. "Don't tell me he's another creepy PI after the dongle."

"Worse." Van leaned away from me. "Ket's informant."

My eyes went wide and a bubble of anger rose in my throat, erupting in a primal scream. I pushed my chair back so hard it slammed against the heating/air-conditioning unit behind me.

"Ballistic. I was right." Van jumped to his feet and headed for the dresser to prevent me from getting my gun.

I had no intention of going near the Beretta. I lunged for the bedside and Old Slugger, visions of a slugger-sized dent in Steve's thick head.

Van registered my change of direction and dived for me, trying to pry Old Slugger loose from my grip. We struggled over the bat. Finally, he pushed me onto my back on the bed and threw himself on top of me, pinning my arms over my head, still holding the bat.

He straddled my hips. "Let go of the bat."

"I'm not going to kill him," I said, panting and getting a nice view of his crotch. "I'm just going to maim him. A little."

"A little?" He rolled his eyes. "I'm not buying that, homerun babe."

Van was sitting on my recreation zone. Which did nothing to fan my anger and a whole lot for my libido. I grinned and did my best to arch up against him. Distraction by feminine wiles. "Let me go and I'll show you a good time."

Van smiled back through his puffy lips. "Let go of the bat first."

"No way."

"Then nothing doing. I like this position. I could sit here all night." He leaned down and kissed the side of my neck, the hollow of my neck, the top of my breast—

There was a knock on the door. "Everything okay in there?" It was one of the Bobs.

"We're fine," Van called back, looking at the door. "Everything's under control." His gaze flicked back to me, his eyes flashing with a devilish light. "Give me the bat." He leaned down and nibbled my ear.

My anger was slipping away, replaced by yummy thoughts of Van and chocolate. And revenge on Steve. Later. I released my grip.

Van grabbed the bat and tossed it away. "We'll get Steve."

"You better."

"Now," Van said and kissed me, "we have better things to do."

As his kisses trailed to the tips of my breasts, my phone sprang to life, playing Mom's familiar ring tone.

My turn for the apologetic look. "I have to get that."

Van swore under his breath. "Our phones have it in for us."

I rolled over, picked up my cell and flicked it open, trying not to sound too breathy. "Hey, Mom."

"Your grandpa's missing." Simple words, panicked tone.

"What!"

"Your grandpa's missing," Mom repeated.

I mouthed, "Dutch is missing," to Van. "You're sure?" I said to Mom. I was grasping for hope.

"No, I'm not sure. I just called to panic you."

"Mom—"

"I've looked everywhere for him. Last time I

saw him he was safely tucked in his room in the guesthouse, cleaning his gun. In case of emergency only."

"Oh, no."

"Oh, yes," Mom said. "I told him to stay put and not get any ideas about patrolling the perimeter. That was half an hour ago."

"You don't think he's pulled a General Zaroff and gone off Ket or Goon hunting, do you?" Grandpa wasn't a violent man, but he had a protective streak that ran bone deep. If he thought he could scare Ket off once and for all . . .

"The cars are all present and accounted for in the garage," Mom said. "Along with the bicycles, the scooter, and the riding lawn mower. Unless he took my garden cart for a joyride, he's on foot."

"Damn!" My heart jumped right into worried warp speed. There was no way Grandpa would go after Ket on foot.

"Damn it to hell," Mom said.

We both paused, waiting for the wrath of Dutch at our blatant cursing. If foul language didn't draw Dutch out, nothing would. And it didn't.

"Have you called the police?"

"About a grown man who's been gone maybe half an hour?" Mom sounded frustrated and as panicked as I felt.

"There are extenuating circumstances. I'll get on it and call you back," I told Mom and disconnected.

I flashed Van an angry, anxious look. "Dutch is missing. Your men were supposed to be watching him. Protecting him!" My pitch rose with each word as I repeated what Mom had told me.

"I'll handle it." As he flipped open his phone to make a call, my cell rang again.

I picked up the call.

"If you want Dutch back in one, big three-hundred-pound piece, you'll give me the dongle."

"Cindy Lou Goon, is that you?" The menace and anger in my voice came out naturally.

Hearing Goon's name, Van cut his call short and motioned for me to put the call on speakerphone. Which I did.

"Nice you recognize my voice. Makes me feel special. Don't like the name. Goon I can live with. Lose the Cindy Lou. I hate those broads."

"You over-accessorizing bastard!"

"Would you stop with the over-accessorizing!" Goon cursed under his breath. "I've learned my lesson. Better too little than too much.

"Darn right." I moderated my language in case Grandpa could hear. "And if you hurt my grandpa, I'm going to use your head for batting practice, Goon, so help me God. A smashed head doesn't go with anything."

"Sticks and stones," Goon said.

"Hey, that was a threat, not an idle promise."

Goon laughed. I pictured him shrugging, and scowled. Van motioned for me to tone down the rhetoric. He didn't understand the special, adversarial relationship Goon and I had. Throwing and receiving insults made it work.

"You're still not getting paid extra to maim and kill?" I said as conversationally as possible.

"Nope. Maybe I can get that in my next contract."

He laughed. "Until then, I'm still pretty much a lazy ass. Doing the minimum for the buck."

There was a thump in the background and some grunting and muffled words that might have been "for cripes sakes." He definitely had Dutch.

"Put Dutch on the phone so I know you really have him."

"Where's the trust?" Goon sighed like he was disappointed in me. "I have him. I definitely have him. No way I'm handing him the phone. He's likely to take a piece of me if I get too near."

Which sounded exactly like Dutch.

"Then put me on speakerphone so I can talk to him. No talking to Dutch, no dongle." Like I had the dongle to exchange in the first place. I'd worry about that later.

"Brave words."

"I'm serious. I mean it. Let me talk to Grandpa."

"Girlie, you forget who has the upper hand. I have the old man," Goon said over the muffled grunts in the background.

"And I have your precious dongle. Which I could easily turn over to the Feds if anything happens to Grandpa," I said with as much menace and bravado as I could muster, trying to keep the tremble out of my voice. "Now let me say a few words to him."

Goon mumbled some curses. "Fine. You've got thirty seconds. Starting . . . now."

"Grandpa, do what Goon says and everything will be fine. No heroics. I'm going to save you."

I thought I heard Dutch's voice mumble my name and maybe the word "no." Grandpa wouldn't want me putting myself in danger, but what choice did I have? I wasn't letting Goon kill him. Much as I might banter back and forth with Goon, I knew he was a dangerous son of a bitch. I wasn't messing with that.

Goon came back on the phone. "Tomorrow evening. Seven. Madam Lou's Martini Bar. You come with those camp buddies of yours. No cops. We make the exchange. No one gets hurt."

The phone went dead.

Chapter 27

I turned to Van for guidance. "Can you trace cell phones? Did I keep him on long enough? What are we going to do?"

For my sake, Van tried to tone down his excitement. Truth be told, he had that kid-in-a-candy-store look about him. "We're going to get Dutch back. This is the break we've been waiting for." He flashed me a look meant to pump me up and into action.

And action I took. I stumbled to the bed and collapsed, all my bravado gone with the sound of Goon disconnecting. "And the call? Can you use it to find Dutch?"

"We can do a reverse cell number trace," Van said. "But odds are he's calling from a disposable cell phone and has already dumped it. I'll get the boys on it."

I could tell from his tone he was appeasing me.

"Give me your cell and call your mom back on the hotel phone," Van instructed, further tempering his excitement. "We're putting her in protective custody. Is your dad home yet? He'll need to go, too."

I shook my head, and handed him my cell. "But he'll dash back when Mom tells him about Grandpa."

"Advise him not to. He's better off where he is."

"What about Dutch?"

"With your cooperation, we'll get him back, safe and sound."

"You have a plan?"

"We do what Goon asked. He wants the FSC team, he gets them. Including me. He won't be expecting the FBI."

I tried to buck up. Dutch wouldn't want me to mope. It was always onward and upward with him. Size up the situation and conquer.

"Nobody expects the FBI," I said in my best Monty Python–Spanish Inquisitor voice. "Our chief weapon is surprise."

"Surprise and ruthless efficiency." Van shot me an encouraging look, tinged with a smile. "Our two chief weapons are surprise and ruthless efficiency."

"And an almost fanatical devotion to the Director?" I sighed, trying to be brave.

"Among our chief weapons are surprise, ruthless efficiency, and an almost fanatical devotion to the mission and the safety of our citizens." Van plunked down beside me and gave me a hug. "Everything will turn out fine. We have an excellent success rate."

"Is it one hundred percent?" I leaned my head back against him.

"No."

"That's what worries me."

"Call your mother. I'll phone my special agents."

"Are they?" I asked.

"Are they what?"

"Really special? I've always wondered why they're special agents. Does the Bureau have any non-special agents?"

"We have janitors and mail room employees," he said. "Call your mom. Just don't tell her about the dongle."

"You mean lie to my mother!" I put on the shocked voice.

"Pretend you're back in junior high. Everyone lies to their parents in junior high." He winked.

"Okay, big shot, what *do* I tell her?" My head hurt. Maybe I needed another dose of painkiller.

"Let her think Ket's behind it."

"And what would Ket want as ransom? Me?" I frowned at him. "That's supposed to comfort her?"

"Snide doesn't suit you," Van said. "Tell her we're sending in an agent dressed like you."

"She watches too many *CSI, Without a Trace*–type shows to go for that."

"Tell her we'd never let anything happen to her baby girl." He gave me a playful nudge and picked up his phone.

Mom took the news better than I expected.

"So they'll make absolutely certain you're safe?" she asked.

"Positively, absolutely." I hoped I sounded brave enough to fool her. "And Grandpa."

"I suppose it can't be helped," Mom said, referring

to the whole substitute-me-for-Dutch situation. "You're a brave girl. I'm proud of you." She sighed and I thought she sounded a little teary and sentimental. "When we get Dutch back," Mom said, changing the subject, Mom was a dwell-on-the-positive person just like Dutch, "I'll make a celebration dinner—bread oxen and sauerkraut casserole."

If there was ever an inducement *not* to rescue Grandpa, sauerkraut casserole was it.

"Sounds great, Mom. The FBI guys will be there any minute to take you in. Tell Dad to be safe."

"I will." She paused. "Reilly?"

"Yeah?"

"Live long and prosper. I love you."

"You, too, Mom."

Van was on the phone to his agents until late in the night, working out *The Plan*. At one point, he went out for several hours. I fell into bed and slept like the dead. The Bobs were guarding me, what could happen?

Turns out a mild concussion is the best soporific around. Dead cold, dreamless sleep beat nightmaring by a long shot. A night of undisturbed sleep had been such a rarity for me these past few years, I decided it was almost worth the kosh on the noggin.

I woke in the wee hours of the morning with Van curled around me. I had a momentary memory lapse and caught a glimpse of what my life could be like in an alternate universe. Then I remembered the Goon-had-Grandpa thing and how I was supposed to be Reilly-to-the-Rescue. I am *not* good with heroics.

Van stirred. Playing the alternate universe game for just a second longer, I turned and kissed him lightly on the lips, brushing the hair out of his eyes and imagining what life would be like with no Ket, no dongle, no Goon.

By mutual agreement, Van and I got up and showered together. Water streaming over our bodies and faces, we kissed and nibbled and meshed and, well, made love like there was no tomorrow. Frankly, I wasn't so sure there was going to be.

"Phenomenal," Van murmured, shuddering to climax as he pressed my back against the steamy tiles of the tub enclosure.

I had my legs curled around his waist. I did my best python imitation and squeezed him with everything from my legs to my kegels. He shuddered again.

"Superman," I cooed, and licked his ear.

He grinned. "Yeah?"

"Yeah, Legs of Steel. Being able to support the two of us in the steamy water after a passion-laced boink is an awesome superpower to have."

He laughed and nuzzled my neck. "You couldn't hold our weight?"

"Right now, I couldn't hold mine." I kissed him again.

All too soon the fantasy shower ended and reality returned.

"Who knew fear is such a potent aphrodisiac," I said as we toweled off and a sudden dread of the day ahead overcame me.

"Not fear, adrenaline." He gave me a playful slap with his towel. "Today we save the universe."

"I'd settle for saving Dutch." My voice shook.

"Yeah, that." Van looked at me with concern. "You all right?"

"I guess I have to be."

He gave me a gentle caress. "You will be."

We finished drying, and dressed.

There was a knock on the door just as I was lacing up my combat boots. Van grabbed his gun, and holding it at the ready, got the door.

"If answering the door these days requires being armed, I'm glad I let you get that," I murmured.

Two bodyguard Bob-clones dressed head-to-toe in black waited to come in. Van put his gun down and ushered them in.

"What happened to the Bobs?" I asked, noting that one of the clones was holding a black case.

"Even Bobs need sleep," Bob-clone One said. "We're their replacements. I'm Larry." He extended his hand and we shook. "And this is—"

"Let me guess. Larry," I said, tongue-in-cheek.

Larry grinned. "Darryl."

"That would have been my second guess," I said.

Van closed and locked the door. "All right, boys," he said to Larry and Darryl. "Let's fill her in on the operation."

My gaze bouncing between them conveyed my confusion. "You guys are . . . ?"

Van grinned. "Special agents."

"And the Bobs?"

Van nodded.

"So FSC didn't hire our protection?"

"They thought they did," Van said. Then, as Larry, or maybe it was Darryl, opened his case of high-tech goodies, Van explained The Plan. "We spent the night with the FSC staff building a mock-up of Madam Lou's—"

"Madam Lou's," I interrupted. "The matchbook I found in my room was from Madam Lou's. I thought Ket left it. Do you think it was Goon after all?" I shuddered. Neither option was reassuring.

Van gave me a sympathetic look. "When we catch them, we'll ask them."

"Doesn't matter," I said.

Van nodded and continued. "Today, when we run through the kidnap scenario and rescue, we'll be practicing for the real event." Van took a blue-print from Larry and spread it out on the bed.

"You got a floor plan of Madam Lou's?" I asked, impressed.

"We did." Van's eyes were twinkling.

Larry and Darryl nodded in agreement.

"Awesome." I looked it over. Having zero spatial ability, blueprints aren't really my thing. I can't imagine them in 3-D. But I pretty much got the lay of the land. "Okay, so what do I do? Commit this to memory and then we eat it so it doesn't fall into the wrong hands?"

"She's a melodramatic one," Darryl said.

"You'll get used to it," Van said to him. "She grows on you."

I turned my attention back to the blueprint. "Bar, light wood, not a lot of grain to it, mirror behind it bordered by decorative pillars, also light wood, and capped with fancy finials? Is that what they call them?" I tapped the blueprint to emphasize my point. "Lots of bottles of vodka and the like on display. Maybe I can get the bartender to place a bottle near me? Just in case I have to hit Goon over the head with it in self-defense."

"I don't think so," Larry said.

"Hey, it works in the movies." I returned my attention to the floor plan. "Black upholstered booths, smoky black glass tables. Red neon lighting around the glass-tiled ceiling. It's a corner position in a corner building so they have windows on two sides, one of which is opposite the bar. Door is at the corner, near the bar for an easy escape. Restrooms in the back.

"Ten-ounce martinis are Lou's specialty. It's not a place for beer drinkers. Cigar smoking is allowed and even encouraged. Bring your own.

"Lou's is known for having a great cover band perform most nights. Probably Goon picked it for the cover noise. And, I'm guessing here, he's a man who likes his stogies. Maybe he even knows the building's history and is hoping for a decor of naked ladies like in the old days when its namesake, Seattle's most famous madam, owned it." I smiled at Larry, Darryl, and Van. "Sorry to disappoint. There are a few photos of Lou and her girls hanging around. But the girls are all clothed. And there's no more going upstairs with the ladies."

"You got all that from the blueprint?" Van shot me a skeptical, amused look.

"What can I say? I'm good." I grinned. "And I've been to Lou's once or twice. Try the Ménage à tini. It's the best."

"Any other observations?" Van asked.

"Why Madam Lou's?" I answered. "Why not Doc Maynard's? It's more squarely in the heart of the tourist district in Pioneer Square. Kids, families, everyone goes there. It's the kickoff point for the Seattle Underground Tour."

"Maybe he doesn't want to get the kiddies involved," Darryl said.

"Old Goon is a softie?" I said. "He did mention he's a family man." I paused, still bothered by Goon's choice. "For that matter, why not some quiet backstreet, deserted alley?" I looked to the men for an answer.

"One, would you be likely to meet him in an abandoned alley?" Van asked.

"Good point."

"Two, with so many civilians around, he's assuming any police action will have to be cautious. He doubts we'd take a chance of an innocent civilian being hurt. He's got a ready supply of hostages."

"Will you be taking any chances with civilians tonight?" I asked.

"About half the patrons there tonight will be undercover cops. We'll take every precaution," Darryl said. "Goon hasn't given us much choice. We can't obviously clear the place."

"How do you think the swap will happen?" I stood and began pacing. "Will he have Dutch in a car outside waiting? Will Goon proposition me at the bar?" Frankly, I was worried about all the possibilities. And all the things that could go wrong. "I won't hand over the dongle until I know Grandpa is fine." My voice broke. "I won't. And what am I going to use for a dongle?"

"This." Van handed me another flash drive that looked suspiciously like the one I had on my key ring. "This? You can pick one of these babies up at Fry's or Circuit City or anywhere. Why would he believe *this* is the dongle?"

"We have reason to believe he will." Van gave me a serious stare. "Will you stop pacing? You're making us nervous." He laughed to take the edge off.

I paused. "What if he wants to check the dongle first to make sure it's real before he gives Grandpa back? What then?"

"Reilly." Van stood and grabbed me by the arms. "We'll take Goon into custody before that happens. Our agents will be posted everywhere in a three-block radius. They'll be looking for Goon and your grandpa, following Goon as he comes to the bar. As soon as he steps in, our agents will release Dutch."

I nodded, but I still didn't believe him. Not totally. "What if something goes wrong?"

"Don't worry about that. We'll have sharpshooters on hand waiting to take Goon out if he so much as sneezes wrong."

I sighed. I had no choice but to trust him. "I thought you wanted Goon alive so you could question him. If he's dead, he can't tell you why he thinks I have the dongle. Without that info, you're at a dead end."

"We want him alive, all right," Larry said for Van. "Let us worry about the details."

We returned our attention to the floor plan and went over several likely scenarios of how Goon would approach. Then Larry returned to his black case. "We're going to put a tracking device on you. We'll be able to follow your every move."

He left the "just in case" part unsaid.

"Great," I said, not warming to the idea in the slightest. "I've always wondered how migrating whales, birds, and seals feel. Now I'll know. Can I have mine in a pretty bracelet? Cayla can help us with that."

Van shook his head. "Your tracking device is going to be practically invisible."

"Do I get to wear a wire, too? While you're invading my privacy, you might as well go all the way."

"Too dangerous," Van said as Larry slapped a tiny transponder on me.

Chapter 28

After a rigorous day of training and preparing for my big night, Van, Cliff, Jim, Steve, Kyle, Ace, War, and I arrived at Lou's at precisely six thirty, accompanied by a box of fabulous trophies in the shape of gun-toting action figures. The FSC trophy was just what I needed to complete the collection on my mantelpiece at home. Six zillion basketball, volleyball, softball statuettes, most often of a girl playing the game, and now one guy with a gun. How phallic would that be?

I would have been more zealous about winning a prize if I hadn't been as nervous as the starting pitcher at the state championships. Completely, petrifyingly nervous, and worried that my fastpitch was not up to speed.

As if it was conspiring to set the perfect gothic atmosphere, the weather had turned from balmy, sunny October to typical Seattle weather—fifty-five with a wind out of the west carrying a waft of impending rain.

I'd changed out of my FSC battle clothes and

into tight skinny leg jeans that made me look tall and all leg. I also wore my spiky party sandals, a metallic magenta cami with spaghetti straps, a shiny black belt, and a black crop jacket. Cliff wore his ubiquitous shorts and a short-sleeved dress shirt. Jim was dressed in a dress shirt and sports jacket. Steve had put on jeans and a polo. Van wore jeans, button-down shirt, and a sports jacket, though I'd been kind of longing to see him in a shirt and tie, like Will Smith and Tommy Lee Jones in *Men in Black* or Agent Jack Malone. Guess that would have been a giveaway. The three FSC instructors had changed into civilian clothes.

We blew into Lou's with a precipitous gust of wind and chose a long booth and accompanying table in the midst of the mixed bag of customers. Seattle is not the fashion capital of the world and has no pretensions to be. It was, after all, the birthplace of grunge. Which meant that people here dressed however they pleased, from fashionable to homeless couture to drag queen. Two of the drag queen variety sat at a table in the corner with their faces obscured.

The hair on the back of my neck stood up. Neither of them were the right size to be Goon.

The Bobs were back on duty and incognito. I recognized them at a booth by the window. I felt like someone in a *Where's Waldo* book. Where are the FBI agents and how can you tell?

War set the trophy box down on the table as the gang took seats and began perusing the menu.

"Sit down, R, and stop ogling the prizes." Cliff motioned me into a seat. "And the prize for eager beaver camper, the girl with the mostest, and I mean moistest"—his gaze slid up my double Ds— "goes to Reilly."

I rolled my eyes and played along. "I'd like to thank the academy and all my long-suffering co-horts at FSC . . ." I remained standing. The seat Cliff had indicated was sandwiched between him and Steve. No way. I could barely look at Steve with-out losing my lunch. And Cliff just wanted to feel me up.

Cliff patted the seat next to him again. "Come on, baby. Have a seat. I'll buy you a drink."

Cheeky, I'll give him that. Van was standing right next to me. It was patently obvious to even the casual observer that Van and I had a thing. We'd dropped all pretenses of feeling otherwise. Ket was already on the rampage. One more inducement might just draw him out.

I gave Cliff a weak smile. I couldn't sit. I just couldn't force myself. I was too fidgety, too jumpy. The door opened and I had to fight the urge to whip around and look for Goon.

I grabbed Van's arm and smiled up at him. "I'm going to go powder my nose."

Van flashed me a look that said, "We just got here." He leaned over and whispered in my ear. "You okay?"

"Preshow jitters."

"I'm going with you."

I couldn't dissuade him. "I'll be right back, boys."

"I'll get you a drink," Cliff said. "What do you want?"

"Ménage à tini."

Cliff looked altogether too hopeful. "You got it, baby."

"I think Cliff has a thing for us," I whispered to Van as we walked off. "Did you see the look he gave us when I ordered the Ménage à tini? He wants me and you. Can you sic your agents on him? I'm the jealous type."

"After this operation goes down, he'll be history."

I did a big, fake, sad sigh. "And so will my movie career."

The ladies' room was opposite the men's room down a small hallway at the back of the bar. It was a one-person affair. I knocked on the door and when there was no answer, tried the knob. The door fell open.

"Are you just going to linger about in hallways?" I asked Van, indicating that no way was he going into the ladies' room with me.

"I'll be here waiting. For you, and you alone, *baby*."

I rolled my eyes. "Oh, man, don't say it like that. Not if you ever want to get lucky again."

He grinned. I stepped into the bathroom. He caught my arm. "Not until I give it the all clear."

I pushed the door all the way open. "One toilet, a pedestal sink, a side table, no cabinets, some soft soap in a pump, folded paper towels. No place to hide. I think we're clear." I pushed past him and closed the door in his face, locking it behind me. Force of habit. Not like Van was going to let anyone walk in on me.

I sighed and did the cliché gaze-at-myself-in-the-mirror routine. The swelling of my goose egg had gone down. My real minerals makeup had done a decent job of covering the purple-green bump left behind. As a woman on the make, I looked pretty good. As the heroine of an action-adventure story, I pretty much sucked. I already had the deer-in-the-headlights, please-don't-shoot-me look on my face and the game hadn't even begun. I tried the sinister *Dirty Harry* sneer. Somehow it didn't come off as intimidating on me as it did on Clint.

My cute little party bag hung from my shoulder on a sleek metal chain. The silver metallic bag held my gun, my super high shine lip gloss, my cell, and the fake dongle. I'd driven to Lou's with a cavalcade of cops following me. When I'd reached Lou's, I jammed my car keys into my jacket pocket. No room for them in the purse, poor things. Now I jingled when I walked.

I snapped open my purse and pulled the gloss from my bag, assessing the odds of wedging my keys in. It was pretty much a no-go. I twisted the lid off my gloss and was just lifting it to my lips when my focus changed from my reflection in the mirror to the reflection of the closet door on the wall behind me. Pulled there by a glimpse of movement.

The closet door had been hidden behind the bathroom door when I'd unceremoniously interrupted Van's inspection. It swung open silently and suddenly before my eyes, exposing not towels and janitorial supplies, but Goon with an evil, triumphant grin on his face.

My gaze darted to the main bathroom door as I calculated whether I could make the quick dash and reach Van and the safety that waited on the other side. I opened my mouth to scream. Before I could move or make a sound, Goon pointed the gun at the back of my head and shook his head in a "no" motion, all reflected in the mirror.

I froze.

In an instant, Goon grabbed me, pressed his hand over my mouth, and a gun to my head. My lipgloss tube slid nearly noiselessly into the sink like a bar of slippery soap. The powder soft gloss applicator hit the floor with all the oomph and volume of a marshmallow.

I was toast. Damned by silent makeup.

As Goon dragged me into the closet, I saw my pitiful life flash before me. The closet was tiny, barely enough space for both of us. Not that Goon intended to linger in tight spaces, not this one anyway. Someone, probably Goon, had cut a hole into the floor. Goon pulled me down it, onto a wobbly ladder lit with an electric lantern and into the pits of hell.

Suddenly the answer to the question I should have pursued hit me, why Madam Lou's? Now the why was easy. Lou's was on the edge of the Seattle Underground, our buried city that spanned a mile and a half circumference and varied in depth from ten to thirty feet. No one expected there to be an entrance to it from Lou's. No one but Goon.

Over a hundred years ago, Seattle burned to the ground. After the fire, the city wanted to regrade the streets to a higher level so that the crapper devices— toilets—would actually flush and not back up and the sewers would work properly. Only the city was slow in going about it, so slow that merchants got overeager and began building without waiting. The city finally got on the ball and raised the streets, but not the boardwalks. The merchants found themselves with first floors that were now basements, ten feet or more below the raised streets.

The guides at the Underground Tour make it all sound like a big joke. Horse teams following off the streets and down into showroom windows. The merchants didn't think it was funny at all. Eventually they resigned themselves to the "first floors as basements" state, all those fancy entrances gone to waste, and built raised sidewalks from the buildings to the raised streets so that people would stop falling off the roads.

Ta da! The birth of the Underground. Today, no one uses the Underground except the Underground Tour, which uses only a piece of it. No one but Goon, who I was certain was leading me to my doom, never to be found again, lying in a tomb beneath the bustling streets of Seattle.

I didn't find the Underground any funnier than our pioneer forefathers. All the way down the ladder, I calculated my odds of success of jumping and running or climbing and running. Neither option seemed particularly viable if I wanted to survive. Goon had one hand on the ladder and one hand with a gun pressed to my head as he climbed down behind me. I had both hands on the ladder and a gun in my purse, but no way to gracefully get it.

I'd played the hostage in several of our earlier game scenarios at FSC. None of them included the Underground. All of them included the cavalry rushing in to save me at just the right moment. What if the cavalry didn't come? Where was Van? Just how long did he think I took in the bathroom?

Goon hit solid ground, grabbed the lantern, grabbed me by the waist, and pulled me off the ladder. "Hurry!" he whispered, shoving me forward.

Lou's sat on the corner, which presented us with four directions we could head. Absolutely diabolical. When Van finally came after me, he'd only have a twenty-five percent chance of making the right choice first off. Goon didn't know about my tracking device.

"Hey! Me hurry? Who jumped the gun?" I was stalling for time, willing Van to get a move on as I tried to get my head in the game. Fastpitch was a mental skill game. Evidently, so was staying alive.

Goon grabbed my arm and thrust me off to the left, gun still pressed to my head. The Underground was pitch-black and smelled every one of its hundred odd years of existence. Dank. Dusty. Depressingly like death. And maybe rats. There had to be rats.

The ground was uneven and not fit for strappy party sandals with fabulous spiky heels. I stumbled. Goon squeezed my already bruised arm and kept me upright. I winced. He ignored me and pressed forward.

"Hey," I said again, more conversationally this time. "Why don't I just give you the dongle right here? You tell me where I can find my grandpa and we're even."

"Not this time, toots."

"Toots?" I said, stumbling again. "You've been watching too many gangster movies."

I felt him grin. In the lantern light he looked sinister and ghoulish. Happy Halloween a few weeks early, Reilly. Stephen King should have set a horror novel down here in the dank scariness.

"What's different about this time?" I asked, still being propelled forward and trying desperately to think of a way to get to my gun and reverse our fortunes. Or remove my belt and buckle him to death.

"This time I stash you while I verify the authenticity of the dongle. Then we talk about Grandpa and returning you to the fresh air above."

"I get it. I'm Persephone now. Instead of six pomegranate seeds, the price of freedom is a dongle."

"You're a sharp one."

"People are going to miss me," I said reasonably. "My friends are going to miss me."

"So what if they do?"

"They'll come after me." I was wearing a tracking device. Not that I mentioned it. Okay, so I had the upper hand. Worse came to worst, I let myself be stashed and Van find me. Assuming I wasn't stashed as a corpse. "What if I tell you I don't have the dongle on me? What do you do then?"

"I strip-search you first to make sure you're telling the truth."

Gruesome thought.

"If you are, I ransom you for it. It's a foolproof plan."

I hadn't counted on Goon being so smart. That's what comes of underestimating people.

"You're still not being paid extra to murder and maim, right?" I asked as I stumbled through a cobweb, stuttering and spitting.

"No, but if I have to off someone, or something goes wrong and someone dies, that's business."

Chapter 29

When the Underground was first built, the people of Seattle used it as a covered walkway. The builders installed glass block skylights at intervals for that cool, natural lighting effect. The lusty, lonely loggers of old liked to linger beneath the skylights and look up the skirts of the ladies who walked at the new street level. The whores, or seamstresses as Seattle liked to call them, used the skylights to advertise their wares, sparking outrage among the morally minded of the city. Eventually the Underground shut down, but the skylights remained. I glanced up, trying to keep track of how many we passed. My own breadcrumb trail system.

Goon kept propelling me forward as if the hound of Baskerville was on our tail.

A rat ran by, his shadow large and grotesque in the lamplight. I screamed. I hate rats.

Goon cupped his hand over my mouth, stifling my scream. "Shut up! Shut up or I'll kill you."

Goon's tone scared me silent. The stench of his rank sweat, not the sweat of exertion, the sweat of stress, mingled with the gloom of the Underground and I felt his desperation. A desperate man was a dangerous man.

This wasn't the same easygoing Goon I knew and hated. Van's warning came to me. The stakes around the dongle reached higher with each day that passed. Someone was squeezing Goon to make good. Which scared the spit out of me.

Escape, escape, escape!

This Goon didn't give a rip about coming back to release me. This Goon was a shoot-and-stow Goon. I'd be dead toast if Van couldn't find me and soon.

I don't know what changed in that instant, but my FSC survival training kicked into high gear and the warrior in me came out. I wobbled forward, looking for a weapon. Goon kept cursing and perspiring. I worried the stench would overpower me.

"Faster, bitch." His voice held all the promise of an itchy trigger finger.

"I'm moving as fast as I can," I hissed back to him. "Have you ever tried running in three-inch heels? I'm not one of Charlie's Angels you know." I stalled.

He nearly yanked my shoulder from its socket.

I tugged back. "Let me take my heels off. We'll move faster without them."

Goon hesitated. I bent to remove my shoe. Shoe with a sharp, pointy heel. Looked like a weapon to me. I removed the first one and dropped it. I took off the second one, twirled around and beat Goon on the head with the heel of my shoe, ignoring the sickening thuds of shoe meets flesh, aiming for his eyes and windpipe. He dropped the lantern. Then he lost his grip on his gun as he tried to protect his head. It clattered into the darkness.

I seized the opportunity and gave him a knee to the groin. Goon groaned and went down on his knees. As he cupped his boys, I grabbed his head, pulled it back, and punched his neck with all the force in me, silently thanking War for my secret spy move, and regretting I didn't have any coins to pack my punch.

Goon gagged and his eyes rolled back in his head. He slumped forward, unconscious or dead. I didn't take time to check.

I grabbed the lantern and did a quick sweep for his gun. I didn't see it. There was no time to lose. I hated to bash and dash, but there you have it. I pulled my cell from my purse. Damn it all! No coverage beneath the city. Wait until I filed my complaint!

My little Berretta sparkled up at me from the recesses of my bag. I pulled it out, slid my shoes back on, and ran back in the direction I'd come, pretending I was Drew Barrymore, Lucy Lui, or Cameron Diaz—one of the Angels, anyway. Those girls kicked butt and ran in high heels as if they were sneakers.

My little bag swung against me as I ran. My keys jingle-jangled with every step I took. The lantern bounced in my hand. Retracing my steps, I screamed for Van. As far as I could tell, the goon and I had made only one turn in the Underground, one turn three skylights back. I screamed and counted skylights, looking for my turn and my way back out.

I found it, spun around it. And ran right into a six-four drag queen with enough force to knock my breath and the lantern away. Soft, feminine curves, he did not have. As I gasped for breath, the drag queen grabbed my arm, wrenched it back, and pulled my gun from my hand.

In the next instant, he pulled me against him and pressed the gun against my head. "Miss me, baby?"

"It's been less than twenty-four hours, Ket." I tried to keep my voice even. Where was Van? Where were my special agents? Evasive action. Stall. "Nice dress. Get it at the Big and Tall Man's Drag shop? Or did you borrow it from someone in the WNBA?"

Ket shook me until I thought my head would rattle off. "See what you drove me to?"

Hard as it was to suppress the obvious smart retort, I kept my mouth shut. I kind of liked my brains.

"Looking for someone?" Ket tipped the lantern upright with his foot. "I wouldn't hold my breath waiting for him." Ket laughed like he was high. "I took him out before I came after you. I left him unconscious with his head bleeding."

"What did you hit him with?" My voice pitched into panicked, hysteria territory. I struggled, wanting to punch a hole straight through his windpipe. "He's FBI. They'll give you the death penalty."

"Such concern." He gave my arm another good wrenching. He would have been good with the rack.

I winced and took a deep breath to keep my knees from buckling under the pain. "You're hurting me, Ket. You don't want to break my arm. You know how good I am with my arms."

"Pick up the lantern, bitch, and let's get moving."

I did as he asked. "Where are we going? We can't go back the way we came."

He laughed. "You think I'm stupid? There's another way out. My limo's waiting in a back alley."

"So it's off into the sunset for us? I don't think so." I winced again as he tightened his grip.

"I do. Let's move." I fought him as he tried to spin me around and point me back in the direction I'd left Goon.

"No! No!" I screamed, struggling. "There's a dangerous mafia goon that way."

He managed to flip me around, bringing us face to muzzle with a submachine gun–toting man who looked like he meant business.

"Hold it right there."

"Huff?" I asked, stunned. "How in the world?"

"I told you I'd be watching your backside, babe." The lamplight gave him a huge, grotesque shadow and lit up his grin like the Cheshire Cat's. I was betting he had the Cheshire's little cat feet, too. "This your boyfriend?"

"Ex," I replied.

"Thought he'd be more masculine. I didn't figure you for the type to go for a cross-dresser."

"The drag queen routine came after we broke up. Personally, he could have used my advice with his makeup. I was a model—"

"Shut up! Shut up, both of you." Ket pressed the gun against my temple with enough force that I could feel a barrel-shaped bruise forming. "Move and I kill her."

FSC had given us only minimal training in

hostage negotiation. Although great sport and satisfying in its own warped way, working the perp and insulting his manhood probably wasn't the greatest idea.

Huff shrugged like what the heck, do it. Okay, so that peeved me. Until I realized his game. Ket pulled the gun from my head and pointed it at Huff.

Both men looked eerie and surreal lit long in shadow.

"My piece is bigger than your piece," Huff said conversationally. "Drop your weapon."

"Drop yours, asshole." Ket sounded furious and crazy.

"You think you can outshoot me?" Huff laughed. "Drop it before I make Swiss cheese out of you."

Desperation made me fearless. While Ket focused on Huff, I knocked his gun arm with the lantern. He squeezed off a shot, but it went wild.

Huff surged forward and pressed the submachine gun against Ket's head. "Let her go. Point blank I never miss."

Ket released me.

"On your knees," Huff ordered Ket.

Ket fell onto his knees. Huff had his gun trained on him.

I collapsed against Huff. "I think I love you," I said, and kissed him full on the mouth in front of Ket, temporarily forgiving him for the whole dongle episode.

He grinned. "What about V?"

"Him, too." Tears ran down my cheeks.

"Hey, don't cry."

I bit my lip and tried to hold back the tears.

"I should have been here sooner. Sal gave me the slip back there." Huff gave me a squeeze.

"S'okay."

"Give me your car keys, babe. I need an escape vehicle."

I shimmied them out of my pocket and handed them over.

"Good girl." He pulled something from his pocket and handed it to me.

It took me a minute to realize it was a flash drive like the one on my key chain. "What the . . . ?"

Huff grinned. "Yeah, you had it all the time," he said, leaving me feeling like Dorothy in Oz. "That one's yours." He nodded toward Ket. "He's been a real asshole to you."

I nodded.

Huff tipped my chin up and gave me a light kiss on the lips. "Things got out of hand. Didn't mean to put you in danger. I'll make it up to you. Promise."

I stared at him and nodded, still feeling his kiss on my lips.

Huff gave me a slow smile. "If only things were different . . ."

I knew what he meant. But he and I would never work out. He wasn't totally tall enough for my tastes. I'd be stuck in flats forever.

"Pick up your gun, R. Take the lantern, and head back the way you came." He pointed the way. "I know another way out. I'll take our boy here and go that way."

Ket was scowling and looking like he wanted to kill both Huff and me.

I nodded. "Huff?"

"Yeah?"

"My grandpa?"

"He's fine. The cops have him. The man's an ox, but he swears like a sissy."

I laughed and a tear of joy trickled down my cheek. Huff really did know Dutch. "Were you . . . ?"

"Watching him? Yeah."

"Thank you," I said, totally relieved. "I really do have a guardian angel."

"I don't know about that," Huff said. "Dark angel, maybe."

I retrieved my gun. "Be careful."

"Always." He pointed again. "Did you kill Sal?"

"I don't know. I punched him in the windpipe and fled. I left him back there." I pointed in the direction I'd come.

Huff nodded as he gave me the up and down. "Hot shoes."

I smiled through my tears.

"Hot woman, too," he said. "Now go."

I took off down the tunnel, running in my heels as if they were Nike Airs.

I'd gone maybe half a block when I heard a gun-shot. I convinced myself it was a car backfiring on the street above. Cars did that all the time on the steep Seattle hills. A backfire didn't bear investigating. Not like a gunshot.

I twisted my ankle and my shoe heel snapped. I stopped to fix my shoe and heard footsteps and raspy, labored panting behind me. I lurched forward, ready to go it lopsided.

"Hold it right there, toots." Only the words came out hoarse and raspy.

I froze and turned to look behind me. Goon had his gun aimed at me. He was holding his throat with his other hand. Even in the dim light he looked green to me. Probably I'd done a bit of windpipe damage to him. He was breathing hard and labored. Why hadn't I heard him before? It may have had something to do with my own heart hammering away in my ears.

"You look terrible," I said to him without a trace of sympathy. "You need a medic. You don't have the energy to take me hostage."

And then in a twinkling, I heard down the path the prancing and running of a dozen FBI agents. More rapid than eagles, the agents came with weapons drawn and bright lights obscuring them from view.

Blinded by the light, I shielded my eyes with my arm.

"Drop the gun, Sal!"

"Van!" I screamed, and started toward him. Or rather, the light. Which I think meant him. Light at the end of the tunnel took on a whole new meaning.

"Stay put, R."

"I'm in the crossfire here, V. I really, really want to go to the light." I imagined him smiling, though he could have been all serious FBI.

"When it's safe, R. Drop your weapon, Sal. We outgun you. We have snipers. Let the girl go. Come in peacefully, and maybe we can cut you a deal."

"No deal. I still have Toots's gramps." Goon's wheeze sounded worse. He gave a big, bloody-sounding cough that made smoker's hack sound melodious by comparison.

"We have Dutch. Safe and sound," Van said.

I almost collapsed with relief as Van confirmed they'd found Grandpa bound and stashed in a nearby alley, giving Goon enough details to convince him of the truth.

Goon hack, hack, hacked again.

"Oh, for heaven's sake," I said, taking some small amount of pity on Goony boy. "He needs a doctor, V. Offer him a trip to Harborview before he hacks his insides up. I gave Goon a good chop in the throat. Goon, take whatever V offers and get help."

"What she said," Van said. "Medical attention."

Goon wheezed out a curse and dropped his weapon.

"Hands above your head where we can see them."

Goon wheezed a second time and held his hands over his head, looking like it took his last ounce of energy to do it. He swayed, ready to go down for the count. Two agents ran past me and cuffed him. They had to hold him up to do it. Several other agents kept their guns trained on Goon.

I ran to the light and Van, and collapsed into his arms. "Boy am *I* glad to see you! Ket didn't kill you, after all."

"I have a hard head."

"Thank God for that."

"Thank God for tracking devices." He paused. "You knew about Ket attacking me?" he asked, suspicion and surprise in his voice. "And I thought I was going to have to apologize for not fully checking the bathroom."

I blushed, but I doubt anyone noticed in the dark. "I *did* slam the door in your face."

"Yeah, that." He looked around. "Ket?"

I did a mental head slap. "Ket! Huff has him."

I hesitated just a second out of loyalty for Huff. I couldn't withhold evidence from Van. That would be wrong, illegal, probably making me an accessory, and probably be bad for our relationship. Huff was on his own with his head start.

"And the dongle! Huff has the dongle. It was on my key chain. And then he asked for my car keys, to escape. And he gave me back my flash drive. The real one. And he said—"

Van put a finger to my lips to quiet me. "We have the real dongle. We swapped it off your key chain yesterday. I just got verification this afternoon—it's our dongle." He gave me a lopsided grin. Half his face still wasn't working real great. "We tried to swap it out at your mom's house, but Dutch interrupted us—"

"What!" I gave Van a shove.

"Hey! I thought you'd be happy."

"What was all this about?" I made an encompassing gesture with my arms. "Why did I risk my life?"

"To get Dutch back," Van said, nonplussed. "And capture Goon." He pulled me close again.

Van's phone rang. He flicked it open. "Yeah . . . yeah . . . yeah . . . okay." He hung up and flashed me a tender, compassionate look. "My agents just found Ket." His tone of voice didn't bode well for Ket's well-being.

I gulped. "Yeah?"

"They found him shot to death in an alley near another entrance to the Underground."

"He's dead?" I didn't know whether to cry or

laugh. I was free. *Free*. I snuggled into Van for comfort. "Huff?"

"Canarino's right-hand man. No sign of him. But your car's fine. He never had any intention of stealing it."

"Do you think he killed . . . ?"

"Yeah, probably. And Jay, too. We think it was Huff who was following you in the warehouse yesterday. When you thought it was me. He's been following you. Keeping an eye on you and the dongle."

My knees buckled as I realized killing Ket was probably the making up Huff had mentioned. I felt sick.

Van caught me and swung me up into his arms. "Come on. Let's get you out of here."

Van carried me back into the safety of Lou's. I blinked into the light. Grandpa sat at a table, being questioned by special agents and fussed over by paramedics.

"There she is! There's my girl!" He stood and ran to us, enveloping Van and me in a big Dutch hug.

"Grandpa!" I hugged him back.

Dutch let us go and took a step back. He gave Van a squeeze on the shoulder. "This one's a good one," he said to me. He turned to Van. "Thank you, young man."

Van nodded.

"You like him?" I whispered to Grandpa. "You are aware that he's not a nerd, and I like him a lot."

Dutch winked at me just as two paramedics came up beside him. He nodded his head toward them. "They want me to go to the hospital for observation."

"Go," I said.

Dutch looked at Van. "I guess you're in good hands."

I leaned over and kissed Grandpa on the cheek. "Go," I said again. He let the two medics lead him through a crowd of reporters to an ambulance waiting for him just outside Lou's. I watched him go.

"I could really use a drink," I said as the medics loaded Grandpa in the ambulance. "Did Cliff ever order me one?"

"Ask him." Van nodded to the corner of the room where special agents had Steve, Cliff, and Jim in cuffs and were reading them their rights.

"They look busy."

War, Kyle, and Ace sat at the table where I'd left them, answering questions for several other agents. Outside, Grandpa's ambulance pulled away, past a horde of news crews and cameramen awaiting our departure.

War jumped up and almost kissed me, he looked so happy. He caught himself in time and handed me one of the FSC trophies instead. "For the last honest camper." He looked both sheepish and grateful.

I took it from him and tried to smile. "And here I was going for Miss Congeniality."

"That, too. You did a hell of a job at camp. We're proud of you, CT," War said and cleared his throat. "On behalf of FSC, I'd like to offer you a free session of your choice at any of our facilities."

"Thanks." I smiled my appreciation, not planning on taking him up on that offer any time soon.

Another ambulance worked its way to the front of the building. Van took me by the elbow. "Your carriage awaits."

"That?" I pointed. "I'm fine."

He gave me a look meant to silence me.

"You're coming with me, Mr. Hardhead."

He did the grin thing again and guided me toward the door. "Ready?"

I nodded, and clutching my FSC statuette like it was an Oscar, made my celebrity-of-the-moment way into the ambulance as reporters jabbed mics in my face and flashes went off.

"I hope they got my good side this time," I said as the ambulance doors closed and a paramedic took my blood pressure. "You know what I could use, V?"

"What?" he said from the stretcher next to me.

"A vacation."

"You're kidding?"

"I'm not. A vacation on a nice, quiet beach somewhere. No guns. No mobsters. No dongles. I might even buy a new bikini." I gave him a significant look, imagining him on the beach next to me.

"I have some time off coming up."

"Do you?"

"How does Hawaii sound?" He squeezed my hand.

"Fantastic."

He leaned over and brushed my lips with a light kiss. All wasn't exactly right with the world. But close enough.

More by Bestselling Author
Hannah Howell

Romantic Suspense from
Lisa Jackson

See How She Dies	0-8217-7605-3	$6.99US/$9.99CAN
Final Scream	0-8217-7712-2	$7.99US/$10.99CAN
Wishes	0-8217-6309-1	$5.99US/$7.99CAN
Whispers	0-8217-7603-7	$6.99US/$9.99CAN
Twice Kissed	0-8217-6038-6	$5.99US/$7.99CAN
Unspoken	0-8217-6402-0	$6.50US/$8.50CAN
If She Only Knew	0-8217-6708-9	$6.50US/$8.50CAN
Hot Blooded	0-8217-6841-7	$6.99US/$9.99CAN
Cold Blooded	0-8217-6934-0	$6.99US/$9.99CAN
The Night Before	0-8217-6936-7	$6.99US/$9.99CAN
The Morning After	0-8217-7295-3	$6.99US/$9.99CAN
Deep Freeze	0-8217-7296-1	$7.99US/$10.99CAN
Fatal Burn	0-8217-7577-4	$7.99US/$10.99CAN
Shiver	0-8217-7578-2	$7.99US/$10.99CAN
Most Likely to Die	0-8217-7576-6	$7.99US/$10.99CAN
Absolute Fear	0-8217-7936-2	$7.99US/$9.49CAN
Almost Dead	0-8217-7579-0	$7.99US/$10.99CAN
Lost Souls	0-8217-7938-9	$7.99US/$10.99CAN
Left to Die	1-4201-0276-1	$7.99US/$10.99CAN
Wicked Game	1-4201-0338-5	$7.99US/$9.99CAN
Malice	0-8217-7940-0	$7.99US/$9.49CAN

Available Wherever Books Are Sold!
Visit our website at **www.kensingtonbooks.com**